Praise for

Story of a Racehorse

"An outstanding debut novel for young people."— Kirkus Starred Review

"A compelling tale of the courage and resilience of a great thoroughbred, my favorite breed."

—Michael Matz, Show Jumping Hall of Fame, Olympic medalist, Trainer of 2006 Kentucky Derby winner, Barbaro

In a quest to fulfill his destiny, Raja bounds from race-track to fox hunt, city police work, and steeplechase, in an adventure that slowly reveals itself to be a love story. Young equestrians will be thrilled by this fine story.

—Alex Prud'homme,
author of *The Ripple Effect* and co-author of *My Life in France*

"Anne Hambleton's enchanting book is fiction, but it might in actuality be true. There is a dark, hidden secret behind the surface glamour of thoroughbred racing. Once a racehorse, especially a gelding, proves insufficient on the racetrack, it becomes unwanted, unappreciated, and unlikely to find a safe harbor. Such is Raja's fate. One moment, a pampered darling, the next a reject throwaway who spirals down, down, down, through a series of failed second chances, until he's face to face with the saddest reality of all, the kill pen at the last chance auction."

"How he is miraculously saved, and how he struggles back to reach the pinnacle of another racing world is the climax of this ultimately uplifting story of destiny lost and destiny regained."

"Raja" is an authentic story. Most authors haven't ridden what they write. Anne Hambleton has. She knows what it feels like to gallop down to the post of the Maryland Hunt Cup, and she conveys those sensations to her readers with a sharp immediacy that is certain to delight and enthrall."

—Denny Emerson, Hall of Fame Three Day Event rider/trainer, Olympian,
Author of *How Good Riders get Good*

"A page turning adventure."

"The voice of an animal is not the easiest of genres to master but Hambleton's lifetime spent with horses gives her an insider's perspective to the psyche of horses of all personality types."

"Readers will want to devour chapter after chapter to see what's next for her extraordinary horse. The book is a natural for young equestrians but as its plot is universal, good versus evil."

—The HORSE of Delaware Valley

"Captivating read! Anne has done an amazing job of putting the reader inside Raja's mind. She takes you on a wild ride through Raja's incredible (but still believable) journey into the varied disciplines that a thoroughbred could take. Very fun read and a great peek into the inner workings of the extreme equestrian sports world. A must read for any aspiring equestrian!"

—Blythe Miller Davies, Two-time National Steeplechase Champion, Winner of the 2011 Maryland Hunt Cup

"Hambleton is a horsewoman who knows all the disciplines intimately, and Raja's adventures unfold believably and with authority. The characters in the story—both animal and human—are well-crafted, and we care about them."

"This is a wonderful book. I read it through in two nights, much of the time with a lump in my throat because it is a well-crafted and well-told story of triumph over adversity—the necessary ingredients of any great story."

—Norman Fine – *Foxhunting Life*

"I come from a racing background and this book is very authentic! Great book for children and adults! (It's) nice to read a horse's point of view!"

—Georganne Hale, Director of Racing, Maryland Jockey Club

"Captivating…and inspiring, it will make you cheer!"

—George Grayson, Chairman, Thoroughbred Retirement Foundation

To Dave, the most patient man in the world
and to “the boys”: Shaddy, Holzmann,
Rather Be, Noco, Salute and Seamus,
who all have stories to tell.

to Gavin,
kick on!

RAJA

Story of a Racehorse

By Anne Hambleton

With Illustrations by Margaret Kauffman

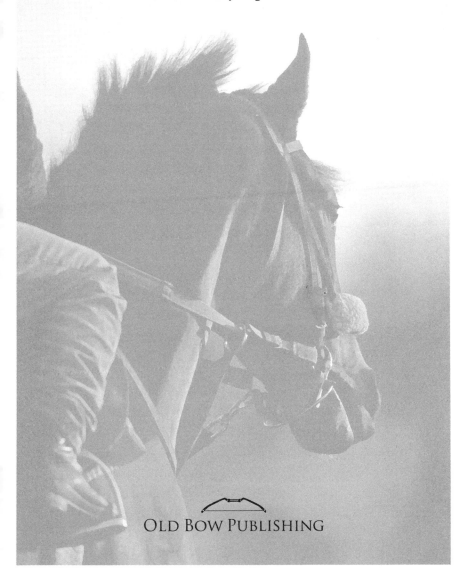

OLD BOW PUBLISHING

First published in the United States of America in December, 2011
By Old Bow Publishing
www.oldbowpublishing.com

For information about permission to reproduce selections from this book, write to
Permissions,
Old Bow Publishing
1816 Morgan Horse Farm Road
Weybridge, VT 05753

Illustrations by Margaret Kauffman
Cover Photo by Cappy Jackson
Book design by Sally Stetson
Text set in Bembo
Printed in the U.S.A., First Edition

Publisher's Cataloging-in-Publication Data

Hambleton, Anne
Raja, Story of a Racehorse/by Anne Hambleton; with illustrations by Margaret Kauffman.
p. cm.
ISBN 978-0-615-54029-0
[1. Horses—Fiction. 2. Horse Racing—Fiction. 3. Horse Shows—Fiction.]

Library of Congress Control Number: 2011942177

OLD BOW PUBLISHING

Table of Contents

Raja

Story of a Racehorse

—Part I—

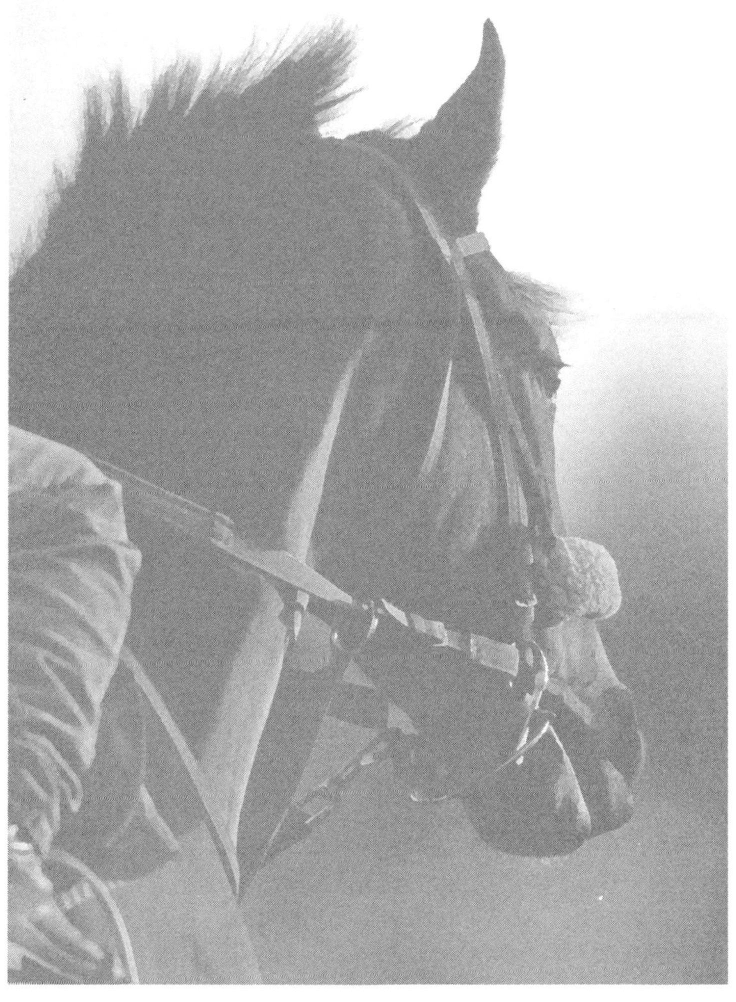

1

The Mark of the Chieftain

September, Ocala, Florida

I could tell something was wrong by the way Princess Ayesha walked wearily across the field toward me, hunched over as she clutched a yellow shawl tightly around her slender frame. A row of glass bangles on her arm stood out cheerfully in a burst of color against the cloudy, grey sky, at odds with the deep sadness I could feel coming from her. She looked tired — defeated, somehow. Her long, glossy black hair, normally brushed neatly, was now loose and uncontrolled, messily framing her tear-stained face. She patted me softly and burst into tears. Her shoulders trembled as she sobbed into my neck, sniffing and hugging me. Putting my head close to hers, I nudged her gently with my nose.

What is it? Why are you so sad?

I heard the gate to the field open once more and looked up to see Bob walking stiffly toward us with an uncharacteristic look of distress on his face, his yellow baseball cap in his hands. He stopped as he reached us and raised a leathery hand to his head in an unconscious gesture, smoothing his straw colored hair. Looking down at his well-worn cowboy boots, he reached into the back pocket of his jeans, pulled out a red bandana and wiped his forehead with it before clearing his throat.

"Princess Ayesha, I'm so sorry. I don't know what to say. The news about the terrorist bombing is terrible. I feel so bad for the families of the people who were killed."

He paused to clear his throat and began again quietly in his deep, soothing voice, as if he were talking to a nervous foal. "Crazy people do crazy things, and then other people do even crazier things. Nothing like this has ever happened in this country before — all those people gone."

Princess Ayesha sniffed, keeping her fingers twisted into my mane. "Father says that I have to go back home, that it's not safe for me here."

"Some people just want someone to blame. And even though you're not from the same country...well...some people don't care. It's insane. People do terrible things to each other — and to horses, too, for that matter. I don't understand evil. But it's out there, no doubt about that."

Bob reached out to pat my neck. "I know you'll miss the horses and Raja, especially. Don't worry. We'll take good care of him. You'd better get inside. We're gonna get some weather. There's a tornado watch in effect. I just heard on the radio that the storm will reach us in about an hour. Are you all set in the big house if we lose power? The generators should be working. They were tested last week. I'm sure the house staff has everything ready."

She nodded. "Will the horses be OK?"

"They'll be fine. Usually they just stay in their turn-out sheds during storms. We put in extra hay so they have something to munch on."

Bob cleared his throat, patted me on the neck, and then wordlessly shuffled off to check a broodmare that had a hoof sized lump on her chest.

Princess Ayesha gave me another hug. She scratched the tickly spot above my eye and whispered. "You are the most perfect thing in the universe and I love you." She gave me one last pat and slowly turned and started walking away. I suddenly realized that this was it.

She's leaving me!

Running along the fence line, I whinnied, again and again. Then I ran to my mother. She nudged me to comfort me. "In a horse's life, special people come and go. That's just the way it is. It's better not to get too attached to a person or another horse or your heart will break."

The muggy afternoon dragged on, slower than an earthworm. Fat black clouds squatted heavily on the horizon and the thick air made me tired. After the mothers were fed their supper, a swirling wind kicked up, steadily growing stronger.

It's a strange day; something is going to happen. I can feel it.

I stayed close to my mother watching as the relentless wind made the bushes and the trees spring to life. Trees dipped and bowed. Branches snapped. Deep angry rumbles of thunder growled their way forward as bright flashes lit up the dark clouds rolling toward us. The wind taunted and jeered as it started to take things with it. First, a peppermint wrapper and a paper feed bag, then an empty bucket. A barn door banged and chains rattled in protest as the gates in our field swung back and forth. A sense of dread, like a stone, grew in my stomach.

This is silly; it's just a thunderstorm.

Feeling as though I was in a dream, watching myself, I pawed the ground in a frantic tempo, digging through the grass, growing more and more uneasy. Suddenly, the wind snapped a dead tree branch, flinging it through the air and onto the fence close to me.

Whoa! What's that?!

I bolted across the field, then skidded to a stop to listen, rooted to the ground, flanks heaving, breathing quick, shallow sips of air. I was trembling in every limb. Shaddy suddenly appeared, nudging me with his nose. Max was behind him. I jumped.

"Are you OK?"

He looked me in the eye, holding my gaze for an extra moment. I just shook my head. The black clouds lumbered toward us, seeming to grow fatter and heavier, until they took over the sky. Illuminated by the lightning flashes, the trees looked like terrible monsters moving awkwardly to the wind's wild beat.

Suddenly, heavy raindrops pelted the ground. After a few seconds, Max, Shaddy and I were soaked. We galloped to the shelter of the shed next to the big oak tree. My mother and some of the other broodmares stayed grazing in the rain, unconcerned. Looking out of the shed at the wall of rain, we watched a jagged yellow streak split the sky followed by a loud CRACK, and a sizzle. Another followed. Then another, all accompanied by the terrifying howls and growls of the wind and thunder. I felt an electric surge and raised my head and tail, nostrils flaring and hair standing on end as the ground shuddered.

CRASH!

A huge bolt of lightning hit the big oak tree. It fell with a wood-splintering groan into the corner of the shed, letting in a torrent of rain through the new gash in the roof. Now a dangerous and unfamiliar landscape, the field was all lightning flashes, rain and thunder, all yellow and grey and black. I galloped out of the shed across the field crying out for my mother. She answered in a loud, clear whinny, "Don't be afraid. Come to me."

Halfway across the field, the sky lit up again, this time an eerie yellow, as lightning stabbed the ground. My mother stood, neck arched and proud, outlined against the terrible sky. I galloped toward her as fast as I could.

But not fast enough.

I watched another bolt burst through the clouds. Her body collapsed in a heap on the damp ground. Skidding through a puddle in front of her, I touched her face with my nose. She was still. Not breathing. Steam rose off her body, accompanied by a strange, bitter smell — burnt hair.

I nudged her.

Wake up! WAKE UP!

I nudged her frantically, again and again, trying to wake her, but nothing I did could help my mother. Deep down, I knew she wouldn't wake, that she'd never come back. A cry of despair escaped out of my body and into the roaring, indifferent wind.

I was suddenly exhausted. I could barely move. I curled up next to my motionless mother, trying to shelter from the driving rain. As I nestled into her still warm body, drinking in her mother smell, trying to hold onto it, memories came to me. All night, with the wind and rain howling around us, I thought of happier moments. I couldn't believe that I would never see my mother or Princess Ayesha ever again.

It was the worst day of my life.

Three months earlier, June, Ocala, Florida

"Pip, pip,...trrreat, trrreat...coo-ee, coo-ee."

In the cool dark of the early morning, when you aren't sure whether it's still night, or if the day had finally made up its mind to arrive, deafening caws, whistles and warbles fill the air. Then the sounds of breakfast — nickering, whinnying and impatient kicking of stall walls from the barns. In the field, our mothers all lined up patiently at their buckets at exactly the same time every day.

A group of shadowy horses and riders jogged out of the morning mist along the endless white board fences past paddocks filled with horses and by our field to the track. After a few minutes, the horses appeared again on the other side of the track, jigging with steam swirling and billowing from their backs as they headed home past the moss-covered live oak trees to the tidy yellow and white barns.

We stood still, watching and snorting. Then, Max stamped. The signal to go! As one, we spun and bucked and raced back to our mothers, where we pulled up to a trot, tails straight in the air, snorting and blowing.

I was scratching my ear with my hind hoof, watching a worm slowly crawl across the ground when I heard them. I looked up quickly, snorted and froze. Half a field away a line of shiny black cars slithered into the farm driveway, passing the big live oak trees and rows of hibiscus before slowing to a halt in front of the main barn.

Something's going on!

Men wearing dark clothes spilled out of the cars and walked quickly across the green lawns. I shivered and played with Max, my best friend, nibbling his neck and rearing up, all the while keeping an eye on the men, watching their every move.

Who is that? Let's check it out — race you to the fence!

A tall man wearing a bright yellow shirt and a young girl with her head covered by a yellow scarf emerged from one of the cars and began to walk toward the barn. The girl slowed her walk and stopped to greet the yearlings in the shed row who were watching her every move, their ears pricked and flicking back and forth, not missing anything. She reached into her bag and fed something to one of the horses who lipped her hand and then tossed his head up and down as he chewed.

"Come along, Ayesha, the foals are waiting for you. Ah, there's Bob." The tall man spoke impatiently, as though he only had a little bit of time before heading on to the next thing.

I looked in the direction he was pointing. Bob ambled out of the stable office and then picked up his pace when he saw the man and girl, covering the ground easily in his relaxed way. Pulling a faded yellow baseball cap off his head, he offered his hand to the man.

"Welcome back, it's nice to see you again, Sheikh." He bowed slightly to the girl. "Princess, it's always a pleasure to have you back at the farm."

"Hello Bob. Wow! Everything looks wonderful. I'm sooo happy to be out of school for summer. That boarding school is a prison! I can't wait to spend time here. I'm only going back home for a little while this year because I have to take SATs here in the U.S., so you'll see a lot of me. My mother and grandmother are coming next week and we're going to the Belmont Stakes. I can't wait!"

"I think that you'll be pleased with this year's foals. That black colt, out of Roxanne, is quite special. Shall we go and see them?"

The Sheikh nodded yes.

Squinting into the sun and using both hands, Bob placed the cap on his head.

"After you, sir," he gestured as he began walking across

the lush green lawn toward the white board fence at the edge of the field.

"Ah, the 'youngbloods.' I have great hopes for you."

The tall man, the Sheikh, is looking at me!

"Bob was right — you're a handsome colt, and big, too. What a powerful hind end. You have the 'look of eagles,' just like your sire. That is an interesting marking on your forehead, like a scimitar, an Arabian sword. Are you ready to win the Kentucky Derby? Maybe the Triple Crown, eh? You'll need a good name."

"Ayesha, any ideas, my girl? A good name for a Derby winner? The chestnut and the bay next to him already have names — Shadrach and Maximillian — after his sire, Millionaire. You were too young to remember, but Millionaire won the Derby ten years ago, when you were six. He's been our best stallion ever since."

Ayesha turned toward me, her dark eyes sparkling with excitement. "They're so cute! The black one is the most beautiful foal I've ever seen." She sighed dramatically, tilting her head and frowning in concentration.

"I hope he wins the Derby! I hope, I hope, I hope…" She thought for a moment. "How about Raja? Raja means 'hope' in Arabic," she explained to Bob, "and in India, Raja means 'king,' or, 'ruler,' so the name has a double meaning." Her eyes lit up as she drew a breath in and held it, waiting for her father's response.

"I like it! Raja, it is. Bob, will you see about registering that name?"

"Of course, sir, I'd be happy to."

One of the men in dark glasses approached. "Sheikh, I'm sorry to interrupt, but the Senator is waiting for you. It's time to leave."

"We'll be right there, thank you."

Princess Ayesha looked at me and smiled warmly, "Good bye, Raja."

The Sheikh, Bob, and the dark-clothed men followed her gaze. Surprised, I raised my head sharply. Pretending to be indifferent but secretly liking the attention, I looked off in the distance at a movement — a man trimming a hedge a field away. All eyes were on me. I stamped, spun and galloped away, causing a stampede of foals and mothers, long broodmare manes flying, hooves pounding the ground like a hundred hammers.

Max, the big bay colt, and Shadrach — Shaddy, he liked to be called — were my best friends. But that didn't mean we were always nice. That's just the way it is in a herd. Someone has to be boss. If one of the other foals tried to butt in, I pinned my ears back and kicked them, or bit their neck — to let them know they were out of line.

"Come here," my mother called in a tone that meant NOW. "You weren't bred to be a bully. Remember, class shows. Our relatives have won every major race in the world. You have greatness in you. It's your destiny. Always remember that."

Her tone softened and her big brown eyes held me. "Always try your best. If you don't, you could be sold."

SOLD?

"Every time you step into a horse van your life could change. You never know, you might be sold. We're lucky, but bad owners and trainers can hurt you. People punish you when you don't understand them, even if you are trying to do what you think they want. Usually you just have to guess."

She nudged me gently. "Remember this always: even when life is hard, never, ever give up."

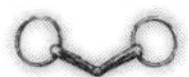

Faster, FASTER!

No one could beat me if I really tried. Sometimes I let Max win, but I was faster and he knew it, always pushing me and trying to catch me out unexpectedly so that he could win. Of course, only winning counts; second or third is losing, every racehorse knows that. That's why we try so hard.

Go hard or go home.

Max sometimes won our play races on sheer willpower. He could outlast anyone. He wanted it so badly. It was quite amazing, really — mental toughness, Bob called it. That's why he was my best friend. He hated to lose.

Shaddy didn't think the same way. An old soul in a bright young chestnut body, he loved to sleep, even more than the older broodmares. Even though he was relaxed — lazy, really, if you want to know the truth — he could get the job done. Every once in a while he would be right there with us as we galloped up the hill, but he didn't see the point in working too hard. He just smiled when we teased him, as if he had more important things to worry about than winning.

What could be more important than winning?

The day after the Sheikh's visit, Princess Ayesha walked into our field. I smelled her first — gardenias and another sweet smell. I stood still, on guard. She walked slowly, holding out her hand, crinkling something.

What does she want?

I held my breath, standing motionless. She came closer, blowing on my nose in greeting. I watched her warily. She inched forward, slowly.

Suddenly she breathed in, holding her breath with a finger under her nose.

A-CHOO!

I spun, then sprinted to the top of the hill.

The next day was the same. She held out a pink-and-white, sweet-smelling offering. I ignored it but it did smell good. I let her get a little closer before snorting and galloping off. On the third day, I let her get close enough to place her hand on my neck. I froze, but let her stroke me. I sniffed the treat in her hand and licked it — delicious — then picked it up in my mouth, letting the sweetness linger on my tongue. Letting out the breath that I had been holding in a rumbling sigh, I rubbed my head on her shoulder.

After that, she came every day. When I saw her, I trotted up to her and rubbed my head on her shoulder, then nosed her hand, looking for my treat.

"Hello Raja, my sweet. Here's your peppermint. Did you have to get gunk on my new white shirt? I should know better than to wear white around horses. Oh well, I don't care, but my mother will kill me. Ugh! I have to have dinner with my grandmother tonight and be formal and polite. All I want to do is to hang out with you and the other foals." I nudged her hand again.

"You greedy thing," She laughed, holding another peppermint out to me. Princess Ayesha flicked her well-brushed, waist-long black hair behind her ear, her row of colored glass bangles on her arm shimmering in the late afternoon sunlight.

She suddenly hugged me, whispering into my ear, "Raja, you're the only one I can really talk to. I never know if people really like me for me for myself or whether they just like me because my father is a Sheikh. We're alike, you know. We're both prisoners. People wish they could have what I have, but I wish I could be a normal teenager. I'm 16. I should have a little freedom." She looked me in the eye, patting my neck gently and hugging me.

"You're my only true friend. You don't care if I'm rich or poor. I can be dirty and silly and it doesn't make a difference to you. You're the most perfect thing in the universe and I will always love you."

She found the shade of the big tree by the gate, sat down on a root and started to sing, lulling me to sleep as the sun tickled grass waved in the breeze and puffy clouds floated across the sky.

"Don't worry, about a thing, 'cause every little thing is gonna be alright,"she sang.

Bob walked up to us and leaned against the fence as the pink and orange sky began to darken, watching quietly and smiling.

Ayesha jumped up, a little flustered. "Bob, I didn't see you; you startled me."

"Cute aren't they? I love watching them."

She reached out gently to touch my forehead. Then she gasped, "Bob, look! Raja has the 'Mark of the Chieftain.' See the way his hair grows? The three whorls? I can't believe I didn't notice it earlier."

"The Mark of the Chieftain, eh? Sounds like some Arabian hooey to me," Bob teased. "In my 30 years with horses, I've never heard of it."

She traced my forehead again, more slowly this time. "It's very, very rare. According to Bedouin legend, horses with the mark change history. They attain great glory or meet great despair. You never know which it's going to be. At least that's what my grandfather told me."

"You should have seen his daddy win the Kentucky Derby, Princess. What an incredible horse. This little fella's got the genes for greatness, there's no doubt about that. He'd better be destined for glory. By the time he gets to the races, a lot of money will have been spent to get him there. If he doesn't show something, he'll be sold."

"My father would never sell him."

"Don't be so sure, Princess. Racing is a business, plain and simple. It's a beautiful sport, but you can't be sentimental if you want to win at the highest levels. Your father knows that more than anyone."

2

Youngbloods

September, Ocala, Florida

"That one. The big black colt over there." Bob pointed toward me. "Of all of the weanlings, he's something special. Watch him trot. He floats — like a ballet dancer crossed with an F16 fighter jet."

I showed off, arching my neck and flashing my feet as I trotted. Bob leaned against the fence watching us, his faded jeans and scuffed cowboy boots dusty from the day and his well-used bandana hanging out of his back pocket. His friend, Michelle, stood next to him, with Piewacket and Muttley, her Jack Russell terriers, at her feet, devotedly following her every move with quick, alert ears.

"He's going to win the Kentucky Derby. It's destiny. Princess Ayesha even told me he has 'special whorls' that say so, see?" He pointed at my forehead, smiling.

"Bob, don't poo-poo that — some people swear by reading horse's whorls. Maybe there's something to it. I don't know much about them, but I agree. He's a nice colt." Michelle's blond ponytail bobbed as she jumped up in a single athletic motion to sit on the fence and watch me. I felt her focus, first uncomfortable at such intimacy, then settling into her admiring gaze. Her intensity surprised me as we connected more like two horses, direct and honest and wordless, straight to the heart.

"Seriously, Bob, he's got charisma. The good ones always do. My horse, Holzmann, has it, and your colt reminds me of him."

"The one who won the silver at the Olympics?"

Michelle nodded. "Raja has the same look of

intelligence. They call it the 'look of eagles.' I think Raja wants to be a jumper and take me back to the Olympics," she laughed.

"Way-ell, now," Bob drawled, a sly smile creeping across his face as he scratched his ear and pushed his cap forward over his forehead, "and how would you pay for the millions he would cost without sending him to stud?"

December, a year later, Ocala, Florida

"El peligroso," the dangerous one. That's what the stable hands called Max after two of them were sent to the doctor with injuries from his well-aimed hooves. I suppose every riding horse has to go through it, but I'm not saying it was fun. Almost everything was just plain uncomfortable: learning to wear tack — heavy, tickly saddles and bridles with heavy cold metal bits in our mouths; having our hooves trimmed by the farrier; and walking up a ramp into a stall on wheels, the horse van.

We tolerated most things now that we were almost two, living in the barn and being "broken in," but it was all slightly trying, especially for Max, who definitely didn't like being told what to do.

"You gotta outwait 'em," Bob told Chris, his new young assistant, who was learning about training. "Sooner or later they come around if they understand what you want them to do. Reward them when they get it right. They're smart; they know."

A familiar, calm smile starting with the crinkles at the corners of his eyes met any high spirits, as Bob waited patiently — no words, just a look that seemed to say, "You really want to make an issue out of this little thing?"

Usually we just ended up doing what he wanted because we were tired of being asked again and again and again. And, of course, there were carrots involved.

Carrots help a lot.

"Vet's comin' tomorrow to tattoo their upper lips. The inside, see here." Bob put his hand on the upper lip of a horse down the shed row from me and rolled it up to show Chris. "See that letter? It's the year he was born. The number after is the last five digits of his Jockey Club registration number. That's the way Thoroughbreds are identified. They have to be registered and tattooed before they race — that's why they all have unique names."

Chris grimaced. "Ouch, sounds painful."

"Don't worry, they only feel a prick."

Soon all of us two-year-olds were training on the dirt track, galloping side by side, four sets of nostrils breathing in stride or bucking and egging each other on.

Starting-gate lessons were the best. We walked into the narrow metal stalls, hearts pounding, muscles taut and ready to go, feeling more alive than I thought possible, knowing it would soon be time to gallop! Watching the gate person intently, filling our lungs with a deep breath. And when you couldn't bear to wait any longer, exploding onto the track, fighting to get out and away first, bodies bumping and hot wet sand flying in our faces.

Max and I galloped head to head. Toward the end, I would look him in the eye.

I dare you to try to beat me.

He always fought fiercely and I always played with him for a while — like the barn cats with a mouse they were about to kill. Then I turned on what Bob called "the afterburners" and blew by him — to keep him in his place.

"Como estas, Raja, how are you today? Are you going to win the Derby?"

Every day, Pedro, my regular exercise rider, greeted me with a grin that took over his weather-beaten face and made everyone in its beam feel as if they were the best thing to happen to him. A mischievous gleam in his eye invited you to share the joke while he innocently rubbed the back of his nearly bald head.

"Only forty years old and I've broken 20 bones — my collarbone four times." He winked at Chris. "I don' think I have any more left to break. I love working with all of the Sheikh's babies. It's so much easier when you start with class. These boys are the top, I'm tellin' ya. You couldn't teach a horse what they've had bred into them — power, boldness, heart. One of these boys could be the next Secretariat or Man o' War."

We had a routine. Pedro usually brought me an apple or a sweet pastry. I greeted him and rubbed my head on his shoulder, trying to find the treat.

"Hey buddy, you look like a big, tough racehorse, but you're just a puppy dog."

Ta-da-da-dum, ta-da-da-dum, ta-da-da-dum.

I felt Pedro's joy, like warm sunlight, as we galloped

together, the two of us chasing down the dirt training track on the mist-filled mornings, with his steady hold and light and even balance floating over my back. By now, I was strong and getting fitter and I wanted to go, go, go.

Sometimes we had a little "conversacion," as Pedro called it, about how fast we should be going. He always made sure that I came around to his point of view sooner or later. When I saw Pedro, I took a deep breath and relaxed. He was interesting, the way he was so calm and easy, but with fire and steel inside, ready if I acted tough, which was often. Mostly, he tried to teach me that the two of us were a team, better together than separate.

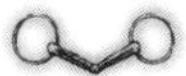

Working! Breezing!

If you really want to understand me, you have to know about working. There's nothing, I mean nothing, better, except maybe actually racing. Most days we galloped or jogged, but on Saturdays, we got to turn it on! First, gallop a turn, around the middle of the track at a two-minute lick. Then, drop to the inside rail — the signal to GO! The wide-open dirt track coming faster and faster until it turns into a blur, no sound but the wind rushing by my ears; Pedro's hold is strong and tight as he crouches lower, moving in rhythm with my longer and longer strides until we begin to fly, skimming the ground.

Then, with a shift of his weight, Pedro stands in his stirrups and the moment is over. Hearts pounding and catching our breath, Pedro laughing, the colors more intense, sounds sharper, I feel happy, more alive, somehow. I know Pedro felt it too. That's why we got on so well. We both loved, I mean, loved, speed.

It was a Monday, our day off, and Pedro and Bob were off with the horse van, leaving Chris and Ken, the second-string exercise rider. Chris moved a little more slowly than usual, cleaning the tack and folding saddle towels as he sang along with the radio. When he finished the tack, he started making his way down the shed row, taking off stable bandages and leading horses out one at a time to hand walk and graze.

"Looks like we might get some weather," Chris pointed to the grey clouds that had taken over the sky. Ken, muttered something angrily to Chris in response. Ken always seemed ready to explode. He stomped around the barn and got all of us horses riled up when he came to ride. Thankfully, I didn't have much to do with him.

"Figures they'd pick a rainy day to leave us to do all the barn work. Typical. That Pedro thinks he's god's gift to horses. Well, he ain't. I'm just as good as Pedro. Better, in fact. He's a tired old man. These people are stupid. I'll show 'em, I'll show everyone."

A wild, cloudy look swept across Ken's darting eyes as he ranted, nervously scratching his scraggly beard, then spitting out his chewing tobacco juice in a long brown spurt aimed at the cat. He walked over to my stall.

I lifted my head suddenly and backed up as Ken jerkily raised his arm toward me, then slapped my neck, thinking he was patting me. I flinched, holding my breath. I stood still, watching him warily out of the corner of my eye.

"Put my saddle on Raja. Ain't no horse I can't ride. What's the big deal 'bout him, anyway?"

"It's the horses' day off. Besides, only Pedro rides Raja, you know that."

Ken glared at Chris. "I said tack him up."

As he put the saddle on, I could tell Chris was worried.

I felt the electricity in the air as the wind picked up, rustling through the bushes lining the stable yard. The sky was greyer than it had been just a few hours ago.

This doesn't feel right. It feels very wrong.

When Ken and I reached the track, we were alone. My skin tingled as the heavy feeling in the pit of my stomach began to grow. I stopped, whipped my head in the direction of the barns, and whinnied loudly, hoping that one of my friends would respond. I wanted to go back. It was dinnertime and everyone was eating. Annoyed, I jigged sideways and let out an impatient buck. Ken hauled on the reins and jerked me sharply, angrily, in the mouth.

"Whoa!"

I tensed and started to toss my head.

Why is he jerking my mouth? Why is he shouting? What have I done wrong?

As we started to jog, then gallop, Ken took a short hold on the reins and, pulling roughly, leaned his weight heavily against my mouth.

Does he want me to go faster? Why is he nervous?

I didn't like this at all. He was heavy and tense, not relaxed like Pedro. He made me nervous.

I want him off my back.

I really want him OFF, NOW!

Head down between my knees, I let out a big, athletic buck, then another, twisting, propping and spinning, then dropping my shoulder and scooting sideways. Ken clung on determinedly and snatched me in the mouth again.

"Here!" He growled in a low voice.

I started galloping, picking up speed, ignoring his

rough pulling. I was stronger than he was, of course. As we galloped, heavy raindrops began to fall, accompanied by deep rumbles of thunder. Black clouds hurried across the sky. Suddenly, I heard a loud crack and then saw a yellow streak dive into the slick dirt track.

LIGHTNING!

My heart began to pound and I heard a loud roaring in my ears. I bolted, running as fast as I could, forgetting Ken, forgetting everything but my desire to get away. Through the driving rain, flowers, bushes and trees all a multi-colored blur. Around and around and around the track, through puddles and slippery wet dirt; sucking in gulps of heavy air until, steamy and wet, flanks heaving, I began to tire and pulled up.

Now that I had stopped galloping, I could feel the wetness of the heavy drenched saddle cloth and the slippery leather bridle. I could smell the damp earth, now covered by puddles and streams. Ken savagely yanked me out the gate off the track, jerking the bit roughly in my mouth. I tossed my head angrily and dropped my shoulder.

I spun again but he clung on. I jigged sideways, then slipped, as I stepped on a rake lying in the path. A sharp, burning pain shot up my leg.

Ken cursed, kicked his stirrups free and vaulted off. Still breathing hard, with rain and sweat running down the sides of his face, Ken clutched the thick, wet rubber reins and hit me across the forehead with his whip.

"You piece of garbage, no horse runs away with me! You're a pig. You need to learn respect. I'm going to teach you a lesson!"

By the time we came back to the barn, the stable hands had gone. Chris walked over to us with a

halter in his hand.

"Here. Let me help you take care of Raja."

"Scram, junior, I'll take care of him myself. This horse needs to learn some manners."

"Bob said I was in charge."

"I mean it. Get out of here. NOW! Before I teach you a lesson, too!" Ken growled. Chris turned and walked away, clenching his fists. Ken put me in my stall, hot and sweaty, without washing me or tending to my cut. After a few hours, I started to shiver. I was burning hot, then freezing cold and my leg throbbed painfully. I was so thirsty. And I was starving! Ken hadn't given me any water or hay.

Sick and weak, I lay down and drifted into a restless sleep. Terrible dreams came to me: my mother, outlined on the hill, calling to me, "Help me. Run faster." I started to run but something held me back, like a giant hand. I was unable to move or help her. I tried to whinny to her, but no sound came out. Then the lightning, and Ken, jeering through his brown teeth, "You're garbage, I'm going to teach you a lesson."

I woke up while everyone was eating breakfast. I was too weak to get up.

I just want to die.

"Bob, Chris, come quick, Raja's sick!" Pedro shouted with alarm. I tried to lift my head, then put it down again as the stall started to spin. I was burning up and terribly thirsty and by now my leg was swollen double its normal size. He pinched the skin on my neck. "See how dehydrated he is. Chris, get him some water with electrolytes. Hurry!"

After I had a drink, several long sips at a time, Bob put something under my tail and held it for a few minutes.

"One hundred and three degrees." Bob shook his head, "He's in shock."

He gently sponged off my sweat and dried me with soft towels before urging me to my feet and leading me to the wash stall, where he cleaned my cut and ran cold water from a hose on it for a long time before giving me a shot and putting a bandage on.

"Puncture wounds like this are the worst. If you don't clean 'em out good, infection gets in and the whole leg swells up," he shook his head grimly.

"It'll be a few weeks before this heals enough for Raja to train again. We'll put him on antibiotics right away so the infection doesn't get worse. Chris, make sure he gets cold-hosed and hand grazed at least four times a day."

"Yes, boss." Chris hung his head, dejected. He looked down at his dusty boots, hiding the tears now running down his cheeks. He sniffed.

"Chris, I don't understand how you let this happen. I'm disappointed in you."

"I'm so sorry. It won't happen again."

"Because you're young, I'll give you one more chance, but that's it. One chance. If ANYTHING like this happens again, I'm afraid we can't allow you to work with these horses. It's not just about allowing a nice animal, any animal, to be needlessly hurt, which is bad enough in itself. Do you have any idea how valuable these horses are? Raja, here, is worth millions. I can't take the risk of something else happening. I told Ken to leave and never set foot on this farm again. Good riddance, I say." He shook his head in disgust.

3

Road to the Roses

July, Ocala, Florida and Saratoga Springs, New York

"The Spa. There's nothin' like Saratoga in August." Bob nodded his head dreamily as he and Chris watched a big shiny van pull into the driveway. "You're lucky to have this opportunity to work for Alex MacLaren. He's a Hall-of-Fame trainer, you know."

We're going racing! It's all we had talked about and dreamed of.

Even Shaddy seemed excited. A tickle of anticipation made me shiver. The thick cotton shipping bandages tickled my legs. I walked and hopped, stiff-legged, for the first few steps before figuring them out.

"How's the big horse training?" Bob's friend, Michelle, was there for the sendoff. She smiled, turning her gaze toward me. I could feel the warm glow of her energy. Her intensity took me by surprise as her green eyes held my gaze. She blew softly on my nose in greeting. I blew back and sighed, rumbling air past my lips, then nickered.

How can she be a person but communicate like a horse?

Pulling a sugar cube out of her pocket, she pressed it to my lips.

Mmmm! As good as a peppermint.

"Like a champ, as always," Bob replied. "He's going to create a buzz up north, although there are a couple of nice young horses out there. Flash Jackson just paid five million dollars for a Derby prospect, Annapurna, at Keeneland. He'll be tough to beat. Wait until they see our "secret weapon." I think Raja will make that horse look like a Shetland pony."

He led me into the van where Shaddy, Max and the others were waiting.

I don't remember much about the journey. Just that it was long — almost two days — and that we slept and nibbled hay nets while the van swayed under our feet.

Shadowy horses and riders and muffled sounds of breakfast — whinnying, nickering and buckets banging — wafted in and out of the cool sun-dappled morning mist. I couldn't believe what I was seeing. So many horses and people and so much activity! The charged air made me jig as I dragged Chris along while he led me on a walk, my ears pricked and head raised as I snorted at the newness of everything.

I want to see it all. I can't wait until I'm in the center of the action, RACING!

We walked past endless green shed row barns. Overstuffed hay nets and well-scrubbed colored plastic feed tubs perched next to stalls shaded by baskets overflowing with pink and red blossoms. Gleaming leather halters with polished brass name plates glinted and winked in the golden sunlight. Horses, everywhere, jigging out to the track to train with their riders laughing and joking, hot walking in circles in front of barns, or standing as they were bathed, with steam swirling from their backs.

Every second I heard something new: music from barn radios, horses whinnying, tractor engines rumbling, hooves thundering on the track or clack-clack-clacking on the tarmac road that lined the backstretch. And the smells, heady and complex: shampoo, liniment, poultice, flowers, fly spray and sweet flowery smells from the ladies in colorful dresses and hats — the owners— who occasionally walked through the barns with their trainer.

The grooms gossiped as they rolled bandages and played cards in the shade of the old oak and maple trees. "Si, Annapurna, el caballo del Flash es muy lindo — mejor que los otros." "Flash's horse, Annapurna, is very nice — better than the others."

"Muy caro — el Flash es muy rico," "Very expensive — Flash is very rich."

"You must be the new crop," a dark bay, almost brown, horse in the stall next to me drawled in a knowing, yet not unfriendly, manner. "I'm Rather Be, also bred and owned by the Sheikh. Everyone calls me 'RB'. For some reason, he still has me out here banging away, even though I've been running for years. I guess I'm good for a stakes win or two despite being an old man of six."

"Stakes win or two!" snorted a nervous, red, "blood" bay on the other side. "RB has forgotten more about racing than most horses, or people for that matter, ever know. He's a race strategy genius. How many stakes have you won, RB? I know you ran in the Triple Crown races — the Derby, Preakness and Belmont Stakes."

RB rolled his eyes, slightly embarrassed.

"Hey, there's Hollywood Bill." He looked across the shed row, changing the subject. We all looked over to the next barn, where a man wearing dark glasses stood next to a very tall man while a group of photographers clicked their cameras.

"I never see him at his barn unless he's with one of his celebrity owners. He usually has his assistants do the training while he chats up the owners. I heard that he just bought Annapurna, the highest-priced horse at the Keeneland sale, for that guy. That's Flash Jackson, a famous basketball player. People give him lots of money to chase a ball around a room. It seems silly. People are funny. But Flash wants to win the Kentucky Derby and he has the money to buy the best horses."

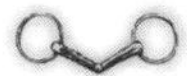

August, Saratoga Springs, New York

"Jog him, please." Alex MacLaren, my new trainer, ran his hand down my legs to feel them, as he did with every horse, every day. He watched me intently and nodded.

"OK, he looks good. Thank you, Chris. Bring the filly out next, please."

Alex looked me in the eye with approval and patted my neck, his manner professional, yet personal, at the same time. Tidy, contained, never without his blue baseball cap covering his short brown hair and penetrating eyes, Alex was constantly in motion, attentive and focused, coffee in one hand and cell phone in the other, noticing and remembering every detail.

"The filly isn't finishing her feed. Try adding Gatorade powder. She did this last year when it got hot. Make sure it's orange, not lime — she only likes orange."

Then Willie, my exercise rider, appeared, and it was time to train! The track was where the action was, the center of everything. Horses jogged next to the outside rail, or galloped in the middle of the track, while owners and railbirds, coffee and racing newspapers in hand, chatted and watched. On the track we always had to have our eyes open for horses spooking or running off with, even dumping, their riders. Alex said that "traffic" got us used to all of the action of a race day.

I still hadn't seen a race, but I couldn't wait.

RB shook his head as we watched the vet use a machine to look at the leg of another horse from Alex's barn who had limped painfully back to the barn after his race.

"Racehorses are athletes and athletes get sports injuries. It sounds as if he's torn his suspensory ligament. He might race again after time off or maybe he'll go to stud. What a shame; he was running well."

"What happens if a horse can't race or gets old?" Max asked.

"Retirement?" RB answered, "I'm not so far away from it myself, you know."

The chatter died down as Max and Shaddy and the others stopped to listen.

What happens to a racehorse after racing?

"Well," RB thought for a while, munching a mouthful of hay, "you know, we're the lucky ones. Most of us are very well bred and will go to stud. The Sheikh is really good about finding homes for his horses that don't go to stud but can do other things. A lot of his horses go back to live in the big retirement field at the farm."

The nervous bay horse next to RB interrupted, excitedly, "It's being sold to a bad owner or trainer that you have to worry about. The ones who think you're an investment that needs to make money."

RB nodded sadly, in agreement. "If you're useful but not especially well bred, you might be sold. Then you keep racing, just easier and cheaper races, and hope that you stay sound enough for another career afterward or that your owners will make sure that you are taken care of." He paused to take a sip of water. "But I hear stories — we all do — racehorses abandoned, even killed for meat."

Meat? That couldn't possibly be true.

"Annapurna won wire to wire and I was second," Max glowed after his first race a week later, his eyes sparkling, words pouring out and running away with him. "Oh Raja, you'll LOVE it. It was so much fun, so different than I expected. Shad, did you see that grey, parrot-mouthed pain in the neck, Sanchez, trying to come up my inside? Dumb idea — I shut him down quick. No one gets up my inside."

Even Shaddy was abuzz from his fifth place finish.

"Raja's entered in the maiden race Saturday," I heard Alex tell Chris.

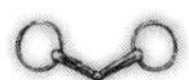

A crisp breeze blew in a glorious morning, all blue and green and red and white, the colors of Saratoga. Sparrows perched on the rafters, darting in and out of the shed row, watching for spilled grain as we ate breakfast. Even the little routines of the morning seemed grand and filled with significance.

Today is race day!

It was a week after Max and Shaddy's race and now it was my turn.

"Knock 'em dead, buddy," Max called as I left to go to the pre-race barn.

"Good luck, my friend," Shaddy echoed. RB smiled and nodded.

From the pre-race barn I heard the announcer rapidly calling each race and saw the runners returning, steam whirling and wisping off their glistening bodies as they jigged and danced. Walking around my stall, I shivered in anticipation, pawing the ground until I had dug a hole through the straw in the dirt floor. Every triumphant note of the buglers' "Call to the Post" before each race stirred my hammering heart:

Da da da dum diggety dum diggety dum, dum dum daa.

Chris led me along a narrow path through a blur of people and colors and food smells until we reached an enclosure shaded by big maple trees.

Let's go, go go! It's time for RACING!

I was so excited, I thought I would explode. I stepped out with my fancy walk, knowing that everyone was looking at me. Alex, now in a suit, wearing a yellow tie, was speaking with a tall woman wearing a yellow scarf and large sunglasses. The curve of her stance seemed familiar.

Is it?

Then I smelled it.

Gardenias and peppermint!

My heart skipped a beat. She reached to tuck her hair behind her ear, a row of colored bangles catching the sunlight in a familiar gesture. As she turned and caught my eye, Princess Ayesha ran to me, trailed by photographers. She smiled and patted me, her smoky eyes shining. She seemed so mature, more dignified. I hadn't seen her for two years. She whispered in my ear as her warm hands traced the length of my neck,

"Raja, I missed you so much. I'm so happy to be back in the United States and especially to see you. You look wonderful — all grown up! You can do it, I know it." She looked me in the eye. "You are the most perfect thing in the universe and I love you."

I barely noticed the tiny saddle, tight girth and even tighter overgirth when Alex saddled me. All I could think of was how I was going to make Princess Ayesha proud.

SARATOGA

I am Raja! Destined for glory.

"Riders up," came the call from an official-looking man. Willie, my jockey, jumped lightly up, with a helping hand under his ankle from Alex, then settled easily onto my back. Then he stood up in his stirrups to test the girths and tied a knot in his reins. Chris led us around and around the paddock, whispering words of encouragement to me, while snippets of conversation floated over to us. I knew that people were admiring me.

"Look at number five, Raja. He's stunning."

"He's my pick. Breeding's impeccable. Class all the way."

We followed the outriders onto the track, past the big stands filled with people cheering and shouting and the announcer calling our names one by one.

Da da da dum diggety dum diggety dum, dum dum daa.

"Go number five!"

"Bring it home, baby."

I couldn't help but jig all the way to the start.

It's time!

My heart was pounding so hard I could hardly hear the crowd. Into the gate, then click as the door was secured. Willie's blood was up, too. I could feel it as he took a deep breath. I looked at the track, poised to go.

Let's go. Let's go.

A reassuring pat from Willie as he gathered the reins into his hold. I took a deep breath.

BRRING! We're off.

Quickly away from the gate, I established myself on the inside rail, sitting fourth.

Ta-da-da-dum, ta-da-da-dum, ta-da-da-dum.

The sound of thundering hooves and jockeys yelling

at each other was deafening. As we passed the stands the first time, fragments of sound from the announcer excitedly calling the race drifted into my ears.

"It's Ice Bullet in front by five, Shimmer Shimmer second, with Natty Boh third."

Thwack, thwack. Clods of hard dirt thrown up by the horse in front of me flew into my face as we ran as a pack, careening around the turn, trying to save ground, bumping and jostling, inches away from each other.

The scrappy, physical, closeness of it all surprised me. Hindquarters in front of me, rising and falling, sharp hooves inches from my legs; and the horse next to me, running head and head, stride for stride, pushing me closer and closer to the rail. We were a moving bubble of churning hooves, clods of dirt, and flying manes, with motionless jockeys hovering atop straining muscles, opening and closing strides as one.

The pace was quicker than our daily gallops, but I felt good and kept an even rhythm to my strides. It all went by so fast, the turns were coming up quickly, the red-and-white striped quarter-mile poles flashed by in a blur; there was hardly time to think.

Coming around the final turn toward the homestretch, the race suddenly turned frantic. Everyone was bumping and jostling, trying to get to the lead. Jockeys urged their horses on, suddenly riding harder and going to the whip. Willie took a shorter hold and started to ask me to go, his hands and legs in rhythm with my longer and longer strides. I knew what to do.

I started to run.

The roar of the crowd filled my ears. I could hear the announcer's excited call, "And it's Shimmer Shimmer by two lengths, Ice Bullet on the outside. Here comes Raja. Raja is making up ground!"

Willie steered me to a gap that had opened up in the pack and asked me again.

"Let's go. Let's go. It's time to go," his hands and body cried. We burst through. I passed the third horse, then the second horse, Ice Bullet. Coming head and head with the leader, Shimmer Shimmer, I looked him in the eye. Then I turned on "the afterburners."

Everything except the track ahead of us disappeared.

"Here comes Raja. Raja moving up on the outside to take the lead. Raja! Raja, followed by Ice Bullet, Shimmer Shimmer, and Natty Boh in fourth. Raja, by one, now two. Raja wins today!"

We passed under the wire with eight lengths between us and the next horse.

"Good boy, Raja!"

Willie stood up in his stirrups to slow me down and gave me a big pat on the neck. The roar of the crowd overwhelmed me as we jogged back to the stands. Princess Ayesha thanked Willie and hugged me again and again. "Raja, I knew you could do it. What a good boy!"

Victory! What a glorious feeling. I am Raja, destined for glory!

Winning was the best feeling imaginable. I jigged all the way back to the barn.

"I knew you could do it," Max confided in me that night. "Of all of us, you're the one who will really make a mark. I know that you can beat Annapurna."

When the Saratoga meet ended and horses began to leave, the electricity in the air faded, leaving us feeling a little sleepy. The crisp September wind whispered of the coming winter as it rattled the yellow-tinged maple leaves. A group of Canada geese came in for a few days, circling the pond in the center of the track with a loud, a-hink-a-honk, a-hink-a-honk, then claiming it with a dramatic, feet first splash landing.

"Go south. Hurry, winter's coming," they seemed to cry.

September, Belmont Park, New York

Grey, that's Belmont for you. No flower baskets, shade trees, or ladies with colorful dresses walking around the stable yard. Grey skies, grey backstretch, grey people, even the other horses looked a little grey after Saratoga.

"You and Max are entered in the Champagne Stakes, a Grade 1 Stakes race," RB told me. "It's a big step up from a maiden race, but Alex thinks you're up to it. You know, you're the favorite. It's because of your win at Saratoga."

Early in the morning the day of the race, I was eating my hay and resting in my stall trying to stay calm, when I smelled it.

Gardenias and peppermint!

I quickly popped my head over my stall door, as a deep nicker escaped me.

"Raja, there you are, my beautiful." Princess Ayesha walked to my stall, gently kissed my nose and scratched the tickly spot above my eyes, feeding me a peppermint as I stretched toward her. She flicked her long black hair out of her face, her row of colored glass bangles catching the sunlight, bringing a splash of color to Belmont.

"I fooled the paparazzi so that I could come and see you. They think I'm getting my hair done, but I sent my assistant, dressed as me, and snuck out the Plaza Hotel kitchen. It was a jail break! Bob's here, too — he drove me out from the city."

She smiled triumphantly, a spark of rebellion in her dark smoky eyes. She likes to be independent, too, I thought, but her life is controlled by others, just like mine.

We're more alike than I had realized.

I was so happy to see her. I contentedly munched some hay, all nerves gone.

Then it was time to go to the paddock.

Da da da dum diggety dum diggety dum, dum dum daa.

I danced all the way to the start, relaxed, confident, floating on air.

BRRING! We're off!

RB was right. This race was a big step up. The pace was quick and every horse in the race was talented, competitive, and out to win. No one was going to let others pass them willingly. I broke out of the gate well, but for the first half of the race, I felt boxed in the middle of the pack. Helpless, I bore it, thundering along with the others.

I can't do anything. I want to go faster but I can't get around the others.

One horse on my inside tried to create a gap and bumped into me, breaking my rhythm. I lost momentum and two horses passed me. Now I was mad. I could tell Willie was frustrated too. He steered me to the outside, the long way around.

Finally, room to move.

He let me out a notch, not full speed, but my running pace. We began to move up and pass horses, sixth, now fifth. Rounding the final turn, Willie made his move, a little early, but I had plenty left. We began to run. The track was wide open, inviting, as if the race, the win, already existed and I just needed to tap into it, to claim it as my own.

Faster, FASTER!

Now we were fourth, now third, now second. I drew next to Max, who was in the lead. Coming into the home stretch, it was Max and me, alone, neck and neck.

OK, Max, this is it. Who is it going to be?

I looked him in the eye, just like all of those times back at the farm. This time I didn't play with him. Every part of me was focused on going forward and going fast.

"Come on, baby," Willie smooched as I blew by Max.

"And it's Raja! Raja wins by six lengths."

The announcer's voice was drowned out by the deafening roar of the crowd. Then we were under the wire, no one else anywhere near us. Willie stood up in his stirrups to pull me up, giving me a big pat, then, dropped the reins to hug me as we jigged back to the finish line.

"Good boy, Raja! You're a machine!"

A woman on a horse accompanied us to the winner's circle. "What a race! What power, what grace! You won this Grade One race by a very impressive six lengths. What was your strategy? Is Raja the new superhorse?"

A new round of cheers burst out to greet us as we approached the stands.

Ah, my people!

I turned and nodded to them. I loved them and they loved me. Everything is beautiful! Perfect, the best it ever was, the best *it ever could be.*

"Nice job, Raja!"

"Way to go, number six!"

Black streaks of tears smudged Princess Ayesha's face as she smiled jubilantly, oblivious to the throngs of people shouting questions at her and taking our picture. She couldn't stop petting me and kissing me. This time the photographers followed us back to the barn. I loved the attention and, especially, I loved being the best.

Winning! There's nothing better!

January, Gulfstream Park, Florida

"I think Raja should run in the Fountain of Youth Stakes in February and then the Florida Derby in March," Alex spoke to Chris as he wrote in a notebook with a look of intense concentration on his face. After a month's vacation at the farm in Florida, we were back in training at a racetrack.

"They're both here at Gulfstream, so there won't be the stress of travel. I'd rather not run him and Max against each other, but I may have to in the Florida Derby since that's an important Kentucky Derby prep race."

The Kentucky Derby!

Here at Gulfstream Park all everyone talked about was the Kentucky Derby, the "Run for the Roses," the first and biggest race in the Triple Crown on the first Saturday in May. Alex was obsessed with our legs, our eating habits, our training schedule, even our poop. The days sped by in a blur of training, sunshine, sand, sweat, baths and the sweet perfume of flowers and horse shampoo.

“Raj, I heard Annapurna’s coming,” Max said the day before the race. “You’re both undefeated. Remember, you’re the better horse.”

Thanks, buddy, I’m going to beat him so bad he’s going to cry for his mama.

“That’s my boy. Bring it home, baby,” Max nickered and tossed his head.

A newspaper page twisted and swooped in front of my stall, held aloft by a strengthening breeze whipping through the shed row.

“Storm’s coming. Make sure the barn doors are secure and everything is tied down,” Chris told one of the grooms as he pulled some hay bales deeper under the roof of the shed row and wrapped a blue plastic tarp over them. After supper, a steady rain began pecking at the metal roof, soon turning into a loud roar as the barn rocked and rattled, straining against the powerful wind gusts.

Something bad is going to happen. I can feel it.

I fretted and stall-walked the whole night, grinding my bedding into a circle. In the morning I was exhausted.

“You look washed out, like someone ‘got your goat.’” RB was concerned.

What do you mean?

“In the old days, if someone was betting against a horse and wanted to make sure he didn’t win, they’d steal his companion goat. The horse would fret all night and lose. Get some rest. You have to beat Annapurna today.”

Da da da dum diggety dum diggety dum, dum dum daa.

Even after the “Call to the Post,” I felt as if I was moving in a fog.

This is an important race and I'm the better horse. I need to focus!

BRRING! We're off.

My body was running but my mind wasn't with it. I ran in the middle of the pack, feeling OK, but not great. Going around the final turn, I saw a grey horse pushing me to the outside of the track.

It's that punk, Sanchez, from Hollywood Bill's stable. He's trying to take me wide to take me out of the race so that Annapurna can win!

Finally, I got mad and snapped out of my stupor. I was on the outside and had a much longer distance to make up, but I was furious and I was on fire. Fifth, now fourth. I passed another horse, moving closer to Annapurna in the lead.

"And here comes Raja. It's Raja, Raja moving up on the outside. Ladies and gentlemen, we have a horse race! Ann-a-PURNA in the lead. But here comes Raja, Raja gaining ground and moving up quickly," the announcer cried excitedly.

Two strides away, then one, head and head, then under the wire, together.

Did I win? It's too close to tell.

The loudspeaker boomed: "The results from the photo finish are final. The winner is number four, Annapurna, with the number-six horse, Raja, in second, followed by Sanchez. Your official winner for the Fountain of Youth Stakes is number four, Annapurna."

Second! Only winning counts, second is losing. I should have won, I'm the better horse.

"Good morning, Chris — you're 15 minutes late. We have a busy morning. Please make sure that Shaddy's mane is pulled and he's trimmed up and looking good." Alex looked up disapprovingly as Chris ambled into the barn with a coffee in one hand and a doughnut in the other. He had been at the barn for two hours already doing paperwork in the stable office.

"Shaddy's going to Maryland. He's been sold. The van is coming at noon."

"Sold! Why?" Chris responded, clearly surprised.

"He isn't racing up to the Sheikh's level. You know he wants his horses to win."

SOLD! Shaddy is sold!

An icy feeling of dread filled my stomach.

If Shaddy could be sold, any of us could be sold.

"Don't worry, the Sheikh sells a lot of his horses to that trainer. I've seen them in Saratoga. They always look well." RB seemed to read my mind. "He's a good horseman. He'll care for him as a horse, not just an investment."

I couldn't understand why Shaddy didn't care whether he won or not. He was content to run fifth or even sixth, even though he had the talent to beat most horses.

I'm going to miss my buddy.

Max, Sanchez, Annapurna and I were finally going to run in the same race — the Florida Derby, a Grade One Stakes, our final prep before the Kentucky Derby.

I can't wait.

Voices from the crowd drifted by us as we followed the outriders onto the track. The vivid pinks, yellows, greens, and blues of jockeys' silks seemed more intense against the darkening grey sky. Jigging to the start, I felt fitter than ever, ready to win.

"Go Raja! My money is on you."

"Bring it home, number three."

I knew that I could beat Annapurna, Sanchez, and every other horse in the race.

A knot of anticipation formed in my belly as I heard thunder in the distance. Big, burly gate helpers in blue shirts led the number one and two horses into the starting gate. Annapurna, in the fifth position and Max, number seven, would be loaded after me. I entered the gate and heard a click behind me as the door was secured. Willie patted my neck and whispered, "This is it, Raja. Let's give it our all."

I'll give it more. I want this win, BADLY.

As Annapurna was loaded into the gate, I heard another rumble of thunder and noticed that the sky was getting darker and the wind was picking up. As the number six horse went in the gate, I felt a raindrop. The gate helpers loaded Max, number seven. I heard another rumble — louder, closer.

Let's get on with it. Let's go!

Suddenly, a bolt of lightning split the sky! My heart started to pump wildly as a loud, sound filled my ears. I had to escape but I was stuck in the gate — I HAD to escape!

Nothing else mattered. Up I went, rearing, catching my leg. My head slammed against a metal pole. Everything went black.

April, Florida Equine Hospital, South Florida

"He has a high temperature. Keep him well hydrated and ice his feet to keep down the risk of laminitis."

"Will do. He's on IV fluids and his vitals are stable, Doctor."

"Good. I'll check in at the end of the day when I make final rounds. Thank you."

Voices drifted in and out of the fog. People moved around me, touching me, but mainly, I slept. I woke up, groggy, in a strange white stall with padded, rubber covered walls. Bandages covered my hind legs, and rubber tubes, suspended from the ceiling, went into my neck as a big strap under my belly supported me.

Where am I? Where are the other horses?

All I could see was an expanse of white. I heard more voices. Was that Chris?

"Hello, I'm Chris. I work for Alex MacLaren. How is Raja doing?"

"I'm Liza, the vet tech. We had to stitch him up for three hours. He was badly cut around his hind legs and he has a fever. He'll need a long recovery, but he'll be OK."

"Raja, you have a visitor," called Liza, waking me, after another long sleep.

I almost didn't recognize her. Hair tucked under a baseball cap, with torn jeans and an old t-shirt. Only the sweet scent of gardenias and peppermint gave her away.

"Be sure to give us warning when the Sheikh or the

Princess come," Liza told Princess Ayesha. "We'll need to beef up security and alert the media."

"Sure. Thanks for letting me come so early in the morning. I have to visit Raja before my job mucking out." Princess Ayesha winked, mouthing the words, "jail break." She came first thing every morning for a week. She sang to me and brushed me and even cleaned my stall.

"The paparazzi would have a field day with a picture of me shoveling manure," she laughed. "Raja, you're going to get better, I know it."

She hummed the tune to her favorite song and sang to me as I rubbed my head on her shoulder.

"Don't worry, about a thing, cause every little thing is gonna be alright."

But after a week, she had to leave to go to college.

"See how many fans you have, Raja?" Chris waded through the pile of flowers, carrots and cards from strangers outside my stall. "Everyone wants you to heal so you can come back and race Annapurna."

Yes, I thought bitterly, I should have won. I could have been a Kentucky Derby contender.

I realized with a heavy, final feeling, that there would be no Kentucky Derby. I was washed up and I was only three.

A crowd of photographers crowded into the aisle, snapping pictures and holding microphones toward a tall, familiar looking man wearing a suit and a yellow tie.

The Sheikh!

Another tall man shook his hand as they posed for a

picture in front of my stall with the crowd of photographers snapping away. As the people began to leave, the Sheikh leaned close to Alex, speaking quietly.

"Take him to the farm and give him time to heal. It's unfortunate that he had to be gelded and can't go to stud. That was a nasty injury, but I hope that we can bring him back to race again. No decisions until we see how he is after some time off."

May, Ocala, Florida

Bob, Michelle and Chris seemed excited as they chatted outside my stall. It was late in the afternoon on the first Saturday in May.

Kentucky Derby day!

Michelle spoke excitedly, "I wish I were there. What are the odds on Max? I can't believe he's one of the favorites. We all have to watch. Bob, bring out the TV. Out here in the aisle — where there is more room so we can all see. I'll make a hay-bale sofa for us all."

"Anything for you, Michelle." Bob rolled his eyes good naturedly.

"Where's that extension cord? I just saw it the other day. Ah, yes, in the wash stall — the vet used it to ultrasound Raja yesterday. I hope this piece of junk will actually work if we move it."

Bob brought the old television set out from the farm office into the aisle outside my stall where I was recovering. Pedro and some of the grooms gathered around and sat on the bales Michelle had set up while she perched on a stepladder, holding Piewacket and Muttley in her lap, absently caressing their ears.

"Oh my goodness, just LOOK at those hats. That's almost the best part. Sh! Shh! They're playing "My Old Kentucky Home." This moment always gives me goose bumps. Who's got a mint julep for me?"

Bob just shook his head, amused.

"They're going to the post. Look, there they are, there's Alex and Max."

As the horses went to the post, the crowd began to sing. Michelle sang along, "The sun shines bright on my old Kentucky home."

We watched as, one by one, they were loaded into the starting gate. It was strange to be watching rather than going into the gate myself, but I felt my heart beat a little faster anyway.

Come on Max, you can do it!

And they were off! Max ran fourth for most of the way with Annapurna in second. Rounding the final turn, Max moved up to third, then, in the home stretch, he burst ahead to reach Annapurna, who had taken over the lead. They dueled it out, head to head, going under the wire together. Pedro and the grooms went wild, while Piewacket and Muttley ran around in circles in a barking frenzy. After a few tense minutes, we heard that Annapurna had won in a photo finish.

Annapurna! Max almost won the Kentucky Derby! I'm faster than Max. I could have been a Derby winner.

"Max isn't going to the Preakness. Alex wants to save him for the Belmont Stakes — thinks he'll do better with the distance. Have to say I agree. Max is a stayer. He's got one lick and that's it. The longer distance should suit him,"

Bob told the vet a few days later when he came to check on me.

"Hey, Bob, you see the Preakness?" Pedro called as he walked into the shed row at the farm a few days later. "I didn't get back early enough from dropping off that broodmare. Dang. I heard it on the radio. I can't believe Annapurna won again. How'd he go? Good enough to win the Triple Crown? I can't believe that no one has won it since Affirmed, 30 years ago. Belmont Stakes gon' be exciting."

The day of the Belmont Stakes, Bob pulled the old television out of the office, banging it with his fist. We could see the rain pouring down hard. I knew that Max would do well. The tougher the footing, the tougher he got. What he lacked in a final kick of speed, he made up for in endurance and grit.

And they were off! Max sat in Annapurna's pocket just off his hind end and close to the two front runners for most of the race. When they started really running after the final turn, he dug deep, keeping up head to head with Annapurna. It was a long and muddy stretch run. Then he looked Annapurna in the eye, the way I used to do with him. Annapurna began to falter. Max dug deeper. By now, even Bob and Michelle were screaming. And he did! He beat Annapurna by two lengths, denying him a Triple Crown victory.

"That was the best race ever!" Michelle raved, red in the face, glowing from the excitement. She hugged and kissed

Bob, who turned to me and patted me on the neck.

"Raja, aren't you proud of Max? You'd have won the whole darn Triple Crown."

I AM so proud of Max, but... I could have won the Triple Crown, I know it!

I fretted all night, crushed that my chance for greatness was gone.

August, Ocala, Florida

"Let's do a little gate schooling," Bob instructed one day a couple months after the Preakness Stakes. By now, I was back in work, jogging and cantering on the track with Pedro in the steamy Florida mornings. We walked up to the starting gate, but when Pedro urged me in, all I could think of was the Florida Derby. Being trapped when I needed to escape, and the blackness.

I just can't go in.

Pedro and Bob worked patiently with me for two hours. Every day it was the same. They covered my eyes, even tried to lure me with grain, but I just couldn't go in.

November, Ocala, Florida

The energy around the farm seemed off. Bob stayed in his office watching the news on his television, more tense than I had ever seen him.

"The Sheikh and Princess Ayesha need to go home to their country because there's political unrest," Bob told Pedro glumly. "The Sheikh's keeping the farm for now but scaling down. He's asked me to start looking for buyers for some of the broodmares and yearlings. We'd love to have you stay on, but you'll have to work part time."

He looked over to my stall. "We have to figure out what to do with Raja. I hate to just turn him out for the rest of his life. What a waste — he's so talented."

Will I be sold? I want to race badly, but I just can't go into the gate. What future is there for a racehorse that can't go in the starting gate?

"Won't you let me try to make Raja into a jumper?" Michelle responded when Bob told her the news. "If he can't go to stud and won't go in the starting gate, what value is he to the Sheikh? He's still an incredible athlete. I'd give anything for him."

"Good idea, I'll ask the Sheikh. He may even give him to you. He'd get a kick out of it if Raja ends up at the Olympics. You might have to learn Arabic, move to the Middle East and change your nationality if he really is Olympic material," Bob joked.

"Hey, guess who's buying Max — Flash Jackson! He's sending him to stud."

Raja

Story of a Racehorse

—Part II—

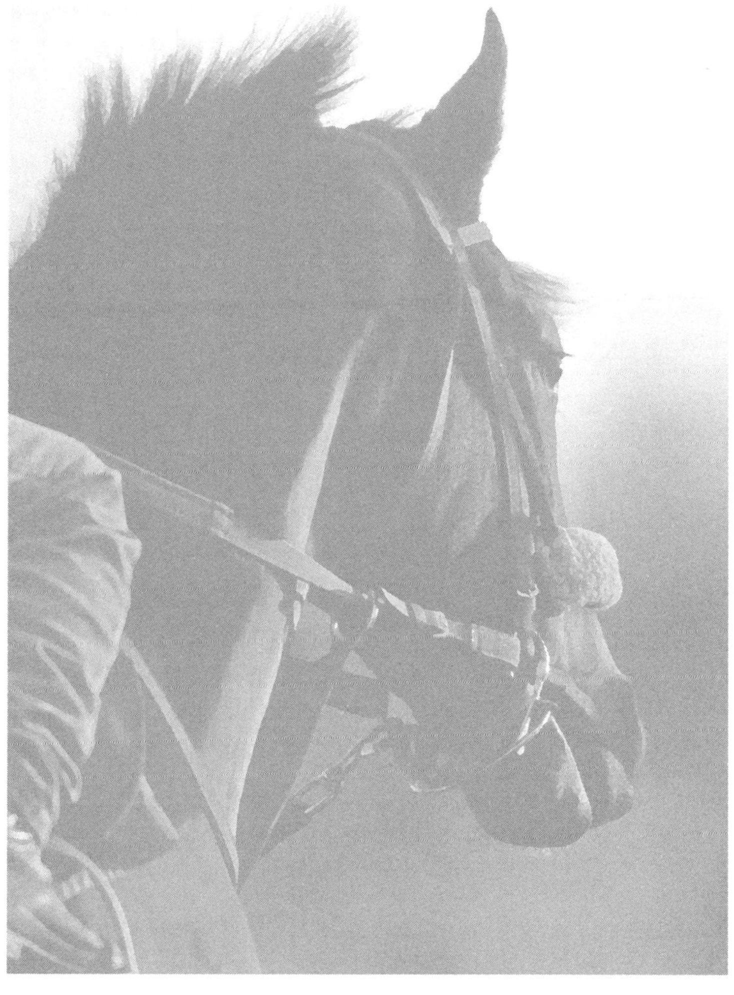

4

Jumpers

January, Ocala, Florida

"He sure is good lookin', ain't he?" drawled Speedy, the stable hand, towering over his broom, thin and lanky as a whip. Five Jack Russell terriers sat around him on the perfectly swept, dark green rubber-tiled center aisle of the long barn, watching in anticipation as he slowly put his hand into his pocket and tossed a handful of corn-smelling goodies to them. The dogs excitedly raced after them, gobbled them up, and looked up at him once more, tails wagging. A row of well-groomed horses looked over their stall doors curiously at me as Bob led me into the barn and handed me to Oakley, Michelle's tanned, fit-looking young assistant. Above the polished brass-and-wood stall fronts, a row of brightly colored shiny strips of cloth, mostly blue and red with gold lettering, fluttered in the breeze that was wafting through the barn.

"He sure is," Oakley replied, pushing his blond hair out of his eyes and wiping his hands on his breeches He lead me past a row of neatly arranged tack trunks, past a big wash stall lined with bottles of shampoo, brushes and a tidy stack of folded towels and past the curious horses, to a woodsy-smelling stall filled with shavings. Bob and Speedy followed, with the pack of terriers close on their heels. After he put me in the stall, Oakley stood with Speedy, admiring me.

"He's huge. And beautiful! Wow! What a powerful looking hind end. I'll bet he can jump. That's an interesting marking on his forehead. Like a scythe. I've never seen that before. Those are some impressive scars on his hind leg, too. It must have been some accident."

"It was a bad one. He's had time off. Now he's ready for a new job."

Bob cleared his throat as he gave me a lingering pat. "I guess I'd better get going. Good bye, Raja. I'm gonna miss you."

Sticking my head over the outside stall door and chewing on a mouthful of the alfalfa that I found in the corner, I watched the van drive away with a frenzied white-and-brown dust cloud of Jack Russell terriers chasing it away, barking furiously.

Speedy shook his head. "Dumb dawgs are gon' get smushed, I'm tellin' ya."

That night after supper, my new neighbor, Holzmann, a small, black, athletic-looking horse, struck up a conversation with me.

"We heard that one of the Sheikh's horses almost won the Kentucky Derby. Did you know him?" He seemed to know that I was a racehorse. I nodded.

Max. He was my best friend.

"Well, you won't ever go that fast again," exclaimed Holzmann, "but those big timed jump-offs can be pretty fun. It's nice to see another Thoroughbred in here. I was feeling a bit outnumbered by the Warmbloods. I started out racing myself, you know. I'm very well bred, but I never really liked racing all that much. I hated all of that jostling and bumping and mud in your face. It just seemed rough and it wasn't intellectually challenging. I'm fast, but I just didn't see the point." He paused to scratch his nose, rubbing it on the side of the stall door. "On the other hand, I love being a jumper. Michelle got me because she had one of my half-brothers. Turns out my family are all amazing jumpers. Lots of Thoroughbreds are, you know." He rubbed his nose again. "We horses figure out pretty quickly whether we want to race or not. No one can force us to run. If we're too slow or don't like to race, we usually find other careers like showing, eventing, foxhunting, trail riding, even polo."

I had no idea there were so many other careers.

What about the horses that can't have other careers, the lame ones?

Holzmann looked at me sadly. "You don't want to know. Usually they move farther and farther down the line, often getting neglected along the way. The lucky ones get adopted as pets, or companions for other horses or go to special retirement farms. The unlucky ones go to the auction and are sold to the killers for meat."

Meat? He can't possibly be right.

"And don't get me started on Warmbloods." He rolled his eyes. "They act so superior. Sport horses, they're called. I have to admit — they're good jumpers." Holzmann stopped to yawn, sighed a deep, rumbling sigh, and continued, "I've been to all of the big international shows: Aachen, Dublin, Hickstead, the World Championships and the Olympics. Michelle and I won the silver medal, second best in the world. I like the concentration and the precision of show jumping. It's a thinking-horse's sport. Now I'm retired and I teach Michelle's better students."

"Don't let him fool you," chimed in a grey almost white, pony in the next stall, "He just likes to show off for the crowd. Give him an audience and he'll go like a champ. At home, with no one watching, he acts like a two-year old. I've seen him buck off more than one of those kids he claims to be 'teaching.'"

"Speak for yourself, Shorty," Holzmann retorted. "You're vainer than everyone."

The pony laughed good-naturedly.

"I'm Farnley Prism. I take kids to big horse shows and win blue ribbons for them. Short stirrup, pony hunter, equitation, you name it. I'm famous. Everyone knows me. I teach kids about winning and I give them confidence. If they can halfway ride, they'll win with me. And if they can't ride, I'll take care of them and teach them. Michelle doesn't usually coach pony hunter riders, but her niece, Grace, is riding me now."

Prism giggled mischievously, as though she enjoyed stirring things up, then winked at me with her white eyelashes and big eyes. "Unlike Lord Holzmann, who finds it amusing to buck off anyone who gets on him, I was taught that the mark of a well-bred horse is kindness and patience. After all, I'm a Farnley pony, one of the best Welsh pony families."

Holzmann rolled his eyes again. "See what I have to put up with? Over there is L'Etoile du Nord — "Toile" for short. She's a Selle Français and used to be owned by someone on the French Olympic team. Michelle has some rich owners who want her to win the gold medal so they buy her nice horses. Toile doesn't say much, but she's a very good jumper and she adores Michelle."

The big chestnut mare looked over at me with a guarded look and nodded slightly. I felt a twinge of jealousy.

Minty-smelling, tingly, warm baths, every day.

Oh, how I love them!

Michelle tried on several of the strange big saddles to make sure that one fit my back perfectly. And the fussing! It made me feel like I was really special. At least 30 minutes a day grooming, boots on for turn-out to protect my legs, and the massage lady once a week to keep my muscles loose. I usually fell asleep when she came.

Speedy sang along with the radio as he flicked the two dandy brushes in a rhythmic motion across my back.

I relaxed, enjoying his singing and the scratchy sensation of the brushes and smelling the delicious salty corn chips he always carried. I reached around and stuck my nose in his pocket looking for them. Speedy just laughed. "You sly dawg. OK, here's a treat."

Thick saddle pad and saddle on. Hoof polish, mane brushed down with water, a wipe with a soft rub rag, a final squirt of fly spray and it was time to train.

"I told you that he'd be good. He's so smart and athletic," Michelle told Oakley as he watched her ride me. The springy sand underfoot, mixed with bits of rubber, made me want to show off my fancy walk and trot. Michelle rode me around the big arena, stopping to show me brightly colored wooden jumps and trot me over the row of poles on the ground. Next, she headed me to two rails crossed in an X. I jumped it.

Fun!

Another X, then a single rail, then two together, like a game. I gave a playful buck.

"Look how balanced he is. How he measures the jump as he approaches it, adjusts himself and uses his back. He's a natural jumper and has tons of scope. Can you please set that oxer up one more hole? Thank you."

Sitting lightly and perfectly balanced, she told me things with the way she sat and used her weight and reins and legs. Stretch my neck and back, bend and straighten my body, change my balance and speed, it was a new language. At first I didn't understand, but she kept asking and asking and when I did it right, she rewarded me with a big pat.

"Good boy! You're a smart one." She turned to Oakley. "The most important thing we can do is to give Raja a good foundation on the flat. Dressage is a jumper's secret weapon. He needs to be working in the right balance and tuned to our aids: seat, hands, legs, voice. Then his natural athleticism can take him where it will, maybe even the Olympics."

I wasn't sure what the Olympics were, but I knew they were big.

"I went to zee last Olympics with l'équipe du France," Toile told me one night when I asked her about them. "Eet ees un grande show. Only four 'orses from each country. Zee best in zee world."

"The Olympics are overrated if you ask me," Holzmann snorted, "but I'll admit that it feels good to know that you are the best in the world. I still get little girls at horse shows wanting to pat me. That's the best part, being a show-jumping legend."

"Oh, great Holzmann, you're a legend all right," Prism giggled. Holzmann pinned his ears and snapped at her, swishing his tail.

"Who's the one with the silver medal, Shorty?"

Prism could barely contain herself, she was laughing so hard. "You, Lord Holzmann, how can we ever forget?"

The best in the world. A gold medal! Those sounds perfect.

A group of Michelle's students sat in the shade of a big moss-covered live oak on the long wooden bench in the corner of the arena, watching her teach Oakley on me. Piewacket and Muttley lay contentedly at her feet.

"Now that he's warmed up, let's start with the red vertical rails to the brush box. Try it in five strides. As my old coach, Colonel Nicolai Belanov, one of the greatest horsemen of our era, used to say: your horse must come to the obstacle in the right direction, speed, balance and impulsion. So...your job is to get him to the fence in the right canter and stay out of his way. His job is to jump the jump. Wait...wait...good, nicely done. Sit quietly... good...again. Now do the in-and-out."

I bucked after the in-and-out.

"I think he's enjoying himself," Oakley laughed as Michelle taught him on me.

"Now, do it again. It has to be perfect. That's what Colonel Belanov drilled into me and I'm going to drill into you. He used to say, 'There are no shortcuts in horse training. It's like watching grass grow, but in the end you have a beautiful lawn.'" She paused to raise the jump a hole. "He was the real deal, a genius, an old school riding master at the Russian Imperial School in St. Petersburg, who came to this country during the war and coached the United States Equestrian Team for years. I was very lucky to be taught by him."

Oakley circled me around yet again, sitting up to adjust my balance as we headed toward the in-and-out in a light, springy yet powerful, canter.

"That was good. That's enough for today. Good boy, Raja. Give him a pat."

March, Ocala, Florida

"The official show time is nine o'clock."

A loudspeaker! We can't possibly be racing. I'm not in shape!

I started pawing the trailer floor impatiently and tossing my head.

"Relax," reassured Prism, along to keep me company for my first show. "It's really easy. All you do is go around an arena and jump. Try not to knock down the rails. You get jumping faults for that and for refusing." She continued, "The worst part is the warm-up area with all of the riders careening around and not looking where they are going. You're going to hate it."

Whoa! What are those horses doing?

I spooked across the arena as three horses came at me. Horses and ponies were everywhere, warming up and jumping in the three arenas, each filled with brightly painted jumps and decorated with flowers. A small dog held by someone driving a golf cart yapped at me as I stared at a horse with his mane tied up in little knots — braids, Prism called them — while a groom carrying a rub rag and fly spray trotted after him.

"More leg, eyes up," the instructors shouted to their students.

"Heads up, vertical," the riders called out to the other riders, heading to a jump.

We were on deck, then it was time to go.

An audience!

I tried harder, showing off my "floaty trot" and "springy canter," knowing they were all watching me. Michelle sat up taller, also basking in the audience attention.

Interesting — I didn't know she was such a showman.

We were alike, Michelle and I. Winning was everything. But winning in style in front of a crowd was best of all.

Let's go! Let's go!

"Easy, love," I felt Michelle's weight suddenly get heavier. "Whoa," she said without words, doing a strong half-halt as I galloped in the arena, on the muscle. Six fences, then across the arena diagonally. Two more, an in-and-out and, finally, four more jumps the other direction.

Easy peasy!

"Good. We've qualified for the jump off." Michelle told Grace, who had come to help out, "I think I'll let him roll on a bit, see how he likes it. I hope I have brakes! He's still pretty green. This might be interesting."

This time, Michelle let me go a little faster.

"A clear round for number 27, Raja, ridden by Michelle Taylor. Raja is our new leader!" The loudspeaker boomed.

We won!

"Well done, Raja." Michelle gave me a sweet, delicious sugar lump and patted my neck over and over as Grace helped her take off my tack, wash me and cool me out before we headed home. "I was only out for a school today, but you were going so well that I thought, 'Why not go for it?' You're a natural. I'm very pleased with you."

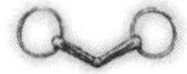

June, Chester County, Pennsylvania

"Those chicken coops in the fence line are for the hunt to jump in and out of the fields when they come through the farm," Prism nodded sagely as we grazed under the weeping willows at Michelle's summer base in Pennsylvania. I looked up at the endless line of post-and-rail fence, interrupted every once in a while by green mesh metal gates or the funny wooden triangles Prism was talking about. Michelle's barn stood shaded by thick-trunked old maple trees. Grassy paddocks and buttercup-filled yellow and green fields dotted with turnout sheds and more shade trees. A row of horse trailers lined one side of the large, jump-filled outdoor sand arena and a knot of plastic chairs huddled under a shade tree at the other end.

We had come here for the summer months to be closer to the big horse shows in the Northeast and it seemed like every day a new student arrived to work with Michelle. Mostly, I loved the big grass fields we lived in every night.

Alfalfa! And clover!

Pink-and-white nectar-filled clover flowers that lingered like sugar cubes on my tongue. Summer days rolled into one: schooling in the cool mornings and afternoons dozing under the weeping willows with Holzmann, my best friend. Telling stories; nibbling at each other; eating clover; standing head-to-tail swishing flies; eating more clover; and watching the tractors next door drive across the big fields, cutting and combing the grass into long rows and dropping neat square bales of hay onto the field.

"Ah, The 'summer girls' are out of school," Holzmann observed as more people and horses started arriving at the farm. "Oakley had better watch out. They all buzz around him like bees to flowers." He gestured toward a tall girl, Mary, who was heading toward Oakley.

"Oakley, can you help me with this figure eight noseband? Do you want to go swimming with us later?" she asked hopefully. Suntanned, with her long dark hair twisted into a braid that swung from side to side when she rode, Mary liked Oakley.

Oakley always smiled quietly and helped, but he never said much.

"Chip...chip...chip," a sparrow warned. Swallows swooped and soared over the endless timothy and corn fields as Oakley on me and Mary on Legato, her big brown Dutch Warmblood, hacked out one summer day after a lesson. I jigged a little. I was feeling fitter from going up and down the hills surrounding the farm. A red-tailed hawk above us glided effortlessly in an arc as a breeze rippled through the hay fields and rattled the tall stalks of corn beside us, now as high as my withers. Mary chatted the entire hack, oblivious to the fact that Oakley was more interested in riding me than listening to her.

Suddenly, we heard a loud CRASH!

Whoa! What's that?

Legato and I both stopped suddenly and stood frozen, hearts pounding. A second later, a six-point buck followed by a doe and fawn burst out in front of us through the corn, bumping into Legato's hind quarters. Surprised, Legato took off galloping across the field. Mary, who had been adjusting her stirrup and chatting, fell hard onto the sun-baked ground and lay still.

She's not moving.

"Oh my god!" Oakley whispered as he breathed in sharply. Almost as suddenly, he vaulted off. I noticed that his hands were trembling as he tried to wake her.

"I'd better not move her — it could be her back or neck. Mary, are you OK? Speak to me! Wake up!"

The hot sun beat down on us silently as a bot fly buzzed around my belly. I swished my tail and stamped. Legato, the buck and his family were long gone.

Mary still didn't move.

I thought of my mother and how still she had been in the field.

Mary! Wake up... Wake UP.

"Rats, where is my cell phone," Oakley cursed, fumbling in his pockets. Then he jumped back on me. "Raja, we need to get back to the barn to call an ambulance, quickly. Now you can show me your speed."

My heart started to spark as we galloped.

This was what I had missed.

I hadn't galloped fast since I was racing, over a year ago. We headed to a big post and rail, part of the fence line. Gallop, gallop. Balance, lock on, one, two, three, fly!

Wow, jumping at that speed really feels like flying.

Over another fence, then down a hill to the farm road at the edge of the field next to the barn. Now I was doing a two-minute lick with Oakley crouched over my neck urging me on. I ran, worried for Mary, but secretly happy to go, go, go!

"Mary's had a fall. She's unconscious. I need to call an ambulance." Oakley jumped off and handed the reins to Speedy, then leaned over, hands on his knees, trying to catch his breath.

"No problem." Speedy took me from him. "I'll send one of the girls to find Legato."

Within minutes we heard a loud whirring sound in the air above the barn.

"There's the helicopter. Those boys're quick," remarked Speedy, as he gently toweled me dry after my bath.

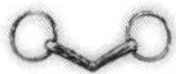

"I just talked to the doctor," Michelle told Oakley later that night as he crouched down, smearing the cool thick clay poultice below my knees, wrapping wet brown paper over the poultice and finishing with a stable bandage.

"She has a concussion and four broken ribs, but other than that, she's OK. She'll stay in the hospital tonight, but she's expected to make a full recovery. Her parents are with her."

Oakley finished the bandage and stood up. "Broken ribs are the worst. It hurts whenever you breathe. Poor Mary." He shook his head. "Thank goodness I was on Raja today. No other horse would have been able to go that fast and jump like that. He's the one that saved her life. The EMTs said that if the helicopter hadn't gotten there so quickly, she could have died. I think Raja liked it — going fast, I mean…Raja, you're the best," he said, giving me a hug, "you saved Mary's life."

Michelle patted my neck and pressed a sugar cube to my lips. "You knew her life was in danger, didn't you, boy." She turned to Oakley, "I swear this horse is a genius."

Oakley nodded in agreement, "Apart from being scared for Mary, that gallop was the most exciting thing I've ever done, even better than the jumpers at Wellington."

I agree. Galloping and jumping across country is almost as good as racing.

"I saw you blazing across the field," Prism grinned at me the next afternoon. "You looked like a timber horse coming up to the finish."

"What's a timber?" I started to say, but was drowned out by the terriers barking loudly as a big hay wagon lumbered into the yard, then the grinding, gravelly creak, creak, creak of the hay elevator bringing the bales up to the hayloft above us, and thump, thump, thump as they were unloaded and stacked.

Speedy wiped his dripping face with his shirt, joking with the farmer as they lifted the bales off the precariously stacked wagon and placed each one on the elevator.

"I'm glad we're gettin' this hay in today. They're callin' for some bad weather. The cows are all lyin' down. We gon' get some RAIN."

He shouted as the bales chugged their way toward the big hayloft door in the side of the barn, "Oakley, ready? You keepin' count? After this load, we're done."

"Ready" a voice replied from the dark opening.

Sinister clouds gathered on the horizon, slowly advancing, accompanied by low rumbles of thunder. The sticky, unbearably heavy air was so thick that you had to push your way through it, if you had the energy. I stood still, head next to the fan on my door, drenched in sweat, not wanting to move.

After the hay was unloaded, Speedy began afternoon chores. He turned up the radio and sang along as he swept the aisle, "Ahhh'm so in love with you." He paused outside my stall to turn on the hose and give me a casual pat. "The Reverend Al Green, ain't no one better."

He moved from stall to stall, topping off the water buckets and singing with a group of interested terriers following him, hoping for a corn chip, then racing toward him each time he casually dropped one.

"BLEEP, BLEEP," the radio interrupted Al Green, followed by a voice. "A severe weather warning for the tri-county region has been issued. A storm is moving east with hail, wind gusts up to 50 miles an hour and possible flash flooding. A severe weather warning is in effect."

"Sounds like we're in for a big one," he muttered, turning off the hose. Several horses heard him as he started measuring out the afternoon feed, and nickered and banged their buckets in anticipation. As another song came on the radio, a heavy rain started drumming an insistent rhythm on the barn roof. I began to paw the ground.

"What is it, Raja?" Speedy went out to close the outside top doors of all of the stalls and then came back to me, "Easy, boy."

CRASH! The thunder sounded as if it were tearing the sky apart.

"Why, Raja, I think you mus' be afraid of thunderstorms. I had an old dawg scared of thunder — he'd hide under the bed until the storm was over."

The big barn door slid open.

"We got soaked," laughed Michelle, leading Toile into the barn, followed by Oakley, both laughing and dripping and making squishy sounds as they walked in their sodden leather riding boots.

"I was on course and the skies opened up — couldn't see anything. It's a good thing Toile could. We won, but I couldn't tell you what the last three fences were."

"What's wrong?" She looked at Speedy, then me, her eyes flashing.

"Raja don' like thunderstorms," drawled Speedy. "I mean, he really don' like thunderstorms. If it's okay with you, I think I better stay here with him tonight." He sat down in his plastic lawn chair and started to sing in a low voice.

Speedy sang to me all night. As the sun's first rays made patterns on the barn aisle, I leaned over my stall door and nuzzled his wrinkled face. He reached up and patted my nose. "You're welcome, Raja, anytime. I know you'd do the same for me."

January, two years later, Ocala, Florida

"Zero jumping faults, zero time faults, a clean round for Raja."

My favorite words!

"Oakley, I can't believe how time has slipped by. Raja looks like a different horse than he did when I got him two years ago as a four-year-old. Look at his topline and the muscles in his hindquarters. He's SOLID. I think he really might be my Olympic horse. This year will tell me a lot about what he's capable of. I'm going to shoot for a Grand Prix this spring and if he's as good as I think he is, the Olympic selection committee will start to pay attention to us. I'm really looking forward to this year. I bet you are, too, aren't you, buddy." She scratched the tickly spot above my eyes and fed me a sugar cube.

At six, I was younger than most of the other horses and I progressed faster, jumping higher and more complicated courses. And, of course, I won for Michelle.

Just like with Pedro and with Willie, we were better together.

Back in Florida now, we trained every day and went to shows on the weekend. At almost every show, we drew an audience and someone offered to buy me.

"Sell my child prodigy? I don't think so. He's the smartest and most athletic horse I've ever sat on. He's not for sale."

"The Olympics are two years away and people are hunting around for talented horses that might be Olympic material. I think you're in that category." Prism told me one day. She always knew the latest about the horses, riders and trainers in the Hunter/Jumper world and loved the gossip traded around by other horses, the farrier, vet and Michelle's students.

The Olympics!

A Brazilian Olympic rider with a funny accent tried to buy me, and a loud, aggressive man with a nasty-smelling cigar, Tony DeVito, wanted me for his daughter.

"Name a price, any price," I heard him say, waving the cigar elaborately in the air, "I only buy the best."

But I wasn't for sale.

"Out of my way, dogs — dang…oww!" Michelle groaned.

"What happened? Are you OK?" Oakley called from down the aisle.

"No! I tripped on Muttley's tennis ball and twisted my ankle. Ow! I think I tweaked that metal plate they put in when I broke it last year." She hobbled over to a hay bale and sat down, grimacing.

"Can you please get me some ice and a bandage? I think there are some ice boots in the tack room fridge. You know, the ones we use on Toile after she jumps. And Speedy's lawn chair? Thanks. Look — It's already starting to swell up and turn purple. Dang! I'd better get an x-ray. It'll be a while before I can ride. I don't think I'll make the big Grand Prix in Wellington this weekend."

She sat for a few minutes, thinking, while Oakley filled up a large wheelbarrow with a bale of hay and pushed it down the aisle, delivering two flakes to each stall.

"Oakley, I think that Raja should take Toile's stall at Wellington and you should ride him in the $10,000 Junior Jumper Classic. It'll be a step up for both of you and you'll be riding against a lot of nice old Grand Prix horses, but I think that you can rise to the occasion."

March, Wellington, Florida

Wellington!

Palm trees waved, golf carts zoomed, little dogs yapped, and colorfully dressed spectators crowded into the stands surrounding the big arena where the showy jumps flashed their colors in the morning sun, waiting for the action to begin. Electricity and anticipation charged the air. It felt a little bit like Saratoga.

As Oakley sat on me, speaking with Michelle while we watched Mary and Legato's round, I smelled something bitter, burning. I looked up sharply. Tony DeVito was a few feet away, speaking loudly, jabbing his cigar in the air for emphasis. He caught my eye, stopped talking and stared hungrily at me with his small, hooded eyes, as if I was an object he wanted to possess. Looking away abruptly, I turned my hindquarters toward him, pinned my ears and kicked the ground in warning, swishing my tail.

"There are 70 horses in the class, including some very good older horses. Every fence is big and unforgiving. You'll need to be precise, especially to the water. If you have even the tip of a toe on the tape along the water, it's four faults."

I swished a fly off my belly with my tail and tried to listen to Michelle, but I was still thinking about Tony DeVito and feeling strangely violated.

"If you open his stride up too much, you won't have time to get him back. Right after the water, shorten your stride. Otherwise, you risk jumping flat and pulling a rail. Remember what we've been working on — rhythm, rhythm, rhythm."

She paused to adjust her crutches and leaned in closer, speaking quietly. "If you make the jump-off, the turn to the in-and-out is where it will be won or lost; whoever makes that tight turn inside the big blue oxer wins, but only if you are spot on. I don't think anyone else will try it. It's too easy to get wrong."

"That big oxer is tough," Mary told Oakley as she

exited the arena, red-faced and out of breath. "It rides shorter than it looks. Everyone's having problems there."

We trotted into the ring and circled, then headed off at an energetic canter to the first fence. Fence after fence I could feel my confidence building. As we headed toward the big oxer, I locked my eyes onto it and, with intense concentration, coiled my body, rocked back onto my hocks, and launched up and over.

Oakley patted me as I landed, keeping his hand on the reins, "Good boy, Raja."

I sped up, wanting to go, but Oakley shifted his weight, asking me to steady. "Whoa, boy, whoa," he whispered under his breath.

I slowed as we turned the corner to the water. Oakley squeezed his legs, asking me to lengthen my stride. We flew it. Then, whoa, whoa, shorten. At the vertical, he squeezed again. I jumped hard, springing off the ground. He steadied me, finishing the easy long way around the outside of the big oxer to the in-and-out.

"Zero jump faults, zero time faults. Clear round for number 20, Raja."

Only five other horses were clean. Now for the jump-off, where the fastest time would win. I pawed the ground and tossed my head. The wait was unbearable.

Let's go! What are we waiting for?

The first two horses had rails down — both went the long way around the oxer. The third horse went clear but slow, also going the long way around the oxer.

A big, white mare entered the arena.

"That's Luna, a former Grand Prix horse. She's very well bred. Her sire, Abdullah, won the team gold and individual silver medals at the Los Angeles Olympics. Sue is a good rider, too. Her father rode on the team with me. Watch how they do that line."

Luna and Sue put in a flawless round. After the vertical, Sue sat up and did a strong half-halt, cutting inside the big blue oxer, and headed to the last in-and-out in six graceful, powerful, perfect strides.

"A clear round for Luna with a time of 28 seconds," boomed the loudspeaker as a huge round of applause arose from the crowd.

We were next. I pawed the ground harder, losing patience, about to explode.

Let's go. It's time to GO!

Michelle leaned in on her crutches toward Oakley. "Even if you're clean and turn inside the oxer, you may not beat Luna's time."

"Why don't we do this the Thoroughbred way?" Oakley responded. "After all, he was a good racehorse, wasn't he? He has a huge stride. I think he can get to the last in-and-out in five strides instead of six."

"Are you sure that you'll be able to get him back for the in-and-out? It's short."

"Are you kidding? Dressage is a jumper's secret weapon," Oakley grinned.

Right from the starting buzzer, Oakley "kicked on" and rode faster. I heard him counting to me, trying to keep the rhythm. I concentrated, feeling like a cat, effortlessly stretching and shortening my strides, turning, balancing, and lightly jumping the fences. After the vertical, Oakley did a strong half-halt, turning inside the oxer.

"Let's go, Raja!" I felt his heels on my sides and sprang forward, opening my stride as if I was jumping out of the starting gate; one, two, three, four. He sat up again. I

shortened my stride, one more stride for five, and up and over the first fence in the in-and-out. One tight stride, then back on my hocks, and up and over and out.

"Ya!!, Raja!"

I galloped fast through the finish flags with my neck stretched out as a huge cheer arose from the crowd.

"A clear round and 27 seconds for Raja, our winner."

Oakley hugged me as we galloped triumphantly around the arena.

"Raja, you have so much power, it's like riding a rocket."

Winning is the best feeling ever.

"I knew you could do it!" Michelle greeted us at the gate, "very nicely ridden, Oakley. Raja, GOOD BOY!" She patted my neck.

"You're a very special horse. You have the talent and brain to be an international horse. I'm sure of it."

"Six hundred thousand," a loud voice interrupted, "that's my offer. It's a nice price for a junior horse. Cash. We can do the deal today."

Michelle recoiled at Tony DeVito's cigar in her face, but smiled politely. "Oh, thank you so much, but this horse isn't for sale." She patted me and smiled, once again connecting in her special, intimate way. "This horse will never be for sale. He's doing the Grand Prix next week."

The Grand Prix! I can't wait. I know I can win it. Finally, my chance!

April, Ocala, Florida

I was resting in my stall watching Oakley organize buckets, trunks, shavings and feed to take to the show.

The Grand Prix is this weekend! I can't wait!

"Oakley," Speedy rushed into the barn, limping slightly, with a worried expression plastered across his face. He didn't pay attention to the pack of terriers that followed.

Speedy never got worried — something is wrong.

"I just got a call from Bob. He's at the hospital with Michelle. She was in a car crash last night. A drunk driver hit her while she was stopped at a red light. The car was totaled. He says it's bad, really bad. Her neck is broken and she can't move her legs. It don' look like she'll ride again. Heck, she might not walk again. She's gon' stay there for a few weeks and then probably move to a rehab hospital." He shook his head dejectedly, "The Lord do test us, don' he?"

Michelle, poor Michelle! When will I see her again?

I missed her so much. The way she listened to me and spoke with movements instead of words, and the way she made me feel like I was the best horse in the world.

5

The "A" Circuit

June, Ocala, Florida

"Tally ho...a hunting we will go!" Prism said in a funny accent, then burst into a fit of giggles. "Has anyone seen a fox? I must chase it. Cheerio!"

She was trying to cheer us up and she was pretty funny, I have to admit. Now that the barn was closing, Prism and Holzmann were going to Pennsylvania to foxhunt with the kids of one of Michelle's owners. Prism was amused by the idea and spent a week speaking with an accent.

Despite her efforts to lighten it, a heavy air hung over the farm. We worried about Michelle and missed her terribly. We had heard Speedy tell Oakley that she was in a special hospital and needed to sell her horses and the farm to pay the bills.

I was now for sale. Tony DeVito came to the farm with his trainer, Karl Arnaquer, to try me for his daughter. Outraged, Prism stamped her hoof angrily.

"Did you know that he offered Michelle a million dollars for you? She can't afford to say no because of the bills. That Karl Arnaquer wants to show you. Mark my words, he'll figure out how to ride you while he pretends that you're there for the girl."

I'm SOLD. I can't believe it.

She pawed at the ground, distressed. "Karl's a fraud. All he's really good at is chatting up rich owners and buying expensive horses. Watch out for him, Raja, I mean it. I heard that he uses drugs so his horses can keep showing when they're lame. Be careful!"

As they walked into the horse van, Holzmann and Prism and I whinnied and whinnied for each other. I thought of my mother's words about getting attached.

Why did things have to change?

June, Fairfield County, Connecticut

"Higher, set it higher," Karl barked to Claire, his groom, as he drilled me every day over the big fences set up in his arena. And the pole — I hated the pole that Claire rapped my hind feet with in mid-air as I jumped.

They don't need that, I'm going to win. That's what I do.

If I had to think of a word to describe my time with Karl and Gabriella, it would be "lonely." Other horses and people were around, I wasn't alone, but I just didn't connect with anyone. Horses are social, you know, herd animals. We need to bond. I thought about the ways I had bonded with the people in my life: Pedro and I shared a love of speed; Willie and I loved to win; Michelle and I wanted to be the best in perfect style.

There's no one here — horses or people — that I want to bond with.

Even when we were at Karl's home barn, we didn't get turned-out much. I spent most of the time dozing in my dark stall. We moved around so much: Wellington in the winter, Connecticut in the summer, living more at horse shows than at the farm. The "A" Circuit, they called it: Devon, Upperville, Saugerties, Lake Placid, and, of course, the Hampton Classic. They were all the same. We lived in stabling tents, with no fields to stretch our legs or have a roll. Grooms tacked us up and groomed us and the kids came and rode and then handed us back to them. Sometimes I got the feeling that I was just another pretty accessory, like the shiny new cars the kids all had.

It was strange. Karl always wore his sunglasses, even in the barn. I never once saw his eyes. He wasn't big on patting and rewarding or trying to hear me. It was as if I were a car or tractor — just turn me on and go. He was always in a hurry, never a moment to take a deep breath and focus. Not like Michelle, who radiated calm and a relaxed awareness of everything I was feeling. All that rushing made me edgy. But he liked edgy, he thought it showed spirit.

"He's going good. Let's think about the Grand Prix at the Hampton Classic." He meant with him riding me, not Gabriella. Prism had been right. Karl was riding me more and more in competition. But I was a winner and I won for Karl, despite the severe bit he rode me in and the way he yanked me around roughly with his heavy hands rather than using his legs and weight subtly the way Michelle had.

"Whoa, baby, whoa." Gabriella clutched the reins, terrified, when she rode me. On course, she panicked, misjudging the fence distances and throwing me off balance, sometimes even falling off just from being loose when I jumped with a little extra spring.

I always felt on edge when her father, Tony, came around the barns. "Come on Gabby, stand up straight, smile! I spent two thousand dollars on that orthodontist — show off those teeth! I bought you a new Hermes saddle. Six thousand dollars — do you like it? It should make you win. After you lose some weight, we can measure you for a custom-tailored show coat — nothing but the best for my little girl."

Gabriella just hunched over more, looking miserable, as if she were trying to hide or blend into the ground. "Thanks Daddy, you didn't need to. I'll try harder."

The other girls teased her so badly that most days she hid in my stall and cried, hugging herself and biting her nails. Often she hugged me and cried into my mane.

How can people be so mean to one another?

I felt sorry for her and I remembered my mother's words about being kind, and tried to live up to them. Now I knew what Prism had meant when she said she gave kids confidence and taught them. I tried to give Gabriella confidence. And we did win, when she stayed on. But it wasn't always easy with all of that clutching and grabbing and yanking my mouth and dropping me in front of a fence and getting left behind.

With Gabriella, I never felt that shared joy from a perfect jump off or fast work — that feeling of being better together. But we won, despite the bad riding. Most of the horses doing the junior jumpers were older campaigners that had already reached the top of their career and were on their way down. I was younger, stronger, and sounder than all of them.

"See here, you behave," Claire shouted when I jigged and danced, full of pent up energy from no turn-out. She jerked a chain lead shank over the soft part of my nose.

What did I do? Why am I being punished?

"What's going on tonight? Heard about any parties?" Claire leaned forward and offered the farrier a cigarette, pulling her frizzy blonde hair with its dark roots out of its pony tail and shaking it loose as she leaned against the side of his truck while he trimmed my hooves.

"Don't tell me you smoke around the barns." He shook his head, disapprovingly.

"Rules are meant to be broken, don't you agree? I'll bet a big strong man like you has broken a rule or two." She winked, sidling closer as he backed up a step.

She broke quite a few rules, but Karl didn't seem to notice. Most days she didn't feed us until quite late in the morning and when Karl was away, she didn't come in the morning at all. When she showed up she wore sunglasses and moved slowly, complaining of a headache. Often, I drank all of my water after I was ridden and spent the night thirsty. She put hoof dressing on so I looked good, but she never picked out my hooves and I got a bad case of thrush, which made me sore.

August, Bridgehampton, New York

"Welcome to the Hampton Classic. The official show time is eight o'clock."

I heard the loudspeaker as two seagulls fought over some old french fries someone had spilled on the ground outside my stall. It was a hot day and a big fan at the end of the stabling tent was making a lot of noise but not helping much. Karl was writing a chart of ride times for his students in the tack stall next to me.

An efficient young woman with a handful of cut pieces of yarn looped through her belt stood on a grooming box braiding a veteran "A" circuit Medal Maclay horse, Wimbledon, who stood patiently in the stall on the other side of me. The woman paused to wipe the sweat off her forehead with a rub rag. Wimbledon took the opportunity to turn his half-braided neck with its row of 30 or so skinny little braids waiting to be pulled up and tied toward me for a chat.

"You're so lucky jumpers don't have to be braided like us "big eq" horses. It's so itchy — especially when it's hot like this. First time at the Hampton Classic for you, eh? The Classic is a special show. It's a big deal, especially the Grand Prix. Rich people and celebrities spend their summers near the beach close by and they come to watch. Half the people here are more interested in watching celebrities than horses!"

Gabriella and one of Karl's students, Wimbledon's rider, paused to watch the braider before walking into the tack stall. "Those braids look beautiful! Thanks! Hi, Karl — what time should I start getting ready? Wow, it's hot out there. This tent isn't much better. We're going to the beach tonight after the show. Oh my god, there are sooo many famous people here. Hey, Gabriella, did you see that Rod McCabe and his royal girlfriend are here? Isn't he your favorite movie star? Paparazzi are all over the place. Maybe you'll get your picture in People magazine if you win," she laughed.

The Hampton Classic did feel different. The fresh, salty sea air permeated everything, overpowering the usual horse show smells. The spectators dressed up more, too — like the people at Saratoga. Big white tents overflowing with food-laden tables surrounded the main arena. High-heeled ladies in colorful dresses and hats with wide, floppy brims chatted with men in crisp, navy blue jackets.

On Saturday, the day of the Grand Prix, I was surprised to see Flash Jackson towering over a group of people in one of the tents. I wondered where Max was.

I miss Max and Shaddy — will I ever see them again?

Later that day, Gabriella and I were walking back to the stabling area after our class and I smelled it...

Gardenias and peppermint!

I stopped suddenly and raised my head sharply, looking into the tent where the smell was coming from. A tall, thin woman with dark hair down to her waist was speaking to a deeply tanned man with dark hair and sunglasses — the curve of her back was familiar. She raised her graceful arm, lined with colorful bracelets, to tuck her hair behind her ear.

It's Princess Ayesha!

I stopped suddenly and pawed the ground impatiently. A high-pitched sound, halfway between a nicker and a whinny escaped from me as I tried to get her attention.

Look over here! Princess Ayesha, I'm here, 20 yards away!

"Come on Raja," Gabriella kicked me forward. "Omigod, there's Rod McCabe. He's even hotter in person than the movies." We stopped once more.

I squeal-nickered again, this time louder, pawing the ground excitedly.

I'm here! Look this way!

But Princess Ayesha still didn't look in my direction. Gabriella gave me a tap with her crop and I walked on, dejected. That night I thought about Princess Ayesha and Bob and Pedro and Chris and Willie and Michelle and Oakley and Speedy.

I'm so lonely. What are Max, Shaddy, Holzmann and Prism doing right now?

My mother's words came back, "Don't get attached to a person, or another horse, or your heart will break."

The next morning, I had a surprise.

"I rode this horse when he was with Michelle. Do you mind if I give him a carrot?"

Oakley!

It was sooo good to see him. He fed me a carrot as I nibbled his fingers and rubbed my head against him, drinking in his minty, liniment smell. Oh, how it reminded me of Michelle and all of my friends! He stopped by every day after that.

"The official show time is two o'clock. There is a hold on course," the loudspeaker boomed as Gabriella and I trotted around the warm up ring. I spooked as a loose flap on one of the sponsor tents billowed then snapped in the wind. Next to us, a woman wrestled to hold an exuberant fat pug at the end of a bright green leash while she carried a cardboard tray overflowing with french fries to a group of junior riders. I noticed dark clouds assembling in the distance. A hat flew off one of the ladies in the tent next to us, whirling and dancing across the arena with the lady in pursuit, struggling in the sand with her high heels.

Something bad is going to happen, I can feel it.

Suddenly, a jagged yellow arrow of lightning hit the stabling tent, followed by an earth shaking boom.

LIGHTNING!

My heart started to pound and a roaring sound filled my ears.

Get out! Now! Run!

I forgot about Gabriella and bolted across the

showgrounds and out onto the road, running as fast as I could. Past a blur of colors and sounds: cars and trucks honking; and big houses hidden by tall hedges. I ran for miles until I reached a big sandy area next to a huge expanse of water.

The sand is deep!

I kept running, laboring through the heavy going. Everywhere I turned, people were sitting on the sand on towels or packing up their picnics as they looked at the approaching storm clouds. I heard a scream as a woman snatched up her child after I jumped over their towel and plastic box. I swerved left, narrowly missing a big pile of sand shaped like a house and kept running, jumping right and left, dodging people and umbrellas. I heard voices shouting, "Catch him! Heads up! Watch out! Runaway horse!"

A man with his nose painted white blew into a whistle and jumped off a wooden stand, running straight at me waving his arms. "Stop! Stop right now!"

I cut left then right, passing him.

Ow!

As I passed him, I twisted my front leg in the deep sand and felt a shooting pain, like something popping.

Ow! That really hurts.

I limped to a stop, suddenly realizing that Gabriella was still on me. She slid off and collapsed onto the sand.

The man with the white nose and whistle came over to us. "Are you OK?" Gabriella just sobbed. "I've called the police and animal control. Would you like to use my cell phone?"

She nodded and sniffed, taking the phone from him and punching in a number. "Claire, hi, it's Gabriella. I'm

OK. Raja ran off with me for miles," she sobbed into the phone, sniffing louder. "We're at the beach and he's hurt. Can you come get us?"

As she and I waited and watched the seagulls circling above us and surfing on the waves and the sandpipers pecking at clumps of green and chasing each other across the sand, I realized that this was the longest time we had ever spent together.

The next morning, I couldn't put any weight on my leg. It really hurt. I stayed in the stall all day until Oakley came over to visit.

"Raja ran for miles and came home lame. Aren't you going to do anything?" Claire just shrugged.

"Well," said Oakley, trying to contain his anger, "would it be OK if I look at him?"

"Whatever," she replied, smacking her chewing gum and lowering her sunglasses slowly with one hand, the other hand on her hip.

"The leg is hot and swollen. It looks like he might have strained or even bowed his tendon. He needs a vet to look at it and may need months, or a year off for it to heal." He looked at her with disgust. "You should be ashamed."

For the rest of the show, Oakley grazed me every day and fed me carrots.

"Raja, you are the most incredible horse I know. These people don't deserve you. I wish I had the money to buy you," he whispered angrily.

Destiny, hah! What was my destiny now? Was I destined for despair, not glory? Maybe I had been wrong all along.

September, Fairfield County, Connecticut

Now that I was on stall rest back at Karl's farm, I didn't see much of Karl or Gabriella. I heard that they were going to Germany to buy a Warmblood.

I was miserable, in pain and lonely. And bored!

Karl was speaking on his cell phone, with an incredulous look on his face.

"What? A crook? Really? He did what? I knew he was a jerk, but a crook?No wonder my bills haven't been paid for months. I guess I'd better cancel my trip to Germany. Thanks, 'bye."

He turned to Claire, clenching his fist in anger. Get this: Tony DeVito has been stealing other people's money, telling them he was investing it and spending it on fancy houses, horses, and even that plane. Twenty-five million, he stole! He's going to jail."

Prism had been right. Tony DeVito was bad news.

The sunlight reflected sharply off Karl's sunglasses as he looked over in my direction, flipped his cell phone closed and tucked it into his back pocket.

"That horse is no use to me. He's just costing me money and taking up a stall that should be filled by a paying client. Get rid of him."

6
Change of Fortune
September, somewhere in Pennsylvania

A loud chorus of cicadas seemed to get louder and louder as I came off Karl's shiny horse van onto a cracked cement pad and looked around at the expanse of overgrown green brambles and vines that crowded an old paint-chipped bank barn. The ominous sound reminded me of the Florida night when my mother was killed. I felt the stone in my belly.

I don't like this place.

I stood for a moment, taking it in.

"He's kind of fragile looking, don't you think?" Tom sneered. He curled his lip while he lit a cigarette with the humid, late August afternoon hanging heavily around us. If my new owner, Mr. Smith, a friend of Karl Arnaquer's lawyer, noticed how rude his neighbor was, he didn't acknowledge it.

Tom shook his head in disgust. "Why would anyone want a thin-skinned Thoroughbred when they could have a real horse like my Belgians, Buddy and Pete?" He tilted his head and squinted, his narrow, icy blue eyes coldly appraising me. His grease-stained fingernails, muck-covered work boots and sour, unwashed smell contrasted starkly with Mr. Smith's polished leather shoes, crisp, clean button-down shirt with a wet patch beginning to show under his arms and clean smell I couldn't identify — a little bit like horse shampoo.

"It's a shame I only get out from the city on weekends, I'd love to spend more time at the farm getting to know Raja. Thanks, Tom, I appreciate your willingness to care for him along with your drafts, and I'm looking forward to enjoying the countryside with him when he's had time off to heal."

"Come on, now," Tom growled, roughly leading me toward a rusty gate that guarded a big weed-filled field.

On edge, I skittered sideways to avoid stepping on the purple thistles bursting out of the cracks in the cement. Tom snatched my lead shank and gave it a jerk, growling again, "See here, now."

I took a step forward and let him lead me across the cracked concrete barnyard littered with peeling red paint and broken glass, past a forest of thistles and burdocks camouflaging the neglected, but once glorious, old bank barn. A big wooden door, pockmarked with holes used by generations of raccoons and squirrels, hung precariously from broken hinges, barely hiding the cobwebbed interior crammed full of old, rusty farm equipment. He strode purposefully through a brown puddle as if to make a point, while Mr. Smith tiptoed behind, trying to avoid stepping in the mud.

Tom opened the gate, and led me into the field. He took off my halter and smacked my hindquarters with the lead shank.

"Yah!"

I stood for a moment, glancing at Mr. Smith, who looked kind, but unsure. He looked back at me, admiringly. "He's beautiful, you have to admit. A thing of beauty is a joy forever. Keats. Welcome, Raja," he smiled shyly.

Tom rolled his eyes as he took a drag of his cigarette, holding it with his thumb and forefinger before flicking it into a patch of thistles by the gate.

"Yeah, whatever," he grunted.

First, a good roll — it felt great. The last time I had been turned out in anything other than a small paddock was at Michelle's. Six months seemed a lifetime ago. After the roll, I trotted over to meet Buddy and Pete.

Whoa! They're giants! Are they really horses?

Long, blond manes spilled, disorganized, over their light brown coats, while their feathery fetlocks topped massive hooves. We sniffed noses for a few minutes, then they squealed, spun around and tried to kick me.

Great. They not just big; they're territorial.

"You pleasure horses don't know about real work," scoffed Buddy. "Pete and I have been the champion pulling-horse team at the state fair three years in a row. We can pull ten times the logs you could. Pete and I don't talk to sissy horses."

Torture. I'm being tortured.

Mosquitoes, deerflies, greenheads, ticks, and big bomber horseflies bit me; gnats and bot flies annoyed me; ground bees, hornets, wasps, and yellow jackets stung me. No fly masks or fly sheets, not even fly spray here.

"What's your problem, sissy horse?" Buddy and Pete taunted. They stood head-to-tail swishing flies off each other, not seeming to mind them with their thick, draft horse coats and long manes. Welts and bites covered my body; sharp, itchy pricks. When the flies were really bad, especially at dusk or after a big rain, I learned to roll in the mud. It helped a little, but not much. My hooves began to crack and my feet got so sore that I had to walk on my toes. After walking around with two shoes clinking from loose nails for weeks, my shoes fell off, one by one.

November, somewhere in Pennsylvania

Giant flocks of geese honked loudly overhead, sometimes landing in our field to rest for the night before heading on, hurriedly, in the morning. Tom's chainsaw whined and complained in a high-pitched growl as he sawed, split and stacked a pile of wood next to the barn. Squirrels rushed around anxiously getting ready.

Ready for what?

Winter! They're getting ready for winter.

I suddenly realized. The trees turned orange and brown and then surrendered their withered leaves to the cold wind that rushed impatiently across our big open field. Buddy and Pete, coats thick and fuzzy, huddled next to each other. My coat stayed fine and thin. I seemed to always be shivering. It was freezing.

One grey, woodsmoke-scented day, I was huddled next to a big oak tree trying to shelter from the bitter wind. Something white drifted in front of me and landed on my nose. Then another one twirled gracefully to the ground. A few more followed and soon there were hundreds of them. I looked up.

The sky is falling! Whoa! What's happening?

Cold, pieces of sky fell until they covered the ground. I stood still, watching and snorting, wondering what to do. Finally, I ran over to Pete and Buddy.

"Haven't you ever seen snow, you thin-skinned ninny?" Buddy scoffed cuttingly, rolling his eyes at Pete.

I wasn't just cold. I was hungry and I was thirsty, so thirsty. My mane and tail were heavy from the burdocks tangled in them. Just grazing was a huge effort for not much reward, pawing through four inches of snow for an hour for only a couple of withered blades of grass. At first, I loved rolling in the light, fluffy snow, but after a few days it got crusty and the snow packed into hard ice balls in my hooves, making it almost impossible to walk. I tiptoed for an hour down to the stream only to find it frozen solid. Walking back up the hill, I slipped, falling to my knees.

I don't want to get up. I just want to go to sleep.

But I got up and walked slowly, dejectedly, to the gate where I stood for hours, head down and hind end into the wind until Tom brought us a round bale of dusty hay and filled a tub with dirty water. Pinning their ears, Pete and Buddy bared their teeth and warned me to stay away from their hay and water.

I could feel myself growing thinner and weaker. Just walking across the snow-crusted field was a huge effort. I couldn't imagine running or racing. That was another life, a dream of a life. All I wanted was food, shelter from the cold wind, and a friend.

I really just want to curl up and go to sleep, forever.

My mother's words circled around in my head, mocking me, "You have greatness in you — it's your destiny. Always remember that."

Then I remembered her other words, "When life is hard, never, ever, give up."

OK, I decided. Like my old buddy Max, I could be tough and dig deep, too.

March, somewhere in Pennsylvania

Thousands of birds passed high overhead, endless rivers of black dots. The sun lingered longer, teasing us with moments of gentle, caressing warmth. The geese came back, this time heading north more leisurely, stopping for a few days to feast on the tender new shoots growing in the field across the road.

One golden day, with the sun lighting up the delicate light green buds on the trees, Mr. Smith brought out an old, stiff, cracked leather saddle — no saddle pad — and a nylon bridle with a big, heavy straight bit.

"Hello, Raja, are you ready to go for a ride? I think your leg must be better now." He took a while to put the tack on, as if he was trying to remember how it went. The leather felt stiff and one of the pieces was backward. The bit was too high in my mouth but he didn't notice. The saddle slipped with the loose girth, but Mr. Smith didn't seem to know that he needed to tighten it to keep the saddle secure.

"Whoa, buddy, steady. Stand." He led me to a fence, climbed up and awkwardly got on. I jigged a little.

"Whoa, Raja, steady."

Seeming nervous, he took a strong hold of the reins. I remembered my mother's words and tried to be kind, even though it was uncomfortable with him bouncing on my back and the loose saddle pinching my withers. We started down the dirt road lining my field.

It feels so good to get out of that field!

May, somewhere in Pennsylvania

"Oo-wah-hoo-oo-oo", echoed the mourning doves as the smells of rich, dark earth, newly mown grass and manure spreading on the fields tickled my nose on warm afternoons. The light green buds on the trees unfolded into leafy canopies as spring greened and deepened into summer. We made a jolly threesome: me, Mr. Smith, and Scrapple, his hyper springer spaniel, sniffing bushes and chasing squirrels as we went out into the golden afternoons with the crickets singing us along.

August, somewhere in Pennsylvania

Late one muggy, grey August afternoon a year after I had first come to live in his field, Mr. Smith and Scrapple came out ready to go for their ride. Fat, dark clouds rumbled in the distance as the heavy air warned of approaching bad weather.

"What do you think, Raja? Can we beat the storm?" Mr. Smith looked up at the late August sky. "I think we can make it in time. We'll just go for a short one today."

We went our normal route around the neighbors' corn field, across the stream, and into the big hay field. As we walked home through the woods, the sky grew darker and darker, almost black. Thunder belched in the distance as the wind swirled around us, picking up and dropping leaves. The trees started swaying and bowing, suddenly restless. I had a strange sense about the afternoon, as though the day was slightly off.

I spooked at a rotten log lying across the path in the woods and felt Mr. Smith slip a little to the side before recovering his balance.

I wish he would learn to do up the girth tighter!

Scrapple raced ahead of us after a rabbit, burning off nervous energy. A branch snapped and a crow's hoarse rasping caw above us seemed to ring out a warning: "Storm's coming! Danger! Danger! Go home!"

I had an odd sense of foreboding.

Something's going to happen. I can feel it in my bones.

I froze, rooted to the ground, head up and ears flicking back and forth.

"Come on, Raja, what are you seeing? Let's get home before the rain starts."

Mr. Smith gave me a nudge with his heels. I stopped again, looking around, then walked on. When we reached the corn field at the edge of the woods, Mr. Smith's farm came into view. I breathed a big sigh of relief and started to walk faster.

We're almost home.

At that exact moment, a long yellow streak scorched the sky, striking the big oak tree in the middle of my field. The tree splintered and crashed loudly to the ground.

LIGHTNING!

My heart began to pound and a roar filled my ears.

Run! Escape!

I shot off across the hay field. Running blindly, I forgot Mr. Smith. I forgot everything except the need to escape! I dodged to the left to avoid stepping in a groundhog hole and felt a movement on my back, then a heavy weight sliding to the side and dragging on the ground behind me. I ran faster through the thick wall of rain, my heart pumping wildly as if being chased by a demon. Another crack of lightning lit up the sky. The fence was directly in front of me. With barely enough time, I rocked back on my hocks and jumped. The weight hit the fence post, breaking it along with the saddle.

Free! I'm free. The weight is gone.

As I ran to the next field, I gradually regained my senses.

Where is Mr. Smith?

I turned and saw Scrapple in the distance next to a broken fence post, sniffing at a heap of clothes on the ground and I trotted back to see what he was doing.

It's Mr. Smith! He isn't moving.

Not knowing what to do, Scrapple and I waited next to Mr. Smith. It seemed like hours we stood in the rain with Scrapple persistently licking Mr. Smith's face, trying to wake him up.

Wake up. Wake UP!

As I was thinking about sheltering under the cherry trees to go to sleep, a flash of headlights, then Tom's voice came through the wet darkness.

"There you are. I've been lookin' all over." He stepped out of his old, red, dented pickup truck.

"Oh LORD! What have you done to him?!" He knelt down and put his hand on Mr. Smith's neck. "He's breathing, thank goodness. I wonder how long he's been lying here?" He wearily pulled out his cell phone. "Mike? It's Tom. Hey, you need to come right away. Got a man down. Fell off a horse and hit his head. He's unconscious. What's that? The Smith farm. You know, Mr. Smith, that city lawyer who bought the old Miller place? Yeah, that's it. I'll be here in the back field. Hurry, looks serious."

Soon the night was filled with loud wailing sounds and flashing lights and vehicles and busy-looking people fussing around Mr. Smith, putting him into a van. I stood watching and waiting, confused.

I couldn't remember what had happened.

The next day, Tom caught me, roughly throwing on a stiff rope halter and leading me out of the field, then tugging me up the ramp of his old, rusty stock trailer.

I don't like this. It's time to stand up for myself.

I reared and pinned my ears.

What makes you think I'll go anywhere with you?

He tugged harder, clipping the chain lead shank over my nose and yanking it sharply three times. "Come on, now," he growled, "get on the trailer. I don't have time for any guff. I'll use the winch if I have to, you stupid Thoroughbred."

I reared again, striking out with my foreleg. Then I felt a prick in my neck and saw Tom throw a plastic tube and needle onto the ground. Clipping my halter to a cable, he started to turn a handle on his truck and drag me into the trailer. It hurt if I pulled back. Besides, I was too sleepy to fight. I was so tired, I could barely stand. Who was that trying to get me in the trailer? Did I know him?

I got on the trailer, weaving unsteadily. A round sweaty face and cold narrow slits of eyes came closer, then faded away, out of focus, like a bad dream. I didn't know where we were going, but as the trailer lurched and banged down the road and I struggled to stay awake, I knew that this wasn't going to be good.

Strange visions flitted into my head: my mother; Princess Ayesha, smiling through her tears in the winner's circle; Bob, Pedro, Michelle, Oakley, Speedy.

Where are you? Take me home. Help me!

I despaired as the dreams floated in and out. I just wanted this dream to end.

But it wasn't a dream. This was real.

7

The Man in the Cowboy Hat

August, New Holland, Pennsylvania

"Tom, haven't seen you in a while. How're your pullin' horses doin'? See they won at the county fair again this year."

The man speaking looked like his belly was about to pop out of his overalls. He scratched a thick ear with a shock of hair bristling out of it, then threw a cigarette on the ground and stepped on it with a boot that looked and smelled like it had been dipped in cow muck.

"Lemme know if you need another horse — I got plenty to sell. What's that skinny nag?"

"Hey, how's it goin'? Can I bum one of those? Thanks." Tom accepted the cigarette and stopped to cup his hand and light it, squinting in the low afternoon sun. He ain't mine. Doin' my neighbor a favor. That sucker's lucky he weren't killed. Dang Thoroughbred ran off with him and drug him clear across a field into a fence post."

Nodding to the man, he continued leading me past a row of old, mud-splattered stock trailers and pickup trucks, then into a long building lined with horses chained to the wall. He clipped me to a metal ring in between a sad-looking Palomino pony and a Percheron with a big, ugly, painful-looking lump on his knee. The overwhelming stench of cow and pig manure mixed with diesel made me light-headed. Another scent I couldn't identify came to me. Then it struck me.

Fear — it was the smell of fear! This is a bad place.

Suddenly a loudspeaker crackled to life, its voice speaking rapidly.

"A registered Paint. Sound, safe for kids, do I hear eight hundred? Five hundred? Four hundred? Four hundred now bid, now four twenty five. Do I hear four-fifty? Four fifty, will you give me five. Four fifty...four fifty. Last chance. SOLD! For four hundred and fifty dollars to the man in the red shirt."

An older lady stopped next to me, shaking her head. "Look how skinny that poor horse is. Look at his hooves. It's criminal. I've never seen such bad rain rot and scratches. How sad."

The Percheron nudged me. "This is my second time through this auction. I was just here last week and my new owner decided that he couldn't handle me after I kicked him and broke his arm when he tried to harness me. He kept me tied in a small stall with a cement floor he never cleaned. You have to stand up for yourself — people can hurt you."

I nodded in agreement. The stone in my belly, that feeling of dread, was heavier than ever. I didn't like this place. Suddenly I felt my skin crawl.

What is it?

Sensing movement behind me, I glanced around sharply, drawing in a quick breath. I smelled something acrid, like the smell when Tom burned trash next to the barn. I looked up. A man wearing a cowboy hat with a jagged red scar down his left cheek and a patch over his left eye stared at me silently as he scribbled on a piece of paper. His single pale grey eye met mine, then moved slowly over my body. I shivered.

"You don't want that one buying you," my draft horse neighbor whispered. "He's a kill buyer. Everyone knows about him. You don't want to end up on his truck."

Holzmann had been right.

The kill buyer had looked me over!

I started to paw the cement floor anxiously, not caring that it made my sore hooves hurt more. I pulled back to test the chain. There was no way I could break it.

My neighbor nodded his head in sympathy. "They're unbreakable. I tried already. We all try. It's no use."

"Wait a second, Diana, I want to look at this one," a minty-smelling woman with kind brown eyes and a no-nonsense tilt to her chin stopped to feed me a carrot and gently pet me. Her experienced, calm hands surprised me. She blew softly on my nose in greeting.

"Hello, my sweet, you look like a nice horse that has seen better days."

I rumbled a sigh, rubbing my head on her shoulder as I chewed the sweet carrot.

Choose me; please choose me.

She ran her hand down my leg. Then she inspected my hind end. "Thick tendon. But it's hard and cold. Those scars on his hind end look old, too.

"Oh no, here we go again," smiled Diana. "How old?"

The minty-smelling woman looked at the tattoo on my upper lip. "He's seven. I wonder what his story is. He looks like a really nice horse. He's skinny and beat up, but in six months, I bet he'd be a picture. Look at his eyes, there's something really special about him. Can we afford another one?"

Diana shook her head, putting a hand on her friend's shoulder. "Beth, I wish we could save them all, but we don't have enough money. We only have funding to rescue that group of racehorses and keep them from the killers. We can't save every horse."

Beth looked me in the eye — this time for several seconds. "This one is special," she murmured. "Look at him, he seems so intelligent. This is a class horse fallen on hard times. Let me make a couple calls to see if I can raise more money."

She stopped twice as she walked away, turning to look at me. Each time, I looked straight back at her.

Pick me, I told her, pick me.

I desperately hoped she could hear.

Ten horses went into the auction ring and then it was my turn. A rawboned young man wearing a straw hat threw an ill-fitting, big saddle heavily over my back and roughly pulled a nylon bridle with a sharp straight bit over my head.

That's the strangest saddle I've ever seen. It's so big.

"You Thoroughbreds aren't used to those Western saddles, are you?" My new Percheron friend commented. "Me neither."

Before I knew it, the young man had vaulted on. With a sharp kick and a "yaw," he slapped the reins on my flanks, turned me down a narrow sand path and cantered down the people-lined channel, turning sharply, down and back several times. His roughness made me nervous.

I don't like this at all.

I watched the crowd, every detail in sharp definition. I felt as if I were in a bad dream that wouldn't end. A man with a checked shirt and a green-and-yellow baseball cap spoke quickly into a microphone.

"A Thoroughbred, seven years old, sound, in the prime of his life. He'll make someone a nice trail horse. Do I hear five hundred? four hundred? three hundred? Three hundred bid, now three hundred. Now three hundred, will you give me three fifty? Three fifty."

He nodded toward the stands. Following his gaze, I noticed a very large woman leaning over and speaking to an equally large man with a gigantic beard. They both looked at me. Then the woman raised the paper in her hand, nodding.

"Three fifty bid. Three fifty, will you give me three seventy five?"

Across from them, a tall, thin man with a pinched face, hooked nose and pained expression studied me and raised his hand. I didn't like him either.

Where is Beth? Where IS she?

I scanned the crowd, desperately searching for her kind eyes in the blur of faces. She must not have been able to get the money to buy me. My head sank down lower, the seedling of hope that had taken root when she walked by me was now trampled as thoroughly as if 20 horses had galloped over it. The stone in my stomach grew heavier, unbearable, as cold fear clutched and pulled at me.

This is really happening — it's not a dream.

Thud, thud, thud.

I could hear my heart beat, could feel my skin tingling, my breath coming shorter.

Keep it together. There must be a way out, a way to escape.

I looked around at the crowd. A small boy next to me wearing a red-and-white striped shirt dropped a green toy tractor he'd been playing with.

Whoa!

It startled me. I snorted, spooking across the path. Then I felt someone's eyes on me, predator-like, as if they were the hunter and I was the prey, exposed and trapped, unable to run away. I froze. Slowly, I raised my head. Then I saw him. The man in the cowboy hat looked at me with his one cold pale eye showing no emotion as it met mine.

"Three seventy five now bid, now three seventy five, will you give me three eighty? Three eighty, for a nice Thoroughbred trail horse"

The man with the cowboy hat raised his hand to bid.

"Three eighty. Now three eighty. Will you give me four hundred? Four hundred? It's a good deal, ladies and gentleman, four hundred? SOLD! To the lady."

Wait — what? What's happening? Am I SOLD?

I looked for the big lady, but she was no longer there. I sighed deeply and hung my head, dejected, as I stood outside the auction ring. I wasn't happy, but I guess it was better than being bought by the killers.

"Hey, skinny horse." I looked up quickly, confused. "I'm glad we were able to save you from the killers." Beth smiled as she patted my neck and fed me a carrot. "We'll do our best to find you a wonderful home."

Beth bought me?

I was so exhausted and relieved that I could barely walk to her trailer with her.

Thanks.

I nudged her shoulder as we walked.

Thanks for hearing me.

It was dusk by the time she loaded me onto the trailer with the three other Thoroughbreds she had bought, first offering me a bucket of water, which I drank thankfully. Bulging hay nets smelling of clover and goodness greeted me as she led me up the ramp and into a stall next to a grey horse. It was getting dark.

"Raja, is that you?" the grey horse nickered in recognition.

Who is that? Do I know you?

Things were getting weird. It still felt like a dream, but it was definitely real.

"It's me, Sanchez. Remember?"

Sanchez! What are you doing here? It's been over four years. I can't believe it.

"I can't believe it either. You don't really look like you did the last time I saw you. The Fountain of Youth Stakes, it was, I think."

Sanchez! You haven't changed a bit, still a skinny, parrot-mouthed, no-talent grey. It's good to see you, buddy.

I smiled warmly, feeling older than my seven years, happy that we were together and able to joke around. I could never have predicted that I would actually be glad to see that pain-in-the-neck horse, but it was truly wonderful to see him again. One of the other horses piped up, "Wow, I'm impressed. A couple of stakes horses! When did you run?"

"What a long, strange trip it's been," Sanchez sighed. "To be honest, I could use a rest. Let's see… I won nine races — second seven times and third eleven times. It all started great. You know what it's like, heady, glorious, exciting. I won a couple stakes races. Probably ran in ten stakes races in all: Saratoga, Keeneland, Gulfstream, Belmont. You name it, I probably ran there."

He gave me a worldly, been there, done that look.

"Then I started to get achy. I wasn't really lame. It just hurt more — my ankle, my hocks and my back. I wasn't winning as much. My owners weren't real horsemen. They just liked the attention from being in the winner's circle at the big races. I was still finishing in the money, but when I wasn't winning, they sold me. My new trainer wasn't as fancy as Hollywood Bill, but he was a kind, decent horseman who tried hard. My new owners wanted to make money — and I did, in the beginning. Up and down the East Coast. I bet I ran everywhere you could think of: Laurel, Pimlico, Philadelphia Park, Delaware Park, the Meadowlands, Colonial Downs, Charles Town. I was getting sore and burnt out, but I was still making money, just in cheaper races."

"I hear you on that," one of the other horses said, "me too, cheaper and cheaper races. Those bad races can be really bad, if you know what I mean. It's demoralizing when they run you against lesser horses when you're sore and know you can do better."

We all were silent for a few minutes, then Sanchez started again.

"They started running me for a tag in the claiming races and I was claimed by a trainer who cut corners — bad grain, dusty hay — and gave me shots that made me feel funny. He ran me hard all year with no break like the other trainers had given me. I started to have problems breathing — it was the bad hay. I was getting allergic. I had to pull up in a couple races because I couldn't breathe. After one of the jockeys beat me up when I really was trying, I stopped trying and stopped making money for my owner. So, here I am."

We stood silent, thinking about our racing days while we munched on the sweet clover in the hay nets. As the trailer rocked down the highway, I realized how deep-down tired I was and fell into a deep sleep.

August, Eastern Maryland

A tidy, freshly painted, green bank barn surrounded by paddocks, each with its own turn-out shed, greeted us as we pulled up the long gravel driveway lined with flower bushes. A teenage girl followed by a pack of mostly three-legged dogs came to help Beth and Diana unload.

"Hi Beth, I heard you rescued an extra horse. You can't resist, can you? I made room for him in the third quarantine paddock. He has fresh hay and water. What should I feed him? A bran mash, like usual? There'll be an open stall in the main barn next week after Seamus and Noco leave so he can move in then if he's ready. Their new owners are coming to pick them up on Monday. Does he have a nickname yet? How about 'Ol' skin-and-bones'? or, 'Slim'? Hey, I like that grey one — he's cute."

"Beth, I got the worst of it, but these feet are in terrible shape. It looks like he was last shod over a year ago and shoes stayed on until they fell off. I think we should wait until they grow out a bit before putting new ones on.

"The farrier wiped the sweat off his brow with his muscular forearm before taking off his leather shoeing chaps and putting his tools away in the rolling box now blocking the barn aisle.

I stretched my nose toward the shelf next to the cross ties where the brushes were kept. A bag of carrots lay just out of reach next to a dandy brush.

Just a little farther…

Beth laughed and took a carrot out of the bag, breaking it in pieces and placing it on her palm for me. "You think you are so clever, carrot thief. You're a smart one, Slim." She turned to the farrier. "Thanks — those feet were unbelievable. Poor thing, he's a bit of a project."

She paused to grab a broom and continued speaking while she swept the hoof trimmings into a little pile and shoveled them into a nearby muck bucket. "We'll fatten him up and get him back to looking like a real horse. I've been waiting to ride him until he's in better shape." She unclipped the cross ties and started to lead me back into my stall. "I have two more for you to do — are you ready for them? Some visitors are due in a few minutes, so I'll get one of the girls to hold them for you."

At that moment, a grey truck pulling a horse trailer crawled up the driveway and pulled to a halt. Two women got out and walked into the barn.

"Hello, you must be Ellen and Katie," Beth smiled, tying her long brown hair up in a ponytail and grabbing a rub rag hanging nearby on a stall door to wipe her hands. She walked over to them and shook their hands.

"Sanchez, the grey horse in the video I sent, is all tacked up and ready for you. He's a lovely mover. I think he'd make a fabulous dressage horse."

I leaned over my stall door, watching Beth ride him around in circles, helping him figure out how to stretch his neck and back and accept the contact with the bit.

I know dressage! Michelle taught me — take me.

They came back into the barn a few minutes later. "You're right. He's a very good mover. We'll take him. He seems willing and smart, too. You know, I have a weakness for Thoroughbreds. They try so hard and have such a good work ethic, such heart. How could you not love that?"

"There's nothing like a Thoroughbred," Beth agreed, her eyes smiling, "Diana and I run this rescue program because there are so many lovely young, sound horses that aren't working out at the track but can go on to have second careers."

She put Sanchez on the cross ties while Katie began to wrap his legs with thick shipping bandages and Ellen fed him carrots.

"I'll bet that you didn't know that a third of the horses entered at Rolex this year are ex-racehorses, off-the-track Thoroughbreds. I looked up their race records for fun. Most of them won about $300 when they raced. Several ex-racehorses are on the short list for representing the U.S. on the national equestrian team."

"Really?" Ellen answered. "I thought eventers were mostly Warmbloods."

Beth nodded in confirmation and smiled. "More and more people are realizing that Thoroughbreds make great event horses, even jumpers. Not as many as 20 years ago, but you have to admit they're great value. You can't buy a nice Warmblood for less than tens of thousands of dollars but you can adopt an ex-racehorse for very little and you might have a superstar on your hands. You'd be shocked at how many nice racehorses are abandoned or sent to slaughter when they don't work out for racing. But Thoroughbreds are so smart and wonderful for all kinds of horse sports. We've placed our rescues with trail riders, fox hunters, polo players, hunter/jumper riders, eventers, you name it."

"Where do you find them?"

"We go to the auction and the track and buy horses that don't want to race anymore and would probably otherwise be sold for horse meat. Then we find them new homes." She grinned happily, patting Sanchez.

"Did you know that 35,000 Thoroughbreds are foaled in North America each year? Most racehorses retire before age six. I've seen some dressage horses still competing at 20 or older." Beth gave Sanchez a pat. "Have fun with Sanchez and be sure to let me know how he comes along. Send pictures. I'll put them on our website. We love to keep track of our rescues' success."

"Will do. Thanks again — good bye."

"Bye."

I have to admit that I was more than a little jealous. I took a drink of the sweet water in the bucket in my cool, dark stall and munched on some clover hay, getting ready to settle into my mid-morning nap. It seemed only minutes later when I was awakened by the sound of barking. I looked out my outside stall door to see another car coming into the driveway accompanied by the pack of three-legged dogs. I drowsily looked out over my stall door. A tall, thin, angular man with a slight limp and the bowlegged gait of a lifetime rider ambled easily into the barn as Beth came out of her office to greet him.

"Good afternoon, Beth."

"Paddy Murphy, thanks so much for coming."

"You're welcome. Glad to be here. Sweet Jesus, it's hot. These are the days I wish I was back in Ireland. Ah, well, it is what it is. How many nags have you for me?" He twinkled, his lips unsuccessfully suppressing a smile.

"Paddy, I can't tell you how much we appreciate you donating your time to the center. You're the only reason these horses can chew properly. People underestimate the importance of a good horse dentist."

"Thank you Beth, we all do what we can. I owe my racing career, my livelihood and the most fun I've ever had to horses, the least I can do is to try to give back."

"I forgot. You were a jockey, weren't you? Steeplechase, right? Didn't you win the Grand National at Aintree?"

He's much too tall to be a jockey!

Paddy nodded, smiling slightly, a twinkle in his eye.

"Let's start with this skinny black horse, Slim. His teeth are in terrible shape. I don't know how he's able to chew anything. It looks as though someone just threw him out in a field and left him to fend for himself."

Diana came into the barn, grabbed a clean rub rag out of the pile of neatly folded towels and wiped her forehead. "Beth, do we have any cold sodas left in the barn fridge? The volunteers and I just unloaded 600 bales of hay. I think I'm going to pass out."

She dunked the towel into a bucket of water and held it to her face. "Oh, hi Paddy. Thanks for coming. It's too hot out there for unloading hay. Shall I hold that horse for you? Would you like a cold soda? Beth, want one?"

"That would be lovely. You two do great work here. It's a good service you're doing these horses and I'm honored to help you with your dentist work."

When Diana returned, Paddy took a long drink then turned his attention to me and started to file my back teeth with a big metal rasp. Beth began throwing flakes of hay into the stalls, speaking while Paddy worked.

"Normally, we try to find homes for them as soon as they come."

She came over to pat me on the nose and pick a burr out of my mane. "With this one, I want to wait until we get him a little fatter and in better health before I get on him and start advertising him. Excuse me. I've been trying to find the time to look up his race record."

She looked at my tattoo, wrote down the numbers and went into her office next to my stall. A few minutes later, we heard a scream.

"Diana! I was right!"

"Right about what?" Diana called to her.

"My skinny horse. Slim. Guess who he is? I can't believe it! I knew he was special. His name is Raja. He was bred and owned by the Sheikh. He broke his maiden at Saratoga and won the Champagne, a Grade One Stakes. He was a close second in the Fountain of Youth. He must have had an accident because he was headed for the Derby and then nothing. He hasn't raced since. I'll bet that's what the scars are from."

Paddy whistled long and low and stood back to take a look at me.

Diana looked sad. "I can't believe that a Derby prospect ended up headed for the slaughterhouse. That's insane. He was worth millions just a couple years ago. Now look at him — sold at auction for $400." She held her thumb and forefinger close together. "He was this close to being horse meat."

"That IS insane," Beth replied. "Normally I try to call the breeder when we take in a horse, but the Sheikh sold his farm a few years ago and I have no way of tracking him down."

"If you two hadn't bought this horse, he wouldn't be alive today." Paddy nodded solemnly, "It makes you angry, doesn't it? You can tell he's a class horse, a diamond in the rough. He looks intelligent, regal, even. It's hard to believe this horse was heading to the Derby judging by the shape he's in now. He looks like he's had more than his share of troubles, poor lad." Paddy shook his head. "Well, his teeth are better now. I filed down the hooks on his back molars. He should be able to chew and start to put on weight. I'll bet the two of you have the most aggressive de-worming program east of the Mississippi."

"You betcha. You should see what comes out of some of these guys."

Diana snorted, "Gross."

He gathered his tools and placed them in a bucket filled with water before giving me one more look. Then he fished a roll of something out of his pocket, unwrapped the paper and held out a round treat.

Mmm, a mint!

He smiled at Beth and Diana. "Polo mints, from England. My niece, Dee, lives in New York City and gets them for me. Horses love them. Now then, I'm ready for the next one."

It's finally time!

"Today we start Raja. I think he's healthy enough to ride. Poor thing, I wonder when he was ridden last. It's been almost four years since his last race. I doubt that anyone has sat on him since then."

Beth came out of the tack room carrying tack.

Racing tack: an exercise saddle, yoke and nylon bridle, it's been quite a while since I've worn that!

She carefully put the bridle and saddle on, adjusting the cheek piece so the fat snaffle bit sat evenly on the bars of my mouth.

"Diana, could you please get me another saddle pad

— one of those sheepskin ones? He has high withers. Oh, and another girth. This one is too small. It's a 52. I think I need a 54. Thanks."

She buckled the girth after making sure the saddle fit comfortably and led me out to the courtyard, walking me around a circle in the driveway several turns, gradually tightening the girth with each turn until it was snug.

She turned to one of the volunteers who had been watching and waiting. "Let's do this in the sand arena. Please keep him walking while Diana gives me a leg up. Watch out. Remember that horse we had that bolted whenever anyone tried to get on him? If he pulls away, just let go. Don't try to hold him. Got it? Horses bolt if they're scared. It's the flight instinct — like rabbits or deer. They're prey animals. I don't want you getting hurt, so keep your eyes open and move slowly to keep him relaxed. No sudden movements. And keep away from his hind end. Even if he kicks at a fly, he could get you instead. Good job. Thanks."

I was slightly amused by all the precaution as the volunteer led me down to the arena dotted with jumps and surrounded by shade trees with a group of plastic chairs and a stone mounting block in one corner.

"Walk another turn. OK, Diana, when you're ready."

Diana put her hand under Beth's bent leg then easily hefted her up and over. Gracefully transferring her weight from her hands on my withers, Beth slowly and lightly lowered herself onto my back, keeping her feet out of the stirrups, then gave me a pat.

"Good boy, Raja."

BRRRINNG! The phone in the barn rang.

"The vet was supposed to call. I'll be back in a sec."

Diana ran for the phone.

Beth slowly put her feet in the stirrups and took up the reins, keeping a couple fingers hooked around the yoke, the "sissy strap," the boys at the track used to call it. She took a deep breath and with a light brush of her leg against my side, urged me into a walk. I rounded my neck, walking straight and evenly, pushing from my hind legs.

Dressage, I'll show you dressage.

Her leg whispered against my side again — up into a light springy trot. She was soft and well balanced. Not as light as Michelle, but close. She took up more contact in the reins. I trotted effortlessly in perfect balance, accepting her contact, enjoying and understanding her signals, speaking her language. I felt her leg gently squeeze against my side more firmly and responded by leg yielding across the arena. That surprised her! Then she did a half-halt. I re-balanced. Next, a figure eight, bending in each direction. Finally, we did a canter–walk transition into a perfectly square halt. We turned at the end of the arena, picked up a trot and headed toward a cross rail. I took it perfectly, showing off my springy trot as we approached the fence. Then, into a light canter, and we headed to a bigger fence.

I'm enjoying this.

"Diana!" Beth shouted, her voice alive with excitement.

"Come quick, you have to see this. I feel like I'm like riding air…or butter...I'm not sure which. Raja has an education! He was schooled by someone, someone good, after he raced. He knows what he's doing and he's perfectly soft, light and balanced. Let's see what he does with a real fence."

Diana came out of the barn to watch as Beth headed me toward a big oxer.

"Are you sure you want to do that?" Diana called. Again, I cantered down to it in perfect balance and popped over it lightly, enjoying myself so much I gave a little lighthearted buck after the fence.

"Wow! That was beautiful. His knees were up to here." Diana held her hands to her face, cupping them.

"I know! Isn't he amazing? What a mystery. Not only was he a talented racehorse, he's had great classical training somewhere along the line. And boy, can he jump!" She patted me. "Good boy, Raja. You're a special one!"

By now, my mane was pulled evenly, my rain rot gone, and I was starting to build muscle. Beth and Diana fed me delicious feed and their field was full of the sweetest clover I had ever tasted. I felt stronger, fitter, more like my old self. Beth rode me every day. She was right. I was starting to feel like a "real horse."

"Diana, it's such a pleasure to ride a horse that's so well educated. I'd forgotten what it's like."

Diana steered the wheelbarrow around a stack of hay bales that one of the volunteers was throwing down from the hayloft.

"Have you decided what you're going to do? Are you going keep him? We should figure out how many stalls we have open before the fall racing season, it's always our busiest. You know how all those race trainers panic about keeping unprofitable horses for the winter."

Beth carried the saddle — the heavier jumping saddle

she rode me in now — into the tack room, returned with a rub rag, and started to rub the spot on my back where the saddle had been. It felt good. I reached around and nudged her, hoping for a carrot. She pulled one out of the plastic bag on the grooming shelf and gave it to me.

Yum!

"I've been wrestling with that for weeks. I'd love, love, love to keep him and get back into eventing. When I ride him, I feel like I could go and do an event tomorrow. Heck, I feel like I could go around Rolex again, but I can't afford to keep him. Eventing is so expensive. All of those entry fees and stabling and lessons add up. I need to spend my money rescuing horses, not competing. Besides, the stall he takes up for a year could be occupied by ten horses that might otherwise go to the killers in that time." She shook her head. "He's really, really special. He can't go to just anyone. He's so talented. I'd commit hari kari if someone got him and ruined him by pushing him too soon. He's been through a lot."

I want to stay!

She frowned in concentration for a while, then her eyes lit up as a smile jumped onto her face. "I think I know just the person!"

"Yuri, it's Beth, how are you?" I heard her speaking on the phone in her office next to my stall. "It's been a while. It seems like yesterday that we were hanging out at the team headquarters with your grandfather." She walked out of her office and started to throw hay into the stalls, continuing the conversation perfectly, holding the phone to her ear with one hand while she doled out flakes of hay with the other. "How's the NYPD mounted unit? Really? I'm good, the farm is great. Yeah, I know it," Beth laughed and smiled, "you too, it's been too long. Listen, I heard that your horse went lame and I'm calling to tell you I have a surprise for you. Come this weekend if you can. I'll pick you up from the train station. The express from New York gets in at six o'clock. You won't be sorry. Good. I'll see you then."

Diana appeared with the wheelbarrow and a pitchfork and started to pick out stalls as Beth swept the aisle.

"I might have found a home for Raja," Beth told her. "Yuri Belanov is an old friend and the most incredible horseman I know. He's coming down this weekend to try him. Do you want to come for dinner?"

"He's a pretty amazing guy — a genuine horse whisperer with a classical education and cowboy attitude. We both had summer jobs when we were 16 working at the U.S. Equestrian Team stables in Gladstone for his grandfather, Colonel Nicolai Belanov, who was coaching the Team."

She blushed a little, a small smile stealing across her face. "I'll admit it, he was my first boyfriend. I think you'll like him. It's hard not to."

Beth began to measure out the afternoon feed, accompanied by a series of low nickers and high pitched whinnies. The horse in the stall next to me banged his stall door impatiently with his front leg. "You'd think we starved them. Anyway, Yuri grew up surrounded by the world's best riders and horses when his grandfather was preparing them for the Olympics and World Championships. Pretty amazing education, eh?" She paused to dump a small bucket of feed into my feed bin.

"Does he train or compete? How come I've never heard of him? I've heard of his father, of course. Everyone involved with horses during the last forty years has."

Beth shook her head. "He could. Easily. He rejected the elite equestrian world to make his own path. He never talks about his grandfather. Don't ask me why. It must be complicated being the grandson of a legend. His father died when he was young, so Nicolai raised him — when he wasn't off coaching at international competitions. Truly, I think the horses raised him. I've never seen anyone communicate with horses the way Yuri does."

"So what does he do? Why does he need a horse?"

"Believe it or not, he's a mounted police officer in New York City!" Beth laughed as she started to unwind the hose to top off our water buckets. "Yuri and Raja have got to meet. Oh my god, I'm late. I'd better go and pick him up at the train station. Can you finish watering for me? Thanks! Dinner tonight?"

"Ah, Beth, you're a miracle worker. This isn't a horse. This is a dream, a poem — out of a legend."

The big, deep, accented voice perfectly matched Yuri's confident, erect, yet loose-limbed bearing and blazing green eyes. He wasn't someone who faded into the scenery. Your eyes couldn't help but be drawn to him — in a good way, I mean. He reminded me of a racehorse: fit, athletic, focused and ready to go.

The minute he stepped onto the farm, we all felt the energy change. Colors deepened, heartbeats quickened, things got more exciting. His hearty laugh and quick smile charmed every person and animal in his path, regardless of age, breed or gender. The teenage volunteers watched him in awe. Even the farm's collection of three-legged dogs followed him around, smitten.

He and Beth and Diana were outside the front of the bank barn where one of the volunteers had led me out to show me.

"Look, Raja has the Mark of the Chieftain! See the whorls on his forehead?"

"What on earth are you talking about?" Beth replied.

"You've never heard of the Mark of the Chieftain? It's an old Bedouin legend. They can read a horse's character and destiny from the whorls on a horse's coat. See the way his hair grows on his forehead? These three interconnected whorls?" He traced my forehead with his finger. "Cossacks read whorls too. This particular mark is extremely rare. The Godolphin Arabian had it and his fastest descendants have it. I'll bet you a hundred dollars that Raja comes from his line, just like Northern Dancer and Secretariat."

Yuri placed his hands on me and stroked me all over in a gentle rhythm. He stopped to push his unruly bangs out of his eyes. "I almost forgot." Winking, he clicked his heels together and bowed from his waist, then reached into his bag and drew out a package with a flourish. "I brought you some bagels and bialys from my favorite Russian bakery. I remember how much you love them."

For the first two days, Yuri just sat in my stall and watched me patiently, quietly learning me, and letting me learn him. First, he blew on my nose, letting me sniff him and his unique and complex smell: saddle soap, leather, cedar and pine. I loved his smell. He smelled like deep, endless woods. Gently touching me all over with both hands before grooming me, a brush in each hand, like Speedy used to, he hummed and sang to me in a low voice. I couldn't understand the words, but I understood the tone and relaxed as if I was being worked on by Michelle's massage lady.

"Russian lullabies, like your grandfather." A wistful smile stole over Beth's face as she walked by us, "The apple hasn't fallen far from the tree."

"Trust me,"Yuri seemed to say with his voice and his stance and his hands, wordless, yet more clearly than if he had spoken, as if he were saying, "I respect you and want you to respect me. We're partners, after all."

From the first moment he stepped in the stirrup and swung his leg over my back, settling lightly into the saddle, we were in perfect sync, as if reading each other's mind. Light, balanced, clear, and precise, like Michelle, with a daredevil streak like Pedro, he made me think. He challenged me. We were better together. I had to pay attention, because I never knew when he was going to suddenly turn and head for a big fence — just to dare me to keep up with him.

Dare away. I'm with you, no matter what you throw at me. I like this game.

I matched him step for step. Walk…to canter. Lengthen, then shorten, the strides…into a gallop. Suddenly Yuri leaned over, one leg over the saddle and fell off, or that's what I thought at the time. Then he was back up, laughing triumphantly and sitting up gracefully, rein contact light, holding me into a motionless halt with his stomach, legs pressed against my sides.

"I can't believe you are still doing all of that trick riding," Beth watched us from her plastic chair by the side of the arena, "you just can't resist showing off, can you?" She shook her head, smiling. "By the way, I checked Raja's bloodlines. You're right. His great-great-grandfather is Northern Dancer. You win the bet."

Yuri urged me up into a hand gallop, heading directly for Beth and the volunteers, then halted me, less than ten feet in front of them. Reins in one hand, he dropped his feet out of the stirrups, lifted them onto the saddle and stood up in a single, graceful movement. Before I knew what was happening, he dropped the reins and sprang off, feet over his head, flipping over backwards and landing lightly on the ground.

"Ladies," Yuri bowed deeply, "you've found Raja a new home. I'll call the police re-mount school to book a training session for the two of us. We'll go next week. I'd like to have him ready for patrol in six weeks or so. Also, I know some say it's bad luck to change a name, but Raja needs a Russian name. Henceforth, he will be Sasha." Break out the caviar and balalaikas. Tonight, we celebrate!"

8

Ten-Foot Cop

October, Manhattan, New York

"So this is our newest mount, eh?" Troop Captain Dennis Rourke patted my neck as I took in the tidy, high-ceilinged, light-filled stable, looked down the two aisles of 20 or so horses, and tried to identify the strange new smells: saddle soap and brass polish mingling with diesel from the boats splashing on the river next to the stables and trucks rumbling along the road on the other side.

"He's a looker, isn't he? What a beauty. He's going to bring this troop up a notch or two. Welcome to the Big Apple and the New York Police Department, Sasha."

Fresh, clean shavings and full hay net waited for me in a large corner stall. After drinking deeply from the slightly metallic-tasting water bucket, I rolled.

Ah! fresh shavings, my favorite.

As I stood up and gave my body a good shaking, a dark brown, dished face with wide eyes and a shaggy forelock popped up and stared at me through the stall dividers.

"Hullo there, pleased ta meet'cha, I'm UVM Oliver. I'm a Morgan and a Veh'montah. I've bin with the patrol for seven years. Welcome to Manhattan, the strangest island, strangest people you'll evah see. By jeezum, when I fust came to the city, I couldn't believe all of the cahrs, and people and noyse. Couldn't sleep fuh weeks. No green grass, ya know. All I knew was mountains and cows. It's a shock, I tell ya — horns, engines, sirens, all day and all night." He took a sip from his water bucket. "Ayuh, not too many of you high-strung Thoroughbred fellas on the force, but the ones that make it are good ones."

He paused to catch his breath, then continued, "Here's what ya need to know: every horse here is a professional, even the ones that don't look like much. In fact, they're the best ones. Whether you're a Thoroughbred, a Morgan, a Quarter Horse, or a cross, your job is protectin' people. They say one mounted officer is worth ten on the ground. 'Ten-foot cops,' they call us."

He stopped to lick the block of salt on the wall of his stall. "Ayuh, since Officer Yuri is your partner, you'll get Times Square and Central Pahrk. I had Central Pahrk for yeah's with my partner, Officer Mike. Loved it."

For two weeks, we walked up and down the bike path outside the police stables down to the big boats docked on the river and back to "acclimatize," as Yuri put it. As if anyone could get used to the traffic, especially the speedy yellow taxis blaring their horns and weaving in and out of the flow of cars, drivers shaking fists and cursing. This was a strange place, with sidewalks that rumbled and steamed, strange people wearing strange clothes and speaking strange languages, and more smells than I could possibly remember. Lights kept the city as bright as day, even in the middle of the night.

A north wind rushed over the river on our first day of real patrol, blowing bits of paper down the street and flapping awnings on the storefronts we passed. Every second I looked at something new, sometimes stopping and snorting, not sure what was safe and what was dangerous. Yuri patiently waited for me to take a good look and spoke to me the whole time.

"See, Sasha, we're on 44th Street and ahead there is the Met Life Building. Wait until you see Times Square. It's really something."

We weaved our way past vans and trucks and honking taxis, past a river of people marching determinedly down the sidewalk, cell phones held to their faces, past carts of food with delicious, complex and mysterious smells.

Whoa! What's that?

I stopped, snorted, and did a double take at the big, smelly, blue plastic box. Yuri eased me closer.

"It's a garbage can." He laughed heartily. "Why is it that every horse in the universe spooks at garbage cans?"

Thank goodness he kept talking to me in a soothing voice and stroking me, because when we turned the corner, I froze. Thousands of colored flashing lights and moving pictures covered the buildings. Strange people smells assaulted my nose. The sounds were worse — so loud, so jangly. Street vendors calling out, music, sirens and car horns. I felt it physically, as if I were being hit. My heart raced as I sharply looked around, left, right, straight ahead. People, so many people, all moving in different directions. It hurt my head to look at it all. I lifted my head up sharply, snorted, and started pawing the pavement and tossing my head, not knowing what to look at first.

RUN!

Yuri, reading my mind, relaxed his body and took a deep breath, all the way to his belly. Then, deliberate and focused, he gently put both his hands flat on my neck, bringing me back to him, the energy from his hands tingling where he touched me.

"Shhh, Sasha," he whispered, cajoling, completely

focused on me. It was just the two of us, alone, with a blur of colors and sounds outside our bubble.

"Trust me," I felt him say.

I took a deep breath and walked forward calmly, held by Yuri's concentration.

Together — better together.

"Will he eat a roasted chestnut?" A man next to us with an interesting smelling food cart offered me a small, round treat. I sniffed cautiously first.

Yum! Delicious — nutty and sweet.

Central Park! Oliver was right. When I saw it, I breathed a huge sigh of relief, not realizing how anxious all the cement and taxi horns and people and energy of the city was making me until I got into the cool, green, leafy park. How could anyone not love Central Park and the grassy fields, trees, boulders, children, bicycles, runners, squirrels and pigeons? Especially the tough city pigeons, swaggering down the pavement like pit bull terriers.

"Ah Yuri and Sasha, the most handsome pair on Park Avenue, good morning!" Yuri's buddy, Maurice, the doorman at the Plaza Hotel in his crisp, spotless uniform greeted us each day with an elaborate white gloved bow and an almond pastry for me from the Plaza's French pastry chef. Then we made our rounds, visiting our friends: Gregor, the carriage driver in his straw hat and wool vest, and Periwinkle, his large red feather-plumed Clydesdale mare, waiting in line for tourists in the row of other carriages; Aunt Betty, the bag lady who fed the pigeons while she scolded herself angrily every morning; Anna, the nanny, pushing her charges in their stroller and gabbing with the other nannies; and Lizzy, the dog walker, with a tangle of six dogs straining and sniffing and peeing on the roots of the big oak trees lining the park, deliriously happy to be outside.

Early mornings when the mist rose from the duck pond and runners and bikers streaking through the park were our only company, we practiced dressage in the Sheep Meadow, a field in the middle of the Park. Yuri communicated subtly and effortlessly; with a slight shift of his weight, a nudge of his leg. I understood him perfectly. Circles, serpentines, figure eights and transitions, exactly like the flatwork I had done with Michelle. Stretching, bending, extending. My favorite was doing a powerful yet contained trot, then bursting into a lengthened stride, feet flashing and body stretching.

Oh, how good it feels to be strong, flexible, and "in training" again!

"Hi, that's the most beautiful horse I've ever seen."

Disheveled chestnut braids framed the earnest, chip-toothed grin of a wiry young girl. She looked as though she might take off running at any moment if startled. Her skinny frame hid behind baggy jeans, ripped at the knees, dirty sneakers with laces untied and a big wool sweater with holes at the elbows. Big hazel eyes found my gaze as she stepped off her bicycle, gently laid it on the ground and walked toward me. She spoke quickly, as if she was afraid that she couldn't get it all out.

"I'm Dee. I grew up on a horse farm in Ireland, so I

know a good horse when I see one. He's a good one," she pronounced with authority, then kept going without stopping to take a breath.

"I'm 14. I hate New York. I had to leave Ireland because my mother died and I live with my dad but I never see him because he works too hard and travels. Did I tell you that your horse is beautiful? May I give him a peppermint?"

Yuri didn't have a chance to respond. She took a peppermint out of her pocket, crinkled the wrapper and held out the offering to me, first letting me sniff her hand. She took a breath and started speaking again.

"My uncle, Paddy Murphy, was a champion steeplechase jockey in Ireland and he won the Aintree Grand National, the most famous steeplechase race in the world."

Paddy Murphy?

"He taught me to crinkle the wrapper so that the horse can hear and know that they're going to get a treat. He's a horse dentist now, in Pennsylvania. I spend my school holidays at his farm and ride his horses."

Yuri laughed his deep laugh. "It's very nice to meet someone else who appreciates a good horse. My name is Yuri and this is Sasha."

Dee finally took a breath, flashing a grin at Yuri. Then she hugged me tightly with abandon, breathing in deeply. "Oh, I love horse smell. I miss it so much."

I nudged her. She was really cute and open, more like a horse than a person who hides their emotions behind words. What you saw was what you got.

I choose her, my new young friend, Dee.

Dee rode her bike to see us every morning after that, watching our dressage moves intently and asking Yuri questions afterward.

"Was that a shoulder-in? Why the leg yield before you cantered?"

"If he steps underneath with his inside hind leg to my outside rein, his transition from the walk to the canter will be in a better balance. See that? That's the canter I'm looking for."

I think he enjoyed having a student. I loved having an audience again.

"My grandfather was a horse trainer," Yuri told Dee. "He used to say, 'There are no shortcuts in horse training. It can be like watching the grass grow, but at the end, you have a beautiful lawn.'"

He sounds like Michelle.

Yuri reminded me of Michelle. The way he spoke with movements and knew when to ask and when to give — as though he knew my mind, sure and calm, listening to me. And his way of patiently asking and asking again when I was trying to learn a move, then rewarding me when I got it. He made me feel like I could do anything.

Some mornings, we added Cossack trick riding to our sessions. Yuri would stand up on me or practice picking up a glove or paper cup from the ground at a gallop. One of his favorite tricks was the "under-the-neck switch."

As we galloped across the Sheep Meadow, Yuri climbed out of the saddle, hugged my neck, then swung under my neck and over to the other side. I helped him, lowering my head as he hooked his leg over my withers, then, lifting my head up at the critical moment to flip him back into the saddle. It became our signature move.

"Hooray!" Dee clapped with joy as she watched a perfect execution.

"I can't help it. It's in my blood. I'm a Russian and a Cossack. Cossacks were the boldest, fiercest, best horsemen of Central Asia. These tricks are all from waging war. The good ones could jump their horses over a single sword stuck in the ground or fire a pistol from underneath the belly of a galloping horse. I'll bet that you didn't know that dressage's origins are in training horses for the battlefield."

"Really? I thought dressage was formal and proper."

"Well, there is that element." He laughed deeply. "I can't deny that. I've known a few 'dressage queens' in my day. The word 'dressage' literally means 'training.' Many of the movements and training methods we use today came out of cavalry schools, like the Spanish Riding School in Vienna. You know, the place with the Lipizzaners. I can't let centuries of tradition die, can I?"

Oliver popped his brown dish-face next to my stall, sneaking a bite of my hay net one night as we waited for supper. It was getting chilly outside and I had started to wear a stable sheet in the evenings.

"Next week's the Macy's Thanksgiving Day parade. Biggest day of the year for a cop horse. Ready for it?"

I had no idea what he was talking about and was more interested in my food and irritated that it hadn't arrived.

"I'm sure I can handle it."

"Just wait and see. First time is always interesting. Especially when you see the balloons and floats coming down the street."

What is he talking about? And WHERE is my dinner?

"Can I pat him?" asked an endless flow of teeth-chattering, runny-nosed, pink-cheeked, bundled-up children as we stood on the corner of Broadway and 45th Street on the day of the parade, watching decorated cars passing by, occupants waving and throwing candy into the crowd and people marching in groups. When a troop of horses ridden by people in uniform passed us, several nickered to me in greeting. I nickered back.

Suddenly, the sky in between two tall buildings started to get dark as a big cloud-like thing passed overhead.

Whoa! What is that?

I stopped, heart pounding, gulping in breaths of air.

"Easy, Sasha, It's OK. It's just a balloon. It won't hurt you." Yuri stroked my neck, singing his Russian lullabies to me in a low melodic voice until I took a deep breath and relaxed, letting the air out in a giant rumbling sigh.

As more balloons and giant cars followed down the street, crowds of people, children carried on shoulders, pushed at the barriers trying to get a better view. Children laughed and parents waved, caught up in the parade spirit. I had a momentary feeling of unease.

Something bad is going to happen. I can feel it.

Suddenly, Yuri froze. I felt his energy focus on a dark alley halfway down the block. A man with a hooded sweatshirt stood facing a well-dressed older couple.

Why aren't they watching the parade?

My ears suddenly stood at attention as I saw the sun glinting off something in his hand, something shiny and metallic. Yuri slowly picked up the reins and nudged me into a walk toward a crowd barrier. He sat up and squeezed his legs. We jumped it from a standstill, then halted. Quietly and deliberately, we weaved our way through the crowd. Ten yards away from the couple, Yuri put his heels sharply into my side. I responded, exploding into a gallop toward the robber, while Yuri kicked the gun out of his hands. We pulled up in four strides, did a perfect pirouette, and galloped back toward him.

This time, Yuri wrapped a leg over the saddle and leaned over backwards, Cossack style, grabbing the gun off the ground and climbing back in the saddle. Another pirouette, then spring off my hind legs — like shooting out of a starting gate — back to the robber, cornering him against a building, like a cat with a chipmunk.

"Car support, Broadway and 45th, code two-eleven, armed robbery, suspect apprehended," Yuri barked into his radio after dismounting, handcuffing the robber and handing their watches and wallets back to the relieved couple. Applause erupted from the people gathered around us, parade forgotten, as they watched the drama in the alley. I nodded my head, waving to the crowd.

They love me! I love them back! My people!

Now I understood the pride police horses took in being "cop horses." We're heroes! Protectors of people — making wrongs right. It felt really good, as though I finally had some control over life's random bad moments.

The next week, school kids came to the police stable to meet the "cowboy cop horse." One of the officers pinned up a picture of me from the newspaper on the front of my stall until Officer Rob, the stable manager, tore it off the door and threw it away.

I got a strange feeling from Officer Rob. A bad vibe,

as Speedy used to say. He wasn't like the other officers: all fit and athletic, efficient and dressed in tidy uniforms with polished boots. Rob shuffled around the barn lazily with his uniform stained and wrinkled and a glazed look in his blank, washed-out, pale blue eyes. He was shorter than most of the other officers but much fatter than the jockeys I knew. Worst of all, he smelled sour, like some of the drunks Yuri and I met in Central Park.

Even though his job was to make sure we were well taken care of, he didn't seem to like horses the way the other officers did. He was nervous around me and the other horses and it put me on edge. I noticed that Yuri watched him carefully, too. Something wasn't quite right.

December, Manhattan, New York

After Thanksgiving, the north wind finally made up its mind to stay. The bare trees stood starkly in relief against the grey skies as the last lingering red, orange and yellow leaves gave up their grasp and floated to the ground. It was strange. I was happy and I loved Yuri, but I couldn't help feeling that something was going to happen, something bad, and that my life was about to change.

"It's getting chilly. Do you think it's time to clip everyone?" Officer Mike asked Yuri as he stamped his feet and wrapped his hands around a mug of steaming coffee, trying to warm up from his morning shift.

"Oh no, not clippin'. I hate clippin'," Oliver moaned. He turned to me, "I'll bet you've nevah bin clipped, 'ave ya? By jeezum, it takes forever and those clippehrs buhrn and pinch and tickle, but the sweat does dry fasteh and you don't sit there with a wet coat, freezin' to death."

"Let's clip tomorrow," Yuri nodded to Mike. "The horses will need to start wearing their heavier blankets indoors and quarter sheets on patrol. We wouldn't want anyone to tie up with all of that stop-and-go and waiting around we do. When are they next due to be shod? They should have borium. It'll snow any day. Those streets are slippery this time of year."

"I'll make sure and remind Rob about the borium. The farrier is due next week," Officer Mike replied.

Borium? What's that?

I made a face at Oliver, who laughed good naturedly. "Come on, Florida boy, winter's here. Get with it: borium, studs on your shoes, keep ya from slippin' on the ice and snow we'll be gettin' any day now. Love this time of year — reminds me of Veh'mont. We had real snow in Veh'mont, we did. Miss it, I do."

A gravelly voice woke me up late one night, accompanied by the shaking beam of a flashlight.

"Hey Rob. Hey, man. Got any more of that horse tranquilizer?"

"Shh! Rocky. Quiet. Wanna get us busted? Be cool." Officer Rob heaved his soft, overweight body into the grooming stall and turned on the dim light. He looked around quickly with his empty blue eyes and unconsciously picked at a mole on his chin before pulling a small flask out of his pocket and taking a long drink.

"I'm tellin' ya, it's good stuff. I can sell as much as you can get, the boys on the street love it."

"Gimme the cash first."

Picking a key out of the cluster he wore on his belt,

Rob opened the equine medicine cabinet and pulled out a small foil packet. He held it in the air and kissed it.

"Top quality. From my special European vet connection. Forty grams. Two grand. OK, gimme the cash and get outa here. And don't come around here again. I don't want to have to hurt you or send my boys after you. You don't want that either."

Overnight the city dressed itself up as though it were going to a fancy party. Thousands of sparkly lights on trees and lampposts twinkled prettily in the early dusk. Woodsy smelling wreaths and garlands with red ribbons appeared, expectantly inviting the city to put on its best manners. Women in long coats and high heeled boots and men wearing hats and scarves slowed their rapid, city walks to catch an eye, smile, nod, and say Merry Christmas.

Every street corner smelled of roasted chestnuts, my new obsession. I loved them almost as much as peppermints. Snowflakes finally came, gently drifting through the sparkly lights, hushing and softening the city, wrapping it in a clean white scarf. In Central Park, the ground was still springy underneath the snow. Yuri and I kept up our early morning dressage and Dee still came out to watch, now wearing an old blue parka with stains on the front. Like swarms of bees, more and more shoppers and tourists happily buzzed around the shops on Madison Avenue. The Plaza, especially, had an air of excitement as more limousines and celebrities arrived daily.

"Good morning, Maurice, looks like there's something going on." More security guards than usual hovered around the entrance to the Plaza, where a small crowd of people had gathered to wait for someone important who was staying there. A group of photographers waited off to the side, blowing on their hands, drinking coffee out of paper cups and fiddling with their cameras. "Paparazzi. Must be a Hollywood star or maybe the President?"

Maurice tipped his hat, bowing, "Good morning to you, Yuri, Sasha. We have special guests — Rod McCabe and his royal girlfriend. They arrived last night, over from London where Rod is filming."

"Ah, Rod McCabe, I loved him in his last movie. He deserved that Oscar. I'd better keep an extra eye on your crowd. It looks like it'll get bigger."

The next morning, as brilliant fingers of pink reached across the early morning sky, Yuri and I worked on flying lead changes. A few remaining snowflakes drifted past. A man bundled up in a big puffy jacket and black wool hat threw a tennis ball for an enthusiastic German Shepherd in the southern corner of the field and a homeless woman with her hand on a shopping cart filled with stuff sat on a bench watching us.

Halfway through a series of lead changes, I smelled it.

Gardenias and peppermint!

I stopped suddenly and pawed the ground impatiently.

Where is that smell coming from?

"Come on Sasha. What's wrong?" Yuri was confused.

A man on cross country skis worked his way across the snowy field. Across from him, two runners chatted as they ran along the path in stride with each other, their breath billowing up, steamy, in the cold air. Not that direction. I smelled another whiff of the familiar scent. It was coming from the east. I looked up and nickered.

A woman wearing a snowflake-dusted winter

coat was silhouetted against deeply blushing sky. She was coming this way with two large men following behind.

Could it be?

Another whiff of the delicious, glorious, scent. A joyful nicker escaped from deep inside me, louder this time.

"I'm sorry to interrupt your session," she apologized to Yuri as she approached, "It's just so beautiful and unexpected. My name is Ayesha. I'm staying at the Plaza and find it very difficult to escape from the paparazzi unless I get up early in the morning. Imagine, wandering upon such a sight of sheer perfection. It's breathtaking. Your horse is stunning. May I say hello?"

I nickered again, tossing my head as she came closer.

Here I am!

Her eyes admired me, then widened, as they found the scars on my hind end and then travelled to my forehead. She traced the scimitar marking with a forefinger.

"It couldn't be," she said quietly. I nickered again and put my nose toward her, overjoyed at seeing her again as she burst into tears, hugging and petting me.

"I can't believe it. Raja. I almost didn't recognize you."

Princess Ayesha, I've found you.

It was so wonderful to see her. She was grown up, a beautiful woman now. My heart felt like it would burst from joy. Princess Ayesha, my childhood special friend!

We're finally reunited!

"I take it you've met Sasha?"

"Sasha? Oh, yes. My father bred this horse and he was foaled at my family's stud. He was a very good racehorse and could have won the Kentucky Derby if a starting gate accident hadn't ended his career."

Ayesha scratched my tickly spot. "Oh, how I've missed you." She turned to Yuri, "Sorry. This is just a bit overwhelming."

"It's nice to meet you, Ayesha. My name is Yuri Belanov. A starting gate, eh? So that's what the scars are from. I suspected that there was a story behind them. My friend found him at the auction. He came close to being sold for horse meat. She had to outbid the killers."

She gasped and started at him, horrified.

"Horse meat!"

"He was in rough shape, must have fallen into the wrong hands. We looked up his race record but couldn't find anything after his last race and tried to contact the Sheikh, but he had sold the farm. You must be his daughter?"

Ayesha pressed her face into my neck. "Yes. My father sold the farm when we left the country a few years ago." She threw her arms around my neck. "I found you, Raja. I can't believe it! He loves peppermints. Don't you my love?" She turned her tear streaked face to Yuri, pushing her long hair out of her face. "He looks wonderful — shiny coat, beautifully groomed, happy expression and muscled-up. And what lovely flatwork. He's incredible — poetry in motion. Belanov... Belanov... that name sounds familiar. You're not related to—"

"Princess." One of the bodyguards moved closer.

At that exact moment, Dee rode her bike toward us ferociously, skidding to a dramatic stop before discarding it on the ground and running closer, eyes more on fire than usual, color high. She struggled for breath as her words spilled out in rapid succession in the general direction of Princess Ayesha.

"Hi, my name's Dee. I don't want to rush you, but I thought that you'd want to know that a group of photographers is heading this way."

We all looked over in the direction Dee was pointing. A pack of about 20 men carrying large cameras was racing toward us.

"I'll create a distraction so that you can get away," Dee cheerfully announced with a chip-toothed grin. "Be careful, there's a big patch of black ice over there." She pointed toward an area on the path next to a big boulder and then took off on her bike toward the photographers, pedaling as though she was possessed by an angry spirit. When she reached them, she fell dramatically, clutching her leg and screaming loudly. "OWWW. Help! My leg! AAHHHH. I think it's broken! Please help me!"

Several of the photographers stopped to help her. Yuri and I knew that she was faking, but we went over, adding to the confusion and allowing Princess Ayesha to escape. When we could no longer see her, or her bodyguards, Dee stood up, got on her bike and rode off, smiling and waving at the paparazzi, messy braids flying behind her.

I can't wait to see Princess Ayesha again!

That night I thought of the afternoons at the farm in Florida under our tree with her sweet voice singing to me, "Don't worry, 'bout a thing, 'cause every little thing's gonna be alright."

The crowd outside the Plaza waiting to see Rod McCabe and Princess Ayesha swelled as people stopped to see what was going on. We were on afternoon patrol in front of the Plaza, special duty crowd control. The late afternoon shadows grew longer as the trickle of people walking home from work, heads tucked into their scarves and hats against the bitter north wind.

"Rod McCabe! I love him. I've seen all his movies."

An excited hush came over the crowd as Maurice opened the door and the couple waded through the crowd toward the waiting big black car.

"Over here, Rod."

"Rod, can I have an autograph?"

People pushed and shoved, wanting to get closer to them. I kept willing Ayesha to look toward me, but I had to keep my focus on the crowd.

I'm here! Over here!

Finally, she looked up through the forest of people and saw me. A beautiful smile lit up her face as she caught my eye. She walked closer, trailed by a pack of paparazzi. Oblivious to them, she focused completely on me as she gave me a kiss on the nose, fed me a peppermint and scratched my tickly spot. A warm glow came over me and it was just the two of us. The crowd faded.

"You are the most perfect thing in the universe and I will always love you."

The crowd surged closer in the twilight and the paparazzi started taking pictures.

Flash! Flash! Click! Pop!

Hundreds of flashes of light blinded and confused me.

LIGHTNING!

My heart leapt into my throat and a loud roaring sound filled my ears.

Run!

I forgot about Yuri, Princess Ayesha and the crowd as I wheeled around and bolted as fast as I could down the sidewalk into the park. I passed the row of carriages and the frozen duck pond and went into the park, blind to the runners, bicyclists and baby strollers in my way, blind to Yuri trying to stop me, blind to everything except the need to escape. The only thing that existed was my body, my breath and heart and the sound of my hooves on the pavement.

Ta-da-da-dum, ta-da-da-dum, ta-da-da-dum.

I looked up rounding a turn next to a big boulder.

SLAM!

My feet went out from underneath me.

Black ice!

Yuri, underneath me, cushioned my fall as the reins came over my head. Still possessed by the flight instinct, I scrambled up, hysterical, leaving Yuri on the ground. I began to run again, reins dangling in front of me. Rounding another corner, I found my way blocked by an enormous crowd barrier, taller than a man.

There was no way around it and I was moving fast. It was too late to stop. I had too much momentum. If I tried, I would slip and fall. I couldn't see the other side, but it was too late. I would either make it or crash in a terrible fall. Five strides out, I measured the distance, rebalanced, gathered myself up, and jumped over it in a giant leap.

As I landed, I swerved, extending my forelegs and picking up my hind legs to avoid a tractor parked on the other side of the barrier, then kept galloping.

"Sasha," I heard a voice. It was Dee. I began to slow down, the possession fading as I pulled to a trot and then trotted back to Dee, still heaving and blowing and catching my breath. "Easy buddy, relax, settle." I jigged sideways.

Dee grabbed my reins and vaulted on using a Cossack

move she had seen Yuri do, then steered me back down a path through some trees around the barrier to a man wearing a battered old tweed cap and a weathered green parka with silver duct tape over a tear.

He smells like the country. Like alfalfa and wood smoke.

"Uncle Paddy," she said excitedly, "This is the horse I told you about — Sasha." Paddy's brown forelock fell over twinkling grey eyes, now aflame with excitement. He looked familiar.

I've seen him before, where?

"Holy Mother Mary! Did you see that? I haven't seen a horse jump like that since I saw Nick Skelton and Everest Lastic win the high jump at Olympia. That fence was almost seven feet high. Incredible! And he jumped a tractor on the other side! That was one of the greatest jumps I've ever seen. And I've seen lots of top international jumpers in my day."

He walked over to me with a slight bowlegged hitch to his gait, energetically, yet smoothly, so as not to startle me, and gave me a friendly pat on the neck with un-gloved, callused, knowing hands as his eyes scanned my body.

The horse dentist! Paddy Murphy! I could tell by his movement, his touch.

"You can trust me," he said with his hands and his movement. I was still breathing heavily, hot and excited from the run. Almost unconsciously, I nudged him, rubbing my head on his shoulder and letting out a big rumbling sigh.

"Uncle Paddy! He likes you!"

"Keep him walking. He's still blowing. 'Tis a very handsome horse. Well bred, judging by the look of him. He looks familiar. I feel like I've met him before. I never

forget a horse. I know I've seen him. Ah well, I'll probably remember in the middle of the night."

He reached into his pocket, found a roll of Polo mints, unrolled a strip and offered one to me, patting me on the forehead. "Hullo, lovely boy." He turned to Dee. "He's certainly not your typical police horse. I see why you are infatuated with him. Did you see him jump that barrier? Incredible! He made it look like nothing. Ah, Dee-girl, you reminded me of your mother just then. That was quite a bit of riding — where did you learn that move? You looked like a Valkyrie, jumping on like that! You have your mother's blood, there's no doubt about that. She was the best horsewoman in County Limerick, God bless her soul. She'd have been proud of you. Now, then, shall we take this horse back and find out what happened?"

He walked beside me, putting his hands on the reins to steady me as I jigged and snorted, still agitated from the run. A crowd of people had gathered around an ambulance at the patch of ice where I had slipped. Yuri lay on a metal bed, awake, joking with the EMTs as they loaded him into the vehicle.

Oliver and Officer Mike were at the scene.

"Thank you. Is Sasha OK?" Mike asked, taking the reins from Dee.

"He's fine as far as I can tell. No scrapes and he feels sound. What happened? Is Yuri OK?" Dee asked, with a worried expression.

"It sounds like Sasha was scared by the photographers. He bolted and slipped on the ice going around a corner. Yuri has a pretty good concussion and he broke his leg — his femur. It'll be a while before he rides again."

Yuri smiled at me through the pain as he was loaded

into the ambulance. "It's OK, Sasha, it wasn't your fault. It was the ice. I'll see you soon, I promise."

Oliver looked at me sadly and shook his head. "Ayuh, boltin' ain't looked on so good in the force, if ya know what I mean. Don't know that I've evah known a bolter. Lucky ya ain't huhrt with that fall an' everythin.'"

When would Yuri get out of the hospital? When will I see him?

Officer Mike spoke again, "I'll take him back. It looks as though Sasha may not be cut out for police work."

A freezing rain started to fall as I walked home through the grey and yellow rain-slicked streets of New York with Oliver and Officer Mike.

January, Manhattan, New York

The New Year came with me still in the stable, unridden, and Yuri still gone. The routine went on around me as usual, but I felt a heavy, uneasy, feeling. The stone in the pit of my stomach was growing. There was a lot of talk about what I would do now that I wasn't cut out to be a police horse.

Rob was speaking to Captain Rourke. "I think Sasha needs to go to the retirement farm. He's too much of a liability for a riding school. I wouldn't want anyone to get hurt riding such a dangerous horse."

Dangerous! So that's what they think. But I'm not dangerous. I'm kind and and I always try my best.

The stone in my stomach got heavier.

Why don't they understand me? Where's Yuri? What's going to happen to me?

"My friend ships horses." Rob snorted loudly before spitting a yellow glob onto the ground, staring blankly at me. "He can come and get Sasha tomorrow. I'll take care of everything."

Raja

Story of a Racehorse

—Part III—

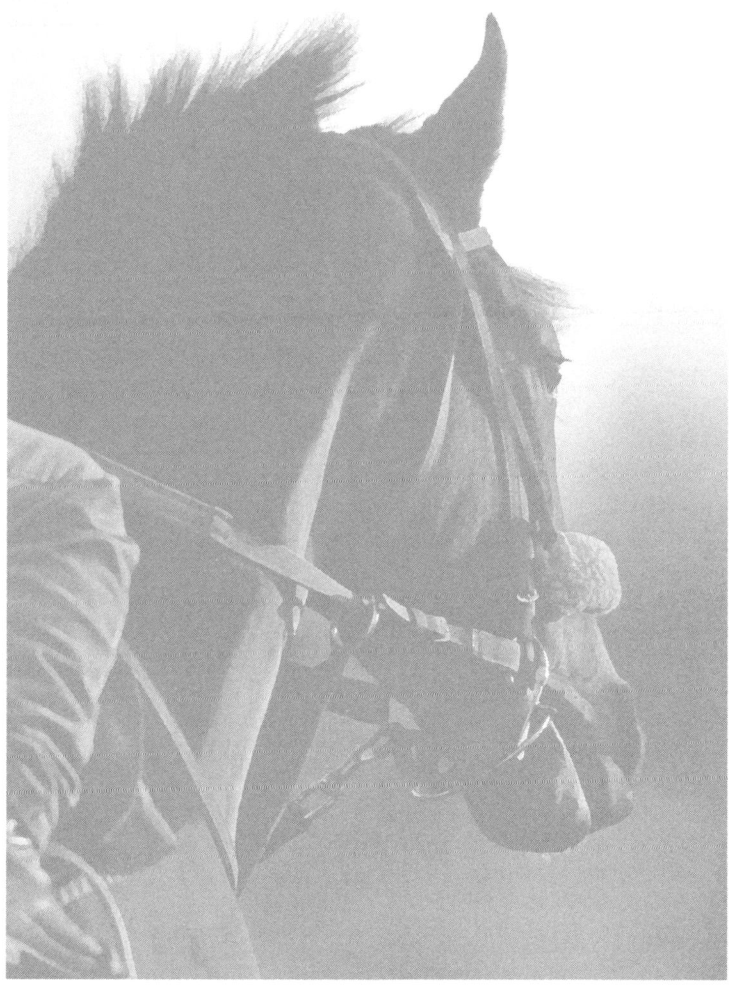

9 The Ice Storm

February, somewhere in New Jersey

The icicles forming around my nose and whiskers made it hard to breathe as a bitter wind blew through the open-sided stock trailer. Every once in a while a huge truck whizzed by, inches from me. Oliver had told me that the farm was seven hours away. We drove for two.

As we turned into the yard of a run-down farm, I saw three skinny horses huddling together for warmth in a small paddock surrounded by rusted barbed wire tied to crooked fence posts with baling twine. A large pile of frozen manure and rusted metal farm equipment sat in the center of the paddock and an old, tired bathtub leaned precariously against a corner, anchored in place by the yellow-and-brown ice that covered the rutted, tire-scarred ground.

I planted my feet firmly while Rob's friend pulled and jerked a chain he had put over my nose and clipped to my halter.

No way am I going into that paddock.

The chain hurt, but I didn't care. Rob's friend tied me to the trailer and went into the truck, pulling out a metal stick, too thick for a whip.

What is it? What does he plan to do?

"Earl, git yer fat butt off the couch and help me," he yelled to someone in the house. While he waited, he took off my warm, heavy blanket and new leather halter, replacing it with an old, frayed nylon halter that smelled bad, like cat pee. Then he placed the chain under my lip and over my gums and gave it a sharp tug.

Ow…that really hurts.

I stood my ground. I was not going into the paddock.

"See here, I mean business," he snarled.

A heavy, bearded man emerged from the house, lumbering down the porch steps as he pulled on a red checkered jacket.

"You owe me one, bro. It's freezing out here and the game is in overtime. Flash Jackson just scored to tie. Man, that guy is good, I tell ya."

Flash? Is he here? Things are getting strange.

"Give me a hand. Hold him."

Earl held the chain while Rob's friend walked behind me with the metal stick.

Whoa!

I jumped high in the air in surprise at the shock. It hurt — a lot. He did it again and I bolted into the paddock, trembling all over and snorting loudly, feeling violated. He nodded, smiling at Earl through brown-stained teeth, before spitting on the ground.

"Cattle prod. Best investment I ever made."

I was so cold, so hungry, so thirsty. By now I knew I wasn't going to the retirement farm. My heart began to pound and my stomach tightened as a feeling of cold dread came over me.

Where am I going?

Rob's friend pricked me with a needle. I was sleepy, so sleepy. I could barely stay awake.

I drifted off into a restless, troubled, dream-filled sleep.

February, New Holland, Pennsylvania

"We made it to the 'retirement farm' OK," Rob's friend barked gruffly into his cell phone, jumping up and down next to the trailer to stay warm.

"It's colder'n sin out here. I'll let you know what he brings and I'll send you a check next week, or would you rather have cash?" He stomped his feet, trying to stay warm.

"We're lucky that meddling Beth ain't here. I'll bet she's stuck in the storm. Glad to see the meat buyers made it. Thoroughbreds are highest quality, Grade A. Your nag's got a lot of meat on him. He'll get a good price."

Are they talking about me? Where are we?

The big cement building and muddy stock-trailer–filled parking lot looked familiar.

The livestock auction!

Rob's friend put me into a small pen with the other three horses and tied us to a metal bar. The frigid wind picked up, biting into my thin, newly clipped coat.

Freezing! It's freezing.

As the other horses and I silently huddled together, desperately trying to stay warm, I smelt an acrid, sickening, bitter smell, like something burning. Looking up sharply, I saw Rob's friend talking to a man wearing a cowboy hat.

He has a patch over his left eye! The kill buyer!

The deal was done in the parking lot. Rob's friend led me to the back of the building where a large tractor trailer idled loudly, belching black clouds of diesel smoke. Inside the open back door, 12 horses stood shivering.

This doesn't feel real. This feels like I am in the worst

nightmare imaginable.

"Git," the man in the cowboy hat growled as he roughly tried to pull me into the tractor trailer. I pinned my ears back and kicked out a warning.

I'm not getting in there.

The crack of a bull whip pierced the icy night air, accenting the terrible sounds of the rumbling truck engine, horses whinnying in fear and men cursing harshly.

"Git, hoss," he snarled louder, stinging my flank with his whip, one, two, three times, each time harder than the last. I skittered sideways, my metal shoes sliding on the ice-covered pavement, and whinnied loudly to the others.

Think! DO something. There has to be a way out.

The stench of diesel fuel mingling with the smell of cigarettes and pig manure from the livestock pens made me dizzy. I suddenly felt weak. I stood unsteadily, pulling back against him, trying to catch my breath.

Oww. OWW!

I felt a strong shock — a surge of electricity — and jumped forward onto the truck, hearing Rob's friend laugh cruelly as I did.

"You need a cattle prod, my friend. It'll save you time."

It was so crowded I could barely breathe. A scared horse slid to his knees, slamming into me. My legs buckled, but I stayed up. Every horse knew where we were going. Several hung their heads low, dispirited. Many were sick or lame, some had open wounds. The ones with fight left in them, who stood up for themselves by refusing to load, were hit with the bull whip or cattle prod.

Behind me, a tall, skinny grey with a big scar whinnied in terror. He reared and slipped on the icy tarmac, then fell over backwards, hitting his head with a sickening thud. I couldn't help but whinny to him in empathy. The men tied a chain around his legs and dragged him into the tractor trailer where he lay breathing heavily, too weak to get up. I moved over, trying not to step on him.

To make matters worse, the freezing rain had arrived, announcing itself with a loud hammering on the metal roof of the trailer. The cold wind bit like an angry dog, growing more and more furious. As hard pellets stung us through the trailer's open sides, a thin layer of ice beginning to form on the floor made it difficult to stand. I shivered uncontrollably, overcome with a deepening sense of dread. The stone in my stomach grew heavier.

This is it. I'm heading to the killers.

It took about an hour to finish loading. Then we began our sad journey. The truck moved slowly, sliding in the sleet that was now falling hard. Struggling up a couple of big hills, we had to stop, back up, and climb again. Each time, more horses slipped and fell. Several couldn't get back up and scrambled on the floor, trying to avoid being trampled. I felt terribly for them, but I could barely stay on my own feet.

The truck lurched up one never-ending hill, reached the top and started down, dragged by the weight of the horses, moving faster. I felt a jerky motion, then we began to slide sideways, gathering momentum. I struggled to keep my footing as more horses went down. Through the sides of the trailer we could see headlights coming toward us on one side and dark woods on the other.

Suddenly, we heard loud voices shouting from the cab of the truck.

"We can't stop! We're going to crash!"

A loud mechanical-sounding squeal filled the air accompanied by a horrible burning smell. We slid faster still, careening out of control down a steep embankment toward the dark woods on the left side of the truck.

CRASH!

Metal groaned and ripped as the truck stopped suddenly and flipped over, flinging us against one side, tearing open the back. For a moment, it was silent. Then chaos — a panicked melee of scrambling hoofs, frantic whinnies and steamy, horse-sweat–drenched bodies desperately trying to escape. Somehow, I managed to right myself and stagger out. I noticed a cowboy hat on the ground, but no people. It was dark, icy and bitter cold, but we were free.

Run! Escape!

We started to run as a herd. Even the lame horses hobbled as best they could. When we were clear of the accident, the truck caught on fire, erupting in a huge fiery orange ball that lit up the sky.

BOOM! BOOM! BOOM!

Three explosions followed, as the flames climbed higher and higher into the dark sky. I ran as fast as I could through the freezing rain and the darkness, blinded by the headlights of oncoming cars. A couple of other horses ran with me but I quickly out-distanced them. Slipping a little on the icy ground, I jumped a guard rail and moved to the middle of the highway. I was fit and soon fell into an easy rhythm. I hadn't galloped, really galloped, since I was at Gulfstream Park. It felt like another lifetime. After a while, I turned onto a smaller road, running past buildings still decorated with colored holiday lights. Gradually, I saw fewer buildings. Clusters of houses became fields and farms. I must have run for over two hours through the darkness and the ice storm, but I didn't feel tired or cold.

I feel good. I feel FREE.

At the top of a hill I saw a light on in a big wooden barn with a stone foundation. I suddenly noticed how tired and hungry and thirsty I was. It was getting late. The excitement and adrenalin had kept me going, but my energy was fading. I stopped on the road, studying the tidy farm.

Should I risk it? Is it safe?

I was so tired and so thirsty. I was dying for something to drink.

Maybe I should just sleep by the side of the road? What if they take me back to the killers?

The icy wind picked up and I shivered violently.

OK, I'll take the chance.

I walked cautiously into the courtyard, then stopped and looked around, alert.

Is it safe?

An old man with a white beard looked up from a sweat-covered mare lying on her side in one of the stalls and smiled.

"Hullo…what a nice surprise. Just in time to see the foal being born."

I was so tired. All I wanted was a warm place to sleep and some food and water

That hay looks really good.

I took another cautious step forward and let the man touch my ratty old cat-pee halter. He slowly led me into a stall filled with deep straw with a pile of sweet-smelling clover hay in the corner and filled a water bucket. Feeling exhausted to my core, I drank deeply. He refilled the water and put a scoop of grain in the other bucket, which I devoured hungrily.

"Hmm…you were at the auction." he shook his head, noticing the tag on my hind end. I'll bet you were in that terrible crash I just heard about on the radio, the tractor trailer on its way to the slaughterhouse. Jeez, you galloped a long time — that was over 30 miles away."

He gave me a reassuring pat. "You're safe here." Then he took a good look at me and whistled, "Wow, you are one good lookin', fancy horse. You don't look like most of the horses that go through that auction — skinny racehorses run too hard, or plow horses off the farm. A mystery, you are. Well, my granddaughter is in the pony club. I'm sure she has a friend who needs a horse for next summer."

I hope I can trust him.

We stayed up to watch the mare give birth to a colt before I gradually nodded off and slept deeply, lying down on the thick bed of straw. It had been a very long day.

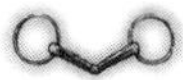

A few weeks later, I was watching a squirrel climb up the frozen tree outside the barnyard on his way to the birdfeeder, when I heard a car door slam outside.

"Good Morning, Paddy. Thanks for coming on such a cold day."

Paddy?

"Good morning to you, Abe. 'Tis brisk, isn't it? My Irish blood just can't get used to these bitter cold days, but I try. This time of year fools you into thinking spring is around the bend and then we have a day like today. Sure, and March is coming in like a lion, just like they say. Let's pray for the warm weather to come quickly, shall we?"

He shivered. "Now then, what have you got for me?"

"The mare, Sierra, you know. Her teeth were last done a year ago so she needs to be done," replied Abe.

"There's a new horse. Come and take a look. I'd like your opinion of him. Do you remember that crash last month? The tractor trailer with the auction horses?"

"Ah yes, the kill truck, I did hear about it, terrible," Paddy replied.

"Well," Abe lowered his voice to a whisper and continued slowly, eyes wide, "that night, a very good-looking, clipped, fit horse appeared at my farm with an auction sticker on his hindquarters — a good 30 miles from the crash. He has heavy shoes instead of aluminum racing plates. I think he's a hunter or an event horse."

He paused, taking a deep breath and exhaled.

"I haven't told anyone. I suspect foul play and I don't want the killers to come looking for him, so please keep quiet. He's very well-mannered and I'm hoping he can be a pony club horse for one of my granddaughter's friends."

I looked over the stall door.

It's Dee's Uncle Paddy — the man I had seen in Central Park and at Beth's!

He was wearing the same tweed cap and weathered green parka with patches of faded grey tape. Overjoyed, I nickered, hoping he would remember me. He came into my stall, his eyes widening in recognition as he looked closely at me.

"There's a good boy," he patted me, whistling under his breath. He opened my mouth and looked at my teeth.

"His teeth are in good shape. They don't need to be done," he told Abe. Next, he flipped my upper lip up and looked at my tattoo. "He just turned eight in January," he continued. He turned to Abe. "Would you mind please fetching me a lead rope?"

When Abe was out of earshot, he looked me in the eye, fished a polo mint out of his pocket, fed it to me, and whispered, "Sasha, so that's where that crooked policeman sent you! Or should I say Raja! Now I remember where it was I had seen you first. It was at Beth's farm. I never forget a horse, especially a horse like you."

Abe returned and handed the lead rope to Paddy.

"Abe, you're right, he's a handsome horse. But I'd make sure he's safe before putting a child on him if I were you. We've no idea why he was on that kill truck."

Paddy took off his cap and scratched the back of his head, cap still in hand.

"You know, my niece, Dee, comes to visit from New York during the school holidays. We've been looking for a horse for her. He might suit her. Would you take 500 dollars for him? I'm sure that if he has any riding quirks, we can sort them out. I rode quite a few devils in my day when I was a steeplechase jockey."

Abe seemed pleased. "You're right. I was wondering what got him on that truck. Frankly, I didn't want my granddaughter to be the first one to ride him." Abe reached out to shake Paddy's hand. "You have a deal."

10
The Murphys

March, Chester County, Pennsylvania

"Hullo, Mac and Angus." Paddy leaned down to pick up the slobber-covered tennis ball one of the two friendly black Labrador retrievers had dropped expectantly at his feet. He threw it far into the field, down the hill, toward the pond, while two streaks of black tore after it.

After leading me into the field, Paddy took off my new halter and stood watching.

A piebald pony trotted up cheerfully and sniffed noses with me, while an older chestnut horse followed him, slowly picking his way across the frozen field.

"Hello there, I'm Snickers and that's Robbie. He doesn't hear very well."

I sniffed first with the pony and then the chestnut, squealing a little as we got acquainted. The chestnut seemed weary as he spoke,

"I'm Robbie. What's your name? What? Sorry, I didn't get that."

"Well, it's nice to meet you," Snickers interrupted. "I'm happy to have someone new to talk to. Ol' Robbie can't hear anything I say. Makes it kind of hard to have a conversation! Come on, I'll show you the good patch of clover. Follow me."

As we pawed through the frozen mud to get the tender new shoots, Snickers began speaking again, clearly excited to have company. "Paddy's two sons used to ride me before they got obsessed with hockey and lacrosse. I don't get out much now unless Dee is visiting, then she rides me. The neighbor comes over sometimes and leads his grandson around on me, but it's pretty quiet around here."

"What's that? Louder, can't hear you," Robbie complained. "Young fella, it's nice to have you here. I'm Robbie. I'm 25. What's that you say?"

He turned to Snickers, who looked at me innocently and shook his head.

"Sometimes Robbie imagines things," he whispered.

"Be quiet, Snickers. I'm talking to the new fella."

Robbie lowered his head and promptly fell asleep.

The skunk cabbage, fiddlehead ferns and crocuses shivered out of the wet ground, reaching out eagerly to the March sun. I smelled black earth, woodsmoke and things growing. As I looked over my stall door, a flock of geese loudly circled the farm and landed dramatically on the pond, feet first, wings flapping and splashing.

This day is different. I don't know why, but I can feel it.

As I sniffed the early spring air, I knew that something was about to happen. Two sets of footsteps creaked on the wooden barn floor.

"I have a surprise for you, Dee. Come, have a look."

Even though it had only been two months since I had seen her, Dee looked taller, more grown up, as she peered into my stall. A chin-length haircut that made her chestnut hair swing as she walked replaced her unruly long braids. Her shaggy wool sweater was gone, too, I noticed. She looked at Paddy, astonished, then threw herself at him, hugging him.

"Where did you find him, Uncle Paddy?" She burst into my stall and hugged me tightly, smiling a wide chip-toothed grin.

There's the Dee I know.

"Sasha! I thought you were at the retirement farm. I went by the barracks and Officer Rob told me you'd been sent upstate."

"There's a story and it'll be told at supper," replied Paddy. "Now, then, these horses need some supper of their own. We can ride tomorrow."

"I'm going to ride bareback," Dee announced the next day as I was finishing my breakfast. "Yuri said that riding without stirrups is the best way to develop a good seat."

"I suppose that's all right. We've been riding him every day; he's been perfect."

Dee rode me every morning that week. We explored the countryside as the meadowlarks and song sparrows sang spring forward and endless clouds of black dots, rivers of high flying birds, crowded the sky. Rabbits and groundhogs roamed the fields, sunning themselves and looking for mates. The world had suddenly woken up.

Dooo…Dooo…Dooo…Doo doo doo doo doo.

That sounded like a bugle, like the call to the post.

It was around suppertime, four o'clock, when we heard it. Dee was riding late. Along with the sharp, quick, urgent notes of the horn, came the stirring sound of dozens of dogs crying in unison.

"Ah, listen to that hound music," sighed Paddy. "It sounds like they're on a good run. If you hurry, you can see them come through."

At the edge of the field we saw an amazing sight. It was

a big race, led by dozens of hounds running and baying. A man wearing a red coat galloped with them. Two men in red coats flanked the pack, followed by another, leading a thundering herd of galloping horses toward the post-and-rail fence surrounding our pasture. Fanning out, each rider picked a panel and jumped into the big field.

This must be the hunt!

A teenage boy with his stirrups jacked up, jockey style, on a handsome black horse galloped past easily, with a girl in pigtails on a grey pony at his heels.

Was it? It's Holzmann and Prism! I can't believe it!

I broke into a gallop and started running along with the other horses.

I have to find out what they're doing. I'm not stopping, Dee.

After trying to pull me up, Dee changed her mind and decided to enjoy the ride as we rolled up and down the hills and through the woods, jumping coops and post-and-rail fences in our way.

"Hello, Raja!" cried Holzmann as I passed him. "Isn't this fun?"

Holzmann! What are you doing here?

"Foxhunting — come on, this is a good run. I'll race you to the top of the hill," he shouted, taking off with a spurt of energy. He looked great — better than I'd ever seen him — all muscled up and fit. It was hard to believe that he was 19. He looked six.

I'm so happy to see him again!

Dee and I galloped with Holzmann, then moved closer to the leaders. Down a steep hill, over a big muddy stream and then up another big hill, passing more horses.

It feels so good to run. I like this kind of race!

The man in the red coat galloped easily toward a huge

four-rail fence at the top of the hill and jumped it in an effortless leap. The next three horses refused. We were next. I measured the fence, gathered myself and flew it while Dee grabbed my mane, following perfectly.

That's fun!

The hounds went silent and the man in the red coat stopped to listen for them. No one else behind us jumped the fence.

"Some fence, eh?" The man grinned at Dee. "I'll bet it's almost five feet high — and you're riding bareback. Nice job! This horse I'm riding, Inquisitor, has won the Maryland Hunt Cup. If I were sitting on any other horse, I wouldn't have attempted it."

He laughed with triumphant glee. "My name is Rick Dunlop; pleased to meet you."

We heard another horn call. This time it was different — long and mournful.

"That old fox has gone to ground. He always gives us a great run whenever we come over here. I guess we should pick up hounds and call it a day. Today was our last hunt of the season. What a great way to end it."

Dee patted my neck as she spoke, a little out of breath. "Thanks, that was really fun. I'm Dee and I live in New York. Paddy Murphy is my uncle."

"Paddy Murphy's a good man and great horseman. He does my horses' teeth. He rode a couple winners for me back in the day when he was still riding races. I'm a steeplechase trainer," he explained. "By the way, I like your horse."

What's 'steeplechase'? It sounds like racing. Why don't I know about it?

Rick opened a gate and we joined the other horses.

"We're a good way from your uncle's farm. Why don't you hack back to my barn? You can clean up your horse and give him some supper. Then we can figure out how to get the two of you home."

At that moment, the boy and girl riding Holzmann and Prism trotted up to us.

"Wow! We saw you jump that four-railer with Uncle Rick. That was amazing! I'm Sam and this is my sister, Harper. I'm riding Holzmann and Harper's on Prism, 'the wonder pony,' as everyone in the hunt calls her, ever since the little squirt beat all the big horses to win overall champion at last year's hunter trials. Thanks, Uncle Rick. That was an awesome day. I jumped all the big fences except that last one," exclaimed the boy happily, cheeks flushed and glowing from his day. His sparkling blue eyes peeked out under unruly straw-colored bangs. "Are you going back to the meet?"

"I am indeed, shall we hack back together?"

"Raja! Fancy seeing you here," bubbled Prism as she jigged up to me. She looked fitter, and a little whiter.

"How about that? Was that fun, or what? This is so much more fun than short stirrup equitation. Holz and I are having a blast. In the fall and winter, we foxhunt and in the summer we do Pony Club. Harper and I do Pony Club games, which are hysterical. She's so cute, I adore her; she gives me birthday parties and plays circus with her friends. She even brings me inside her house." She nodded with emphasis, shaking her perfectly white mane. "It's true! Inside the house! Isn't that funny?"

She took a breath, "Sam's 14 and wants to be a steeplechase jockey, so he jacks his stirrups up and gallops Holz all over the place and finds big jumps to jump. You love it, though, don't you, Holz?"

"Sam's a good kid," Holzmann agreed, grudgingly. "We get along well."

As we hacked back to the meet, I told them my story, all of it: Gabriella DeVito and her crook of a dad; Mr. Smith; the auction and Beth; New York City and Yuri; the kill truck and my escape and the lucky meeting with Paddy Murphy.

It seems a lot longer than three years.

"Wow, that's incredible. How lucky that you ended up here. Paddy Murphy does our teeth. I hope Dee does Pony Club with Sam and Harper so that we'll see you."

Holzmann trotted up to keep up with me. Sam laughed. "I think my horse likes yours," he beamed at Dee.

Is foxhunting a race?

"You know, all they're interested in is chasing the fox," Prism explained. "They get all dressed up, take the hounds out and spend a couple of hours finding and chasing a fox across the country. Some people like watching hounds work and others just like to run and jump. The foxes are so much smarter than the hounds that it's sometimes funny," she chortled. "I know their tricks. If they want to get away, they just go up a stream, or run through a herd of cows, or along the top of a fence line to throw the hounds off the scent. I see them sitting on top of a hill watching the hounds, laughing at them. We usually run around in big circles and then the fox finds a den and goes to ground. Galloping with a big group of horses is fun. It gets your blood up."

"Good night, Sam and Harper," Rick waved goodbye when we reached the trailers. He glanced at his watch. "We'd better keep moving. It's getting dark."

"Thanks, Uncle Rick. See you around, Dee."

Soon we reached a tidy green bank barn.

I'm starving.

"There's the wash stall. You can put him in the corner stall after his bath. Here's a wool cooler for him. I'll make up a couple bran mashes after I clean up Inky. What a great day! I think your horse should stay here tonight. I'll bet he's tired. I'll give you a ride home after you're done and Paddy can come and get him tomorrow."

Dee gave me a drink of water and nice warm bath, turning on the heat lamps in the wash stall and rubbing me dry with a towel, speaking to me all the while.

"Sasha, you were awesome. Wasn't that fun? I loved today. I think you did, too."

Mmm — I feel cozy and warm and good. Those heat lamps are wonderful!

Dee and I definitely bonded today, I reflected contentedly as I struggled to stay awake. That must be why those horses and riders like hunting. It's a way to share the fun of running across country.

Better together, I mused, sleepily.

Dee led me to a stall bedded thickly with straw and I dug into the warm, wet, bran mash hungrily, not noticing the other horses in the barn.

Delicious!

"Raja, what are you doing here?" came a voice from the stall next to me. Startled, I looked up from the mash. My gaze met a familiar set of eyes smiling at me.

Shaddy! What are YOU doing here?

I can't believe it. It's soo good to see you!

"I live here. Rick trains me. I'm a steeplechaser. I race over hurdles."

"And he's very good," piped up a horse with an English accent. "You're looking at the champion hurdle horse for the past two years."

You like to race? I knew you had the talent, but I thought you didn't like it.

"After I left Alex, I came to a trainer in Maryland. I ran at all of the Mid-Atlantic tracks but, you're right, I wasn't interested and didn't really win much. He put me in a claiming race and Rick claimed me. He said I was very well bred and I wasn't running to my potential and maybe I'd like running over jumps. He was right, I do like it. I've been steeplechasing ever since. The jumps keep it interesting and I really like training across country instead of around and around the track every day. It turns out I'm a really good jumper."

That's funny. I'm a really good jumper, too.

"I heard about Max. He's a big stud — that's great. Hey, ask that young buck in the corner stall his name."

Excuse me, hello, can you please tell me your name?

The horse, who hadn't been paying attention to our conversation, replied self-importantly, "My name is 'To The Max.' My sire is the famous Maximillian, winner of the Belmont Stakes and my grandsire, Millionaire, won the Kentucky Derby."

Max's son! Wow! I couldn't believe it.

Shaddy stifled a giggle. "He's such a snob about his breeding that I haven't had the heart to tell him I'm his uncle. We're getting old, my friend," he said quietly. "He's headed for the three-year-old hurdle races and will be tough to beat. Next to him is Admiralty Bay from England over here to show us how it is done. This will be his second season over timber. He's shooting for the big sticks: Maryland timber."

"Pleased to meet you," nodded Admiralty Bay with a British accent.

Shaddy, please tell me WHAT steeplechasing is?

"It's racing, but over jumps and for longer distances than the races we used to do. In fact, most steeplechase races aren't even at a track, they're over fields in the country. Jockeys are bigger, too. Hurdle races are faster, racing over brush fences. That's what I do. Timber horses race over wood post-and-rail fences. Those races are slower, longer, usually three- to four-miles long, so those horses are not only good jumpers, they have stamina. Max would have been good at them," he grinned.

Max! I miss him so much.

"Most steeplechase horses start out racing at the flat track, then race over hurdles first and if they are really good jumpers or a touch slow, they convert to timber. I've seen horses win timber races at nine or ten years old or even older. Young Dubliner won the Maryland Hunt Cup at 12 and was second at 14. Then he won two more timber races at 15."

A fifteen-year-old winning a race? The racehorses I know are retired at five or six.

Shaddy continued, "A lot of timber horses go foxhunting to learn how to jump solid fences at speed and to get the core fitness they need to race for three or four miles. Inky, 'Inquisitor,' who Rick was hunting today, is really good. He won the Maryland Hunt Cup last spring and is headed there again next month. It takes a really special athlete just to make it around the Hunt Cup course, let alone win."

By now, my head was spinning. It had been quite a

day. Seeing Prism and Holzmann and discovering my new favorite sport, foxhunting, was wonderful. Bonding with Dee was also great. Best of all, seeing Shaddy and hearing about steeplechase racing was amazing. I liked these horses, and steeplechasing sounded like it was the best of racing and jumping.

I'm good at both!

"What stinks in here?" Tricia, Dee's aunt, wrinkled her nose. "Dee, I think it's those nasty sneakers of yours! You can't possibly take them back to New York with you!" She held out an empty feedbag that was being used as a trash bag, "put them in here. They need to go to the dump! Honestly!" She shook her head, "I thought I was a tomboy, but you're ten times worse! I bought you pair of proper paddock boots, some Blunnies, as a thank-you present for all of your help. See if they fit. The horsey look is always fashionable in the city!"

"Wow! Thanks! They're awesome. I wish I didn't have to go back to New York. Spring break was way too short this year. I'll see you in the summer, Sasha."

Dee gave me a final hug. "Take good care of him, Uncle Paddy and Aunt Tricia. Thanks for everything. This was the best break, ever."

"You have a deal," replied Paddy. "By the way, he needs his old name back. 'Tis bad luck to change a horse's name. He needs only good luck from now on."

“It’s starting to feel a bit more like spring around here. Everyone wants their horses’ teeth done before the racing season starts,” Paddy commented one warm March evening as he and Tricia did the barn chores. “It’s fun to see who’s getting ready. I went to Rick Dunlop’s today. Between Shaddy, To the Max, Inquisitor, and Admiralty Bay, he’ll be hard to beat. It’s too bad Dee will miss the spring races. I think she’d enjoy them.”

I wish I could see them. I’m very curious about steeplechasing.

“Hey, I almost forgot to tell you, Rick has asked me to be an outrider for the hunt point-to-point.”

“That’s great, Paddy. I wonder if those young jocks will know there’s a ringer in their midst. You can ride circles around all of them, even if you are 30 years older.”

Paddy smiled, “I was thinking that I could take Raja. What do you think? Would Robbie be better?”

“Take Raja,” Tricia answered, putting down the pitchfork and taking off her well-worn leather gloves to tie her long blond hair up in a knot. “Don’t forget, he was a police horse. He’s used to crowds. He’s so beautiful he deserves to be worshipped by all of us mere mortals. I’ll braid him for you. I used to do a pretty mean braided tail in my day. The two of you will be the most handsome pair in the history of the point-to-point.”

March, Unionville, Pennsylvania

It was the kind of day where everyone is your best friend, sharing a giddy secret with you, a robin's-egg-blue sky perfect day. The sunlight glowed golden green through the new leaves on the trees and a warm breeze sent a ripple through fluffy pink-and-white-blossomed crabapple and dogwood trees that welcomed us up the farm road to the field where the trailers parked. Beyond the trailers, I saw another field filled with cars, people chatting with each other, kids tossing balls, dogs sniffing other dogs and car tailgates covered with plates of food.

"Hi Paddy, who's that you're on? He's beautiful."

Everyone knew Paddy.

Our job was to lead the horses to the start and catch loose horses. I had been led to the start by outriders at the track and it was funny to be on the other side. We walked to the paddock with Admiralty Bay, Rick Dunlop's English horse, then stood to the side as the horses walked single file around the paddock.

"Riders up!"

The colorful silk-clad jockeys, all bigger than the jockeys at the track, I noticed, went to their horses and lightly hopped up, helped by a leg-up from their trainers.

Da da da dum diggety dum diggety dum dum dum daaa.

The Call to the Post!

My heart started to quicken as Paddy and I led the horses to the start field away from the crowd on the hill. The course, marked with red-and-white flags, snaked across several fields and up and down a hill over post-and-rail jumps that looked just like the fence at home.

Where's the starting gate?

After stopping to show the horses the first fence, we led them at a canter across the field to a knot of people. A man in green rubber boots, a tweed cap and a bow tie raised a big red flag in the air as the horses walked, head-to-tail, in a large circle.

This must be the start. How strange — no gate?

"Tighten up guys, come on. Number three, pay attention — closer to two please, thank you. One more time around…now turn your horses."

They turned in a line, facing forward.

The loudspeaker crackled and sputtered, "They're all in line…the flag is up."

Then, waving the big flag downward with a flourish, the starter jumped aside to get out of the way of the seven horses that were now heading toward the first fence.

"And they're off in the three mile open timber race!" The loudspeaker barked.

I want to go!

Paddy just laughed and circled me as I started to gallop with them.

"Easy Raja, I know. I want to go, too."

They're crawling. Why so slow?

I remembered Shaddy telling me that timber races were long — three miles — and I thought of the day Mary fell and Oakley had galloped me to call the helicopter.

This isn't very different. These races look fun. And NO starting gate!

The second time around, the pace picked up. As the horses approached the last fence, the race took on a sense of urgency, now fast and furious. As the crowd surged close to watch, two horses ran at top speed into the stacked wooden rails, head-to-head, nostrils flaring, straining toward the finish.

Wow! I love this! THIS is exciting!

Admiralty Bay, on the inside, took off to jump from what seemed impossibly far away, flying over the fence in a powerful leap. The horse next to him, who looked a little tired, took off with him, cleared the fence, barely, and stumbled upon landing, dislodging his jockey, who fell to the ground. The ambulance that had been waiting beside the course wailed to life, lights flashing, as it drove onto the course to retrieve the jockey.

The riderless horse ran through the finish, through the crowd and into a big field next to the course, heading toward the top of a hill where cars and trucks rushed back and forth, oblivious, along its crest.

He's going to get hit by a car!

"Come on, Raja. Time to go to work." Paddy urged me into a gallop.

Down a hill, then up. By now we were doing a two-minute lick. When we reached the crest, Paddy turned me toward a fence line. It was a shorter distance to jump a big four-rail fence and head him off. As we approached the fence, Paddy shifted his weight slightly, still staying up off my back. I rebalanced, set up for the fence and pinged it.

Perfect! Like a bird flying.

"You're amazing, Raja!" Paddy shouted as he patted me. He kicked me on and we galloped faster toward the loose horse, now dangerously close to the cars and trucks flying along the road. "Come on, Raja, show me what you have."

I turned on the afterburners.

Faster, FASTER!

We ate up the ground, quickly reaching the horse, then slowed to run alongside him, matching stride for stride. Orange, rubber-covered reins slapped against the runaway horse's foamy, sweat-covered neck. In a swift motion — so quick I didn't realize it was happening — Paddy reached out, grabbed the reins and turned us both from the road in a big circle. Gradually, we slowed as a pair, then made our way to the trailers, blowing hard and jigging.

"Nice job, Paddy! You haven't lost a thing!" Rick Dunlop grinned as we reached the trailer area with the loose horse. "That's a nice horse you have there. He jumped that big post and rail beautifully and what a turn-of-foot. Good lookin', too. Have you thought about running him?"

"He's a nice horse, all right," Paddy replied. "He belongs to my niece, Dee. She'll decide what she wants to do with him. Knowing her, she's happy just riding bareback around the farm."

"Hey Raja, nice to see you," Shaddy called from Rick's trailer, where he was being readied for his race.

I still can't believe that you actually like racing.

"These point-to-points are fun and easy. I'm here for a 'work' before my first big money race of the season, the Carolina Cup, in Camden. You should be out here, but I'm glad you're not in my race," he teased.

We led the horses to the paddock and then the start. The flag was up and they were off! Shaddy hung in the back of the field, saving his energy, looking lazy and slow. I was sure he would finish last.

What kind of a race is he running? Get going!

The second time around he started casually passing horses, one by one. Approaching the finish, he suddenly found another gear and powered into the lead.

"That was for you, Raja." He jigged triumphantly next to me as we accompanied him back to the judge's stand for the win picture and trophy presentation.

"I'll bet you're just itching to do this. That was pretty easy compared to the races you're used to winning." Shaddy smiled knowingly.

I just looked at him and nodded my head.

Yes, indeed. Steeplechasing looks perfect.

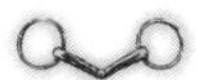

June, Chester County, Pennsylvania

One hot green-and-blue day, a couple months after the excitement of the point-to-point, Dee ran into the barn and flung her arms around my neck,

"Raja, I missed you so much. I can't wait to ride. I'm so psyched it's summer."

Some summer days Sam and Harper and Prism and Holzmann came over.

"That's five foot three — I'll bet you can't do that bareback," Dee challenged Sam, setting up the jump standards to the highest hole. She and Sam loved to jump big fences and practice Cossack tricks, egging each other on, even though Holzmann didn't much tolerate the trick riding and usually bucked Sam off when he tried them. Sam just climbed back on and tried again. Dee's favorite was heading me at the big post and rail fence next to the barn riding bareback with a lead rope tied to my halter.

I don't want this to sound ungrateful or spoiled or anything, because I was happier here than I had been since Michelle's. The Murphys were truly wonderful, caring and fun. And I WAS grateful. But...something was missing. I needed a goal, a big, ambitious goal. It's just me, I guess. Something kept gnawing at me. I felt....UNFINISHED.

Every evening after supper when we were waiting for the heat of the day to cool before going out for the night in the big field, Paddy brought me a dark, sweet drink.

"'Tis an old Irish secret — a Guinness a day helps with digestion. In Ireland we give it to the racehorses and broodmares," Paddy nodded, pouring it into my feed tub.

Dee finished brushing me then put me in my stall and sat on a hay bale, her face dappled pink and yellow by the setting sun, while Angus dropped a slime-covered tennis ball at her feet and looked up at her, wagging his tail, wiggling and grunting.

"Red sky at night, sailor's delight,' Paddy mused. "What a beautiful sunset."

Dee nodded and sat, thinking, then casually tossed the ball out the barn door. Mac and Angus bolted after it, Angus wrestling fiercely for it when Mac reached it first.

"'Steeplechase,' that's a funny name. Why's it called that?"

Paddy wiped his forehead with a rub rag and stopped sweeping the aisle. "The first steeplechase race was in County Cork, Ireland, in 1752, between two friends, Cornelius O'Callaghan and Edmund Blake. To decide who had the best horse, they raced to the closest church steeple, St. Mary's in Doneraile. So they 'chased the steeple,'" he smiled, "and they had so much fun, the idea spread. 'Tis still most popular in England and Ireland, but you'll find it all over the world. In this country, the oldest race still going is the Maryland Hunt Cup, first run in 1894.

By the way," he added, "Rick Dunlop's horse, Inquisitor, won the Hunt Cup for the second time this year. I wish you could have been there. It was quite a race."

How good IS Inquisitor, really?

Paddy continued, "Rick called to see if you'd like a summer job galloping for him. Sam'll be riding for him, too. I'll bet you didn't know that Rick's a Hall-of-fame trainer. Last year he was leading trainer. His horses are very nice, and Jed and Wyatt, his stable jockeys, are the best jump jockeys around. It's a great opportunity."

Dee crept into the barn hunched over, walking slowly, like the old ladies I used to see walking their poodles in Central Park.

What's wrong with her?

"It's only my second day riding out at Rick's, but my arms and legs are so sore," Dee complained, "I can't lift these water buckets."

"Galloping racehorses will get you fit," Tricia smiled, "I was an exercise rider for years. That's how Paddy and I met. It's different from regular riding, isn't it? Once you get your strength and balance, it'll be easier to learn how to settle the strong ones and get them to relax, but it takes practice to learn."

For our next few rides, Dee jacked up her stirrups and took me to the big hay field across the road. She was a good rider, but this was different. She tried, but she didn't have the right balance and she wasn't relaxed, like Pedro or Willie or Paddy. I remembered Prism's words and tried to be kind and a teacher and help her to learn.

It felt good to gallop but I wished I was training for something, something BIG.

August, Chester County, Pennsylvania

As we hacked through the misty cornfields to the meet, a glorious, red-streaked sky broke the steamy August day. I smelled a musky scent rising from the warm ground. A fox was around. We followed a worn path around the corn to the crest of the hill just in time to see a huge orange sun appear and paint a golden light over the rolling hills of hay fields and fieldstone barns.

"Wow! There's our reward for getting up at four o'clock. Makes you glad to be alive, doesn't it?" said Tricia, flicking her fly whisk on Robbie's flank. "It was so nice of Rick to invite us cubbing."

Rick rode Inquisitor. This time, I took a good look. He was a big, powerful-looking dark bay. I noticed that he had a special presence — 'the look of eagles,' Michelle had called it. My eyes were drawn to him and I noticed that other horses and people watched him, too.

How good is he, really?

"Dee, Tricia, ride up front with me," Rick invited.

As I walked next to Inquisitor, he turned toward me.

"Shaddy tells me you won some good flat races."

Was there a hint of arrogance in his tone? Competition?

He continued, "I won some races on the flat before I turned to jump racing. Flat racing is definitely a challenge, but I believe that the ultimate test of a great horse is the Maryland Hunt Cup. Not only do you need to be fast and a good jumper, you have to have stamina to make it over four miles and twenty-two of the stiffest timber fences in the world. Making it over the third fence of the Maryland Hunt Cup at speed and in company of a group really separates the real horses from the ponies."

He strode confidently, almost as if he wanted to challenge me at the walk. I increased my pace, catching up to him then walking slightly ahead of him.

Oh, you want to play games? I can play, too.

November, Chester County, Pennsylvania

"Dee's father called me this morning," Paddy announced one blustery, wet-leaved fall day as he and Tricia planted flower bulbs along the fence next to our field.

"Did you tell him how much we loved having Dee last summer? It's lonely now that she's back in New York. Poor Raja must be so bored."

I am bored. Bored, bored, bored!

"His company is transferring him to London. He thinks it would be a great opportunity for Dee, but he's worried that he'd never see her. His work schedule is very demanding — he's always travelling to the Middle East for weeks at a time. He knows she hates New York and the only thing that keeps her happy is coming here to work with the horses during the holidays."

A look of sadness transformed Tricia's normally cheerful blue eyes.

"Oh, no! Dee will be crushed if she has to leave Raja. She'll be 16 soon. That's a tough age to move to a new place, especially another city, without horses. She's had a hard enough go of it already with her mother's illness and then having to leave Ireland to move to New York."

She jammed the shovel into the ground with a bit more force than usual. "I know her father has an important job and that he's a kind and decent man, but I wish he spent more time with her, poor girl. No wonder she loves Raja so much. He's her family."

She paused, thinking. "Paddy, do you think Dee could come and live with us? She was so happy this summer. The boys love having their cousin around and so do I. It's nice to have another female around. I could use the help in the barn and the garden. She could spend holidays in England with her father."

A smile crept across Paddy's face. "Sure I was hoping that would be your response, but didn't want to be the one to suggest it. Shall we call him?"

December, Chester County, Pennsylvania

Dee flew into my stall one dark, frost-rimmed afternoon, throwing her arms around me.

"Raja, I missed you so much. I can't wait to live here and ride you every day!" She fed me a handful of peppermints. "I bought a big bag of them for you, my beautiful."

A big bag of peppermints? Things are looking up.

Everyone busied themselves getting ready for the Murphy's annual Christmas party. The barn smelled of pine from a huge wreath the Murphy boys spent two hours hoisting up the side of the barn through a small window in the hayloft and the apple tree by the barn twinkled with white sparkles of light. As the cars started to roll in the driveway the afternoon of the party, one drew to a stop by the barn while Dee was feeding.

"Merry Christmas, Dee. Welcome back. I saw that the light was on, so though I'd stop in. I always think that a barn is the best place to be during a party."

"Thanks, Mr. Dunlop. I'm happy to be back. Merry Christmas to you."

"How's Raja? He's a very good horse. I looked up his race record. He won a very tough Grade One stakes race impressively, beating a horse that won the Belmont Stakes. I'm guessing he could have been a serious Triple Crown contender if he hadn't had that starting-gate accident."

You bet I would have!

"Have you thought about racing him? I think he'd be tough to beat over timber. There's a Ladies' race at the hunt point-to-point the end of March. You should consider it. You need to be 16 and the race committee has to approve your entry."

"I'll be 16 on March 15th!"

"Give it a thought before you talk to your uncle about it. I can help you train if he doesn't kill me for encouraging you. I'd better get down to the party and butter him up."

"Absolutely not. It's too dangerous. How would I answer to your father if you got hurt? Everyone does, you know. It is a matter of when, not if, in jump racing, I know that first hand. The matter is closed. You can event, or even do the jumpers if you want, but I will not allow you to ride races." Paddy climbed up the ladder next to my stall and threw down three hay bales from the hayloft with a little more force than usual.

"But Rick said…

"End of story. I won't talk about it anymore."

"I think Sam is sweet on you," teased Tricia.

Dee's face turned red. "He's just a friend."

Tricia smiled slyly. "Uh-huh, yep, he's a friend all right, poor guy."

Sam appeared every day after the party to ride with Dee. "You're so lucky your birthday is in March. I don't turn 16 until November. I won't be able to ride anything other than the junior races until next year."

All Sam talked about was the horses that would be running over timber in the spring. His favorite topic was who would run in the Maryland Hunt Cup.

"Uncle Paddy isn't going to let me race. He says it's too dangerous — but he rode when he was my age. You're so lucky that Rick is your uncle! It's too bad Holzmann isn't younger. He'd have been a great timber horse."

I'm with Sam on this one. I want to race over jumps!

I need a goal. Badly.

11
Timber!

January, Chester County, Pennsylvania

"New Year's Day," announced Paddy, "…time to get going if we're going to win that point-to-point."

"Uncle Paddy! I thought you weren't going to let me ride races."

"I might change my mind again, but you're catching me on a good day. After all, I started when I was your age. It was all because someone gave me a chance. I dreamt of your mother last night and thought it must be a sign. I'll bet you didn't know that when she was your age, your mother rode all the rogues no one else dared to. I realized then that it's in your blood, so why fight it?"

He stopped to look at her, a serious expression taking over his face.

"Raja's a good jumper and if you can hold him when he's fit, you should be all right. But you need to take it seriously. Steeplechasing isn't a game; it's a very dangerous sport. I'm willing to help you, but you need to commit to train hard. The two of you must be properly prepared."

He held her gaze, looking serious and intense.

"I want you to gallop as many horses as you can. You need to get experience, get galloping-fit and learn 'feel.' And you'll need to train Raja. This week you'll start a fitness program to build your strength and your wind — weights, squats, lunges, wall sits, running — 20 miles a week, minimum. The boys can help you; they're getting ready for lacrosse, so you can train with them. There'll be no time for a social life. I expect you to keep your grades up or we'll stop."

Wow, he's intense. Now I see why he won so much.

His steely eyes flashed as he looked firmly at Dee, wanting to make sure that every word was understood. "For Raja's first start, an experienced jockey will ride him. Then we'll make the decision about whether you go to the race. It's never a good idea to have a green rider and first-time starter together."

"It's a deal," replied Dee with a big smile on her face. "I'll call Rick this morning."

Every morning after that, no matter the weather, the headlights of the car swung out of the driveway while it was still dark, following Dee as she ran or rode her bike up the big hill on the dirt road behind the farm. After school, we trained, often when the daylight was beginning to fade. We spent hours jogging up the big hay field hill in the grey-and-orange winter dusk and when the ground froze, we jogged up the dirt road, sometimes in the dark, with Paddy following us again in the car with his headlights.

I was so happy to be training again that I didn't care about the cold.

"Uncle Paddy, how did you get into riding races?"

Paddy blew on his hands to warm them as he sat on a hay bale, picked up a clean bandage out of the laundry basket and started rolling it, pressing it straight along his thigh. "I was your age when I started. I left school at 15 to be an apprentice at a big racing yard in Ireland. I rode one very good horse, Black Adder. It was sheer luck, really, but we got on famously and won a lot of races. People started calling me and I was very lucky again to get on some good horses and win more races. It's a tough business, you know, especially in Ireland. Plenty of jockeys are breathing down your neck, ready to replace you. Success comes from luck and perseverance and ability. In that order. Perseverance, especially. Keeping trying and always hoping."

He stood up, dramatically, gesturing with his hands. "Winston Churchill was right: 'Nevah give in. Nevah, nevah, nevah.'"

At the end of January the days were so cold it felt as if they would crack and shatter. The ground was frozen — locked up and rutted — and Dee and I could only jog up the dirt road hill with a biting wind in our faces, burning our lungs with every breath.

"Thanks for the ski pants and ski mask from the boys. I think I have six layers on! I don't know what we would do without the dirt road hill. What do other people do?"

Paddy paused, thinking. "Most trainers go to the training track if the ground freezes. I was thinking that we should. I'll call one of my clients there and see if we can come and have a gallop."

February, Fair Hill, Maryland

Steamy-breathed horses wearing colorful quarter sheets jogged next to the outside rail of the big dirt track, surrounded by open fields and long wooden barns. Others galloped in the middle of the track and one horse breezed next to the inside rail.

A track!

I couldn't stop jigging and letting out excited bucks.

I'm ready to go, go, go!

"Jog once around next to the outside rail clockwise, then turn and gallop SLOWLY once around and pull up at the wire. Stay in the middle of the track. Remember, he hasn't been galloping, so we don't want to do too much too soon. That's a sure way to break down a horse," Paddy instructed.

Ta-da-da-dum, ta-da-da-dum, ta-da-da-dum.

It feels so good to gallop! I'm so happy to be galloping again. What a great day!

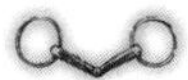

February, Chester County, Pennsylvania

"Happy Valentine's day, my love." Paddy grabbed Tricia in a bear hug and kissed her decisively on the cheek as they did barn chores the first morning of the storm.

"Isn't this snow romantic? One foot on the ground and another foot on the way — time to read by the fire, have a cup of tea, and pop a roast in the oven. The boys and Dee will be out sledding as soon as they get up and I'll bet Sam'll come over with his snowmobile for some fun."

Tricia smiled as she handed Paddy three small buckets filled with grain. Snickers squealed and whinnied in anticipation, pawing the floor impatiently.

"We'd better get the toboggan down from the hay loft. I'm glad we let Dee sleep in. She's been training hard."

As Paddy opened the barn door to dump Snickers' water bucket, a soft pile of snow blew in the barn. "Wow, there's a lot of snow! It just keeps coming. I don't think we'll be riding any time soon. Now, if we had six inches of snow, it would be perfect for galloping. Do you remember those days?"

"Of course," Tricia laughed. "We wore ski goggles and tried not to get hit in the face from the snowballs kicked up by the hooves of the horse in front of us. The horses hated getting hit in the face, too. Remember Damaselle? She used to take off every time a snowball hit her."

The next morning dawned pink, blue and still. Tree branches bent over, transformed into creatures by the snow. Huge icicles hung down from the sides of the barn and towering snow drifts buried the fence. From time to time, a new pile of snow slid off the roof with a loud thud. Everything sparkled.

Paddy stomped into the barn, knocking snow off his boots, followed by Dee.

"I'll need to dig out the tractor and get plowing. It was a quite a job just walking to the barn. I wonder if those snow shoes are still in the hayloft. Will you please take a look when you throw the hay down, Dee?"

The roads were plowed but icy — unjoggable — and the snow was too deep to gallop. Even the training track was shut down.

"I have just the thing for us to do," Paddy announced. "I think you should have an indoor jump school. I have a wonderful client with an indoor arena not too far away. She was on the U.S. Equestrian Team and she coaches now. She's won just about every big international show jumping title in the world, including an Olympic medal. I'll call her to see if we can go over there today if you help me dig out the trailer."

Thump!

A pile of snow slid off the roof of the big indoor arena. I snorted loudly and spooked, bucking, past the brightly colored jumps set up inside. It was cold and I was fit and feeling good. Paddy's voice floated over from the barn attached to the arena.

"Dee's already on and warming up. The horse is a beautiful jumper and he's had a very good education. She's a good natural rider but she needs some schooling. They're working toward riding in the point-to-point."

Whoa!

I spooked again, across to the other side as a wheelchair rolled into the arena.

"Easy, Raja," whispered Dee, patting me and giving me a loose rein.

"Hello, Dee, why don't you come over here. Let's see what we have," called the woman in the wheelchair. I stopped suddenly.

I know that voice!

She looked the same, happy, pretty and smiling.

MICHELLE!

Dee walked me across the arena to the wheelchair and I reached my nose down. Michelle opened her eyes widely, then drew in a quick intake of breath and patted me gently on the nose.

Oh, I remember her knowing and kind touch.

In a quiet voice, she asked, "What did you say this horse's name was?"

"I didn't," Paddy responded. "He's a very good horse, a Derby prospect in his youth. He was rescued from the killers. His name is Raja."

By now, tears were streaming down Michelle's face.

"What did I say wrong?" asked Paddy, concerned.

Michelle smiled. "Raja, it's so good to see you again. You were the one I missed the most. When that awful man went to jail, no one could tell me where you went. Paddy, of course this horse has a good education. I gave it to him!"

She wheeled quickly to the door of the barn. "Speedy, Bob, come here quickly! I have a wonderful surprise."

Dee and I stood still as Bob, then Speedy, appeared.

"I can't believe it!" exclaimed Bob, "I broke this horse. He was bred by the Sheikh," he told Paddy.

"Raja," drawled Speedy, "the good Lord must've been listenin' when I tol' him how much I miss you."

He reached into his pocket, then gave me a salty corn chip, patting my neck. "It's a miracle to see you."

For the next 30 minutes, everyone just talked. Paddy and Dee told their story: Beth, Yuri, New York, the kill truck, finding me in Abe's barn, training for the point-to-point. Then Michelle and Bob told theirs: racing, the starting-gate accident and show jumping. Speedy even told them about Mary and the wild gallop for the helicopter.

"After the Sheikh sold the farm and moved back to his country, Michelle and I were married and we moved up here," Bob explained. Michelle coaches young riders and I break-in youngsters. We run a therapeutic riding program here, too. Of course, Michelle has started riding again and she's thinking about trying out for the Para-Olympic Equestrian Team."

He smiled, "she's always gotta have a goal and be shooting for the stars. That's my girl, like ol' Winston Churchill — never, ever, ever, ever give in. That's why she's an Olympian."

Paddy smiled and raised his eyebrows at Dee, as if to say, "See?"

I remember how much I missed Michelle and how alike we are.

It was quite a reunion, but I was getting antsy. Of course, Michelle noticed. "Dee, I think we better get on with things before Raja loses interest. Why don't you trot him around a bit to warm up, and then we can run through the gymnastic?"

After the lesson, Michelle laughed, "He's still the most phenomenal jumper I've ever known. He has so much power and scope! I hope you come again."

She stopped for a moment. "Funny, I just remembered that my old coach, Colonel Belanov, had a grandson named Yuri when we trained at the USET. He was a very good rider and loved to show off trick riding. He did incredible moves, like picking things up off the ground at a full gallop. He must be the same Yuri. Who else would do dressage in Central Park?"

As we walked out the door, Speedy turned to Dee. "Is he still afraid of thunderstorms? Sing to him, he likes reggae. Bob Marley."

"He's afraid of storms? That's very interesting," Bob said thoughtfully, scratching his chin. "You know, when he was a foal, his mother was killed by lightning — right in front of him. She was the Sheikh's best mare. Maximillian, another colt by Raja's sire, won the Belmont Stakes and came pretty darn close to winning the Kentucky Derby."

The same father? That means Shaddy and To the Max are related to me!

"Ah, the February thaw, 'tis lovely with all of the mud and dirty snow banks," Paddy sighed as he looked at the heavy grey snow drifts that were turning into muddy new streams and ponds. He took off his sweater as he turned us out, watching a bright red cardinal land on the fence by the barn.

"I saw Wyatt Rogers when I did Rick's horses' teeth yesterday. Rick's a lucky man to have both Wyatt and Jed Steele working for him. They're both very good jump jockeys. Anyway, Wyatt said he'd be delighted to ride Raja for his first start. I think we should aim for the Blue Ridge Point-to-Point the first week of March. Your race is two weeks after that. Let's go to the training track this weekend and give Raja his first 'work,' an easy one, more of a pipe opener. After that, Wyatt can work him the following week and school him before the race. If the ground is good, I'd like to take Raja over to Rick's and school over his timber fences in company."

February, Fair Hill, Maryland

Working! We're WORKING!

The cold, crisp, windy day made me jig. I let out an excited buck.

I'm so excited to be on the track.

Several other steeplechase trainers were at the training track with the same idea. Everyone was busy getting ready for the rapidly approaching spring racing season. When Dee and I stepped onto the track, I saw Shaddy, To the Max, and Inquisitor finishing up a work with Sam, Wyatt and Jed aboard.

"This is his first work in a very long time," Paddy instructed Dee, "so go easy. Gallop once around, slowly. When you pass the wire, open him up a little, more of an 'open gallop.' Whatever you do, don't let him go too fast! Pull up when you pass the wire the second time."

I could tell that Dee was nervous, especially since Rick, Wyatt, Sam and Jed were watching. We jogged once around the track, then Dee turned and eased me into a slow gallop.

I feel fresh, fit and strong — sharp!

When we reached the wire, she steered me to the inside rail.

"OK, Raja, let's go."

I opened my stride, punching the track with my hooves in a faster and faster rhythm, the cold wind whistling past my ears.

Ta-da-da-dum, ta-da-da-dum, ta-da-da-dum.

We rounded the turn, approaching Rick and Paddy. I went faster, showing off.

I love feeling athletic again. Look at me!

As we passed Paddy, Dee stood up in her stirrups and tried to pull me up.

I kept going, faster, ignoring her.

I'm having too much fun. I haven't gone fast in years.

"Raja, what's gotten into you? Slow down!" Dee stood up again, leaning back and pulling as hard as she could.

I feel good. Speed, glorious speed!

We came around the turn a second time, heading toward the stretch. Dee was breathing hard, tired, unbalanced and loose in the tack, feeling like she might come off. After we passed Paddy a second time, I let her pull me up. I jigged all the way back.

That was the most fun I'd had in years!

"I said GO EASY! Were you trying to break him down?" Paddy's eyes flashed in anger. I had never seen Paddy this angry. "If you can't hold him, you shouldn't ride him in a race. Only bad things will come of that and I won't be responsible for getting you or Raja hurt. You have three weeks to learn how to hold him or we're not going to race this horse." He turned and walked stonily down the path.

Jed, watching on Inquisitor, laughed scornfully, "You don't want to get run off with in a race, little girl, you'll get yourself, or someone else, hurt."

"That was awful," Dee wailed as we walked back to the trailers with Sam on Shaddy and Wyatt on To the Max. "I'm so embarrassed! I got run off with in front of everyone. I've been running three miles every day. I thought I was fit. How can I get stronger?"

Wyatt grinned. "Don't worry, it happens to everyone. You'll be fine. Hold your reins in a cross, or double bridge, like this. Then you can plant your hands on his neck or withers. It settles them and they pull against themselves, not you. Use your legs and core for strength and leverage, not your arms. And, whatever you do, don't change your hold! That's a clear signal for the horse to go. Stay quiet. Think of balancing a teacup on your back."

Wyatt demonstrated as he spoke. "You should get Tricia to help you. She used to hold all of the tough ones, even the ones the guys couldn't. She finessed 'em. Lifting weights and sit-ups, lots and lots of sit-ups, will help, too. Hey, Raja looks cool! I'm looking forward to riding him."

March, Chester County, Pennsylvania

"I just love a cozy barn with the horses munching their hay and tucked in for the night," sighed Dee as she fed me a peppermint.

Wyatt had come over to school me over jumps and stayed to help Dee with the afternoon chores. The early spring sun cast a golden glow over the apple tree and forsythia bush, whose tiny green buds seemed bigger and greener with each day.

Paddy, followed by Mac and Angus, came in the barn carrying three brown bottles and handed one to Wyatt before pouring the third into my feed tub.

Yum! Guinness!

"Thanks." Wyatt took the bottle from Paddy and sat on a hay bale, scratching Angus behind the ears. Dee and Paddy each pulled a hay bale closer to Wyatt and sat down, pulling the freshly washed bandages out of the laundry basket, smoothing them on their thighs and tightly rolling them, before throwing the rolls back in the basket.

"Wyatt, what's the deal with the Maryland Hunt Cup? Why is Sam so obsessed?"

"Well, now, let's see..." Wyatt rubbed his chin. "The Maryland Hunt Cup. I've tried it seven times. I finished the race four times, won it once, was second once, and had a helicopter ride to the hospital once. The only other races as tough are the Aintree Grand National in England, which your uncle Paddy, here, has won, and the Great Pardubice in the Czech Republic, which is insane."

"Insane is right — I've ridden at the Pardubice. That was quite an experience," Paddy agreed, raising his eyebrows and taking a long drink.

Wyatt laughed. "Believe me, the Maryland Hunt Cup is 'quite an experience', too. For over a hundred years, at four o'clock on the last Saturday in April, America's best jumping timber horses have been battling it out," Wyatt drawled. "It started as a bet between two hunts — sometimes it still seems like that."

"Really?" Dee seemed mystified.

"People get addicted. The purse is good, but it's not about the money. It's about the glory. It's a big deal just to make it around the course, kind of a badge of honor. Two prep races, the My Lady's Manor and the Maryland Grand National, different from the Grand National in England that your uncle Paddy won, are run on the two weekends before. It's sort of a Timber Triple Crown. Inquisitor is headed to the Hunt Cup for the third time with Jed. If he wins again, he'll go down in the history books with some of the greats like Mountain Dew and Jay Trump."

"It sounds amazing. Uncle Paddy, can we please go and watch this year?"

"Sure thing. I haven't missed a Hunt Cup in years. I like to go down to the third and thirteenth fence to watch. That's where the excitement is. You'll see some good-jumpin' horses, that's for sure. You never know what's going to happen in the Hunt Cup. That's why everyone's addicted, isn't that right, Wyatt?"

"Yes, that's very true. There's no sure bet in the Maryland Hunt Cup." Wyatt stood up, "Thanks, I'd better be going. Rick wants us there at five thirty tomorrow morning to go to the track. Good night."

Rick's schooling field was dotted with several sets of big wood-and-plastic hurdle fences framed by white wings. A row of five post-and-rail timber fences, each four panels wide, lined the back side. Wyatt jogged me around the field once and then we started over the hurdles, single file, with Shaddy leading at a quick gallop.

Gallop, gallop, gallop, jump.

It feels like flying!

I can tell that Wyatt is enjoying it, too.

"He's a very good jumper, powerful, and clever — cool horse," Wyatt told Paddy as we jogged back to him.

Next, Shaddy, Inquisitor, Admiralty Bay and I jogged to the timber fences then galloped head-to-head, in pairs, and jumped over them, picking up speed for the last.

"Let's have just Raja and Admiralty Bay go again," Rick shouted over the wind.

Gallop, gallop, gallop, jump! Gallop, gallop, jump!

At the last fence, Admiralty Bay slipped as he took off. I moved over in midair to get out of his way and hit and broke the top rail. I stumbled down on my knees and recovered awkwardly.

"You want to be a timber horse?" Inquisitor scoffed in a withering tone. "Poor Wyatt, I can't believe he has to ride all of you bad-jumping first-time starters. Just don't get him hurt when you fall. Rick needs him to ride his real steeplechasers."

That night, with my legs smarting and poulticed, I wondered. Is nine too old to be starting a timber career? Is it silly to be chasing dreams of glory? Maybe I should just settle into being a teacher, like Prism and Holz.

But... I just want to try.

12
The Big Sticks

March, Berryville, Virginia

The cold wind under my tail goosed me as I skittered off the trailer, ready to go. A crowd of people, bundled up to watch the races, huddled around their tailgate picnics. Paddy put on my stiff timber bandages, then held me while Tricia and Wyatt saddled me. First, the nonslip pad, then the lead pad, number cloth, saddle, girth, and overgirth.

I'd forgotten how tight those girths are. That lead pad is heavy!

Dee led me to the paddock and we walked around with the other horses: Hawker Hurricane, ridden by Jed; The Dynamiter; Another Look; and Notable Contender.

"Riders up!"

Paddy gave Wyatt a leg up. "Remember, just hunt him around. Go easy. This is just to get him used to the timber fences and jumping at speed and in company."

We cantered down to the start following the outriders. Wyatt stopped to show me the first fence, a post-and-rail, then gave me a short gallop. As we walked in a circle, head-to-tail, the riders joked with each other good naturedly.

"Jed, are you going to give us all a lead?"

"Heck no, I'm on a first-time starter, I need a lead."

"The Dynamiter is the pace in this race."

"Watch out, guys, this horse jumps to the left."

The flag was up. Wyatt gathered his reins. The starter dropped the flag.

We're off!

I was irritated. Why was Wyatt holding me? The pace seemed way too slow.

Isn't this a race? Doesn't he get it?

"Easy, buddy, save it for the finish." Wyatt stayed steady and tucked me in behind Hawker Hurricane as we headed to the first fence.

Five sets of hooves pounded the cold wet ground as we streaked across the field toward the first fence, all fighting for position. I shook my head as mud kicked up by Hawker Hurricane hit me in the face. I inched closer to his heels, almost on top of him.

I want to GO!

Wyatt held me directly behind his churning hooves, while The Dynamiter led the field, followed by Another Look. We were sitting fourth.

As we rounded the corner, the first fence came into view, a post-and-rail. Not too high — easy peasy. I strained against Wyatt, edging closer to Hawker Hurricane.

Let's go!

We were at the fence. The Dynamiter flew it like it was another gallop stride. Another Look and Hawker Hurricane, now head-to-head, were next. I saw their bodies rise in the air, but couldn't really see the fence or measure my distance.

Whoops! THERE it is!

Awkwardly, I popped over very high, dwelling a little in the air. I was now several lengths behind Hawker Hurricane. I noticed that he and the others had gained ground on me by jumping flatter, using the momentum from their speed.

This is harder than it looks!

Jumping at speed in a pack of horses was very different from jumping a course by myself in a ring or racing at the track. It was difficult to pay attention to the fences when I had to think about all of the other horses and where they were. And it was hard to think about race strategy when I had to worry about making it over the fences.

At the second, Hawker Hurricane, in front of me, jumped to the left, cutting me off. I couldn't see the fence and didn't have anywhere to go. I put in an extra stride before jumping and twisted in the air.

That was awkward.

After the fence I was even farther behind — six lengths now. Wyatt eased up and let me run faster, settling into a rhythm. By the fifth fence, I began to figure out how to jump at the quicker pace. It was like the day Oakley had galloped me to call the helicopter or chasing the loose horse when Paddy was an outrider at the point-to-point. I started pinging fences, flamboyantly, gaining ground over each fence.

Gallop, gallop, gallop, jump! Gallop, gallop, jump!

Different from show jumping, I felt as if I could use my power and speed to get into a rhythm and stay there. This felt better, less confining, freer.

THIS is the sport I've been waiting to find. I love this. It feels great to run and jump.

"Good boy, Raja, you're a smart one." Wyatt reached down to pat me as we thundered across the field, now third behind The Dynamiter and Hawker Hurricane.

Ta-da-da-dum, ta-da-da-dum, ta-da-da-dum.

We passed the crowd and the cars, going out in the country for another circuit.

Three miles is FAR!

I took a deep breath, then picked my head up. The crowd was a field away. As we thundered around a beacon, leaning sideways, and headed back toward the crowd, the pace picked up and I felt the horses behind starting to come to me. The Dynamiter was still ahead but we were gaining. Hawker Hurricane dropped back, tired.

Three more fences to go and I feel great.

We waited. After the second to last fence the other jockeys started to ride harder, using their hands and bodies to urge their horses to go faster. The pace picked up. It still felt slow, compared to my races at Saratoga and Belmont and Gulfstream. Wyatt held me steady but kept up with the faster pace, easing me forward head-to-head with Hawker Hurricane as we jumped the last. The Dynamiter was five lengths ahead of us.

What are we waiting for? Let's go!

Up, and over. The finish was now in view. Finally, when I couldn't stand it any longer, Wyatt changed his hold and smooched to me, asking me to go. I exploded forward in a powerful burst, roaring past The Dynamiter.

I won! I won! What a great feeling winning is!

"Good boy!" Wyatt patted me on the neck as we pulled up and jogged back to the finish for our win picture.

"Good boy, Raja! Yay, Wyatt!" I heard Dee screaming as she ran toward us, halter and wool cooler in hand. "You made that look easy."

March, Chester County, Pennsylvania

"Right, Dee," Paddy called, "Are you ready? We're off to see if you can hold that wild animal. Today's the big test. But there's no pressure, none at all." He grinned crazily. "Let's go. Load 'em up."

I came off the trailer at an endless field with a strip of mowed grass running up the crest of a big hill. Rick, Jed, Wyatt and Sam waited with Inquisitor, To the Max, and Admiralty Bay.

"Thanks for letting us work Raja with your horses."

"No problem, Paddy. I'm glad for the company," Rick replied, tipping his faded red baseball cap.

"You know how I like the work to go. Single file until you pass the orange cone two thirds of the way up the hill, then finish head-to-head."

Dee listened intently and nodded at Rick before leading me to a post-and-rail fence, stepping on the bottom rail, gathering her reins in her left hand and hopping on.

"Keep Raja covered up behind Admiralty Bay until the cone. Then you can show him some daylight," Paddy instructed, "but don't let him pass Inquisitor."

I let out a playful buck.

I feel FIT.

"Settle, Raja," Dee admonished. I could tell she was nervous. If she didn't ride well today, there would be no Ladies' race for her. In single file, with Inquisitor and Jed leading, then Wyatt and Sam, we jogged, then cantered, around the big field before heading to the bottom of the work strip.

"All tied on?" shouted Wyatt.

"Ready," Dee and Sam both replied.

Dee gathered her reins, made a double bridge and firmly jammed her hands into my neck.

"Let's go," Wyatt called to Jed.

We picked up a gallop, rounding the bottom of the hill, and started to climb. Dee kept my head directly behind Admiralty Bay's hindquarters even though I was pulling hard. She felt good: balanced, strong and tight. Tricia's exercises must be getting her fit. At the plastic orange cone on the ground, she steered me to the side slightly, showing me daylight, and we opened up, moving up next to Admiralty Bay, who came with us to join To the Max. Then, stirrups clanking, hooves thundering, and breathing loudly in unison, the three of us moved up to Inquisitor, reaching the top of the hill together.

"Perfect," yelled Rick, "that should have us all tuned up. I almost forgot, Dee, Happy Birthday! It looks like you're going racing. Nice job holding Raja."

March, Unionville, Pennsylvania

Race day dawned grey, wet and raw: a sloppy, squishy-ground kind of raw that chilled the bones, stripped the apple blossoms, and bullied the sun into hiding.

As Tricia led me up to the paddock before the race, cozy and warm in the fleece cooler that I had won at Blue Ridge, I was surprised to see Dee in her silks.

She looks like a real jockey!

"Riders up," came the call. Dee put her reins in her left hand and hop-walked alongside me, bending her knee. With a hand under her ankle, Paddy hefted her easily onto my back while Tricia kept me walking.

"You have three sets of goggles. The top set is covered with plastic wrap. Take the plastic off right as you are starting so that you can see. You'll get muddy today. As the goggles get dirty, pull them down and use the next pair. Keep Raja covered up and try to get him to settle. Whatever you do, don't let him see daylight until you're ready to go. Follow Hallie on Silver Squire. He's a great jumper and she has a good sense of pace. Stay close and don't make your move until the end. You have a long finish, so make sure you have a good last fence before you ask him to run. Good luck! Remember to breathe!"

They're off!

Two horses, Weybridge Hill and Tucktuckerman, went right to the front early, going fast. It looked as if their riders were getting run off with. They hooked up and battled it out for the first circuit, 15 lengths ahead of us.

They're definitely getting run off with!

Dee, using all of her strength, strained to hold me, placing my nose directly behind Silver Squire, a little too close to his churning hooves, almost, but not quite, clipping heels. I was keen for the first two fences, jumping them huge and almost landing on Silver Squire the second time. Soon we settled into a rhythm.

Gallop, gallop, gallop, jump. Gallop, gallop, jump.

After the first turn the front runners began to tire and came back to us, then dropped back, their races already run. We galloped the second circuit easily, over the post-and-rail fences, up a big hill, then down, gaining speed as we rolled downhill. With four fences to go, the pace picked up. We jumped the second to last as a group.

It's time to go! What are we waiting for?

"Steady, steady, not yet," Dee panted, beginning to tire

and standing up a little in her stirrups to hold me.

She's definitely getting tired. Should I be worried?

Out of the corner of my eye, I noticed that Weybridge Hill was now riderless. As we rounded another beacon and started heading up the hill to the final fence, galloping faster now, Weybridge Hill suddenly cut in front of Silver Squire toward the horse vans. Hallie pulled on her right rein firmly to keep from missing the beacon, cursing loudly at the loose horse. Dee, seeing Hallie, jerked her rein as well. As she pulled, I slipped and stumbled in the soft going, losing momentum and almost going down. Dee lost her stirrups, then grabbed my mane, disorganized, but still on — barely. Silver Squire pulled ahead toward the spectators gathered next to the last fence and the finish.

There's the finish! We're running out of time!

Ignoring Dee's efforts to steady me, I galloped faster in pursuit of Silver Squire.

I know what to do.

Close to the fence, Dee, stirrups regained, reins reorganized and back in the tack, but still out of breath, urged me on between breaths.

Just stay on. I'll take care of everything.

I sprang forward powerfully. Thundering to the last fence, we jumped together, head-to-head, stirrups clinking. In a final burst of speed, I surged forward, spraying mud in Silver Squire's face with five lengths to spare.

"Good boy, Raja!" Dee patted me after pulling me up. She slid to the ground, exhausted, and out of breath.

Winning! I love it! I'm so happy, but it all seems EASY. Is that all there is to it?

“Ugh, spring cleaning is so gross,” Tricia complained, wiping a cobweb out of her hair and leaning on a broom outside my stall. “I need elves to come and do this.”

Paddy smiled as he wiped his grease-covered hands and concentrated on replacing the chain on the bars of his saw. “Right now, chain saw elves would be perfect. Hey, I forgot to tell you, Rick Dunlop called yesterday. He thinks we should take Raja to a sanctioned race, maybe to the My Lady’s Manor or the Grand National. He thinks that Raja’s jumping is good enough for the big Maryland timber races. I have to say I agree.”

Tricia grunted as she knocked down another cobweb with her broom. “Dee’ll be spending her spring break with her father, so she’ll miss the My Lady’s Manor races. The maiden timber race there would have been the perfect spot for him. Too bad. The Maryland Grand National is a big step up. Do you think he can handle it?”

Paddy thought for a while, absentmindedly leaning over to pick up and throw a dirty tennis ball that Angus had dropped on the ground in front of him. “You’re right. It is a big step up, but Raja isn’t your average horse. I’ve seen him jump a very big fence and I’ve galloped him over a pretty big four-railer myself. He’s talented, powerful and smart — and a very clever jumper. He seems to like jump racing and the point-to-points are very, very easy for him. Let’s see what Dee has to say about it. Wyatt gets along well with him and if he’s available to ride him, I think we should give it a try. I’ll see if Bob and Michelle can help us hunt down his papers.”

April, Butler, Maryland

"Most of these horses are going to the Maryland Hunt Cup next weekend," Paddy told Dee as they saddled me before the Grand National. "See how solid they look. I always think of timber horses as the hockey players of the racing world. They're just big, powerful, athletic bruisers you wouldn't want to get in a fight with. Raja fits right in, only he's more beautiful than all of them. Have you noticed how everyone's admiring him?"

Dee led me past a river of waving daffodils to the crowd-lined paddock.

Inquisitor strode by, big, dark and impressive, full of cocky confidence. Jed, in his green-and-yellow silks stood confidently next to Rick. Next was Admiralty Bay, his chestnut coat gleaming with a deep coppery sheen. Silver Squire, the shorter, stocky, steel grey horse I had beaten at the point-to-point was next, with Hallie smiling and joking with her trainer. She looked over at Dee and waved. The last horse, Cove Warrior, was a tall, lanky bay, whose red-silked rider was equally tall and lanky.

"Riders to your horses," came the call from the Paddock Judge.

Da da da dum diggety dum diggety dum dum dum daaa.

My heart started to spark.

Let's go, go, go!

Red-coated outriders, manes braided and tack polished, cantered us down to the start past the rows of shiny cars and crowds of colorfully dressed spectators, then stopped for us to look at the first fence.

It's a lot bigger than the point-to-point fences. This is a whole different game. I began to worry. The other horses had been racing over timber for years.

Am I experienced enough?

Admiralty Bay, on my left, read my thoughts. "I hope you realize that this is a timber STAKES race."

Inquisitor, on my other side, looked over and said, condescendingly, "Aren't you out of your league? Are you sure you're ready for this, flat boy?"

Wyatt patted me reassuringly. "Good boy, Raja. Let's have some fun."

We were all in line, the flag was up, and we were off, heading for the first of 18 fences over three-and-a-quarter miles. Inquisitor burst to the lead, setting a quick pace. Every horse in the race was talented, competitive and out to win.

This is a lot faster than the point-to-points.

We crowded to the first fence as a pack, hooves thundering.

It's hard to see. Where is the fence?

I flew it, hoping I wouldn't land on anyone, and stumbled on landing. Wyatt helped me rebalance by shifting his weight back.

"Easy, Raja, settle — we have a long way to go."

We jumped the second as a group, still jostling for position. After the fence, I relaxed. By now, I knew to save my energy for the real race: the last half-mile and last three fences. I galloped easily behind Inquisitor with Cove Warrior next to me and Admiralty Bay behind. I was surprised to notice that it was easier to jump the fences at the faster pace. The momentum from galloping made me feel as though we were flying when we jumped.

Gallop, gallop, gallop, jump. Gallop, gallop, jump.

Wyatt rode quietly, shifting his weight very slightly

and squeezing his legs against my side, six strides before each fence. I rebalanced, opened my stride to the fence, and pinged each one perfectly, gaining ground on Cove Warrior every time. Another circuit, then out to the back fields on the course. As we rounded the far turn, Inquisitor picked up speed. I stayed with him as we headed to the fourth fence from home.

OK, let's go. I'm right there with you.

I could tell that Cove Warrior was tiring. He was strung out and starting to stab at his fences. I picked up the pace, heading for the finish, hot on Inquisitor's heels, head-to-head with Cove Warrior.

Let's see what you've got, Inky. I'm with you.

By now we were galloping fast. There was no room for error. The jumps had to be right or someone was going down. Wyatt shifted his weight slightly to rebalance me. I locked on to the fence, saw a perfect distance six strides away, and opened my stride to meet it. Cove Warrior, next to me, struggled to stay with me. He met the fence wrong and put in a short, awkward stride before the fence, hitting his legs and pecking on landing and pitching his jockey clear of the oncoming horses. Riderless, he ran up next to me as we headed to the final two fences.

As we approached the next fence, I noticed an outrider out of the corner of my eye, heading toward Cove Warrior and pushing him back into the race.

There's no room. You're going to push him into me.

Inquisitor went faster. I stayed with him, all energy focused on the fence.

Bring it on, Inky. I've got plenty left!

One stride before I took off, Cove Warrior crossed in front of me.

BAM!

He bumped into me, knocking me sideways.

Oww!

Wyatt flew over my head and into the fence as the others jumped around him and headed toward the finish.

Darn! I could have won. I was certain that I could have outrun Inquisitor in a stretch duel. Darn Cove Warrior and darn that outrider.

I saw the lights of the ambulance weaving through the crowd and onto the course. An outrider on a big grey caught me and led me to Dee, who had my halter buckled across her chest and was out of breath from running.

"Good boy, Raja, you were amazing! You could have won that race."

What about Wyatt? Is he OK?

As Paddy grazed me in the van area after the race, his cell phone rang. "How's he doing? Broken collarbone? Oh, no, that's unfortunate, but I'm glad it's not worse. He should be back riding before the end of the spring season. Great, thanks for the update, Trish. I'm sure he's glad you're at the hospital with him. Rick's on his way there now. He said he'd bring the two of you home. See you later. Love you. Bye."

Legs poulticed and bandages on, we were about to load up and head home when the jockey who had ridden the winner of an earlier race swaggered up to Paddy.

"Tough luck. Your horse jumped well, I thought he had the win. If you're looking for a rider for the Maryland Hunt Cup, give me a call. My ride won't be going. Stupid trainer got him hurt." He smiled at Dee. "Hello, darlin' what's your name?"

Dee turned red and stammered, "D-D-D-Dee."

"We hadn't thought of going, but I'll give you a call if we do. Can you come up and school next week if we decide to go?" asked Paddy.

"Sure thing. You should send this horse. He has 'Hunt Cup Horse' written all over him. Here's my number, Ben Kidd, great to meet you."

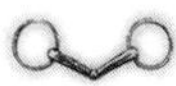

April, Chester County, Pennsylvania

"He looked good out there today; jumped like a stag. I think Ben might be right. I think he could do the Hunt Cup. He seemed to like the bigger fences. What do you think, Tricia?"

"I agree," Tricia admitted, "but I wish Wyatt could ride him. They get on so well. I'm not so sure about Ben."

"He did a nice job on that winner today and he's been around the Hunt Cup course. Besides, Dee thinks he's cute, don't you, Dee?" Paddy teased.

"Oh, those jump jockeys are all charming when they want something, isn't that right, Paddy?" Tricia smiled, giving Paddy a playful shove.

"Let's get these horses turned out and go and have some supper. It's been a long day. I think it's a frozen pizza night. Sorry."

"Where could he be?" complained Paddy. "He's over an hour late."

It was four days before the Maryland Hunt Cup. I stayed in the barn while we waited…and waited. After another 30 minutes, a red sports car came roaring up the driveway and skidded to a stop, spraying gravel into the lawn. Ben sat for a moment in the car to finish a cell phone conversation. Paddy and Dee came out to greet him and waited some more. As he opened the car door, his Doberman Pinscher jumped out and started growling threateningly at Mac and Angus.

"Hiya, darlin'." Ben flashed a smile at Dee and kissed her hello on the cheek. She turned red. Then he turned to Paddy. "I'm ready. Is he tacked up?"

Paddy just glared at him and handed him my saddle and bridle. Paddy rode Robbie and Dee came out on Snickers to watch.

"Gallop him once up the hill and then we'll jump," Paddy instructed.

I hadn't galloped since the race and I was feeling sharp. At the bottom of the hill, I let out a big, happy buck.

I'm back! Ready to go, go, go!

Ben smacked me with his whip and snatched me in the mouth with the reins. "Stop it, you pig," he cursed.

Whoa! What's THAT about?

I didn't know what to make of it. As he pointed me up the hill, I took off, ready to show off my speed.

I'm feeling GOOD.

"Hey, slow down, we're not working," he yelled, as he stood up in his stirrups and pulled against me. I just pulled more; I wanted to run.

This guy is annoying.

I ignored his pathetic pulling and went faster up the hill. Three buzzards sat on the fence at the top watching us. As we approached, one of them took off suddenly. I saw him, but spooked anyway, jumping first right, dislodging Ben, and then, for the fun of it, dropped my shoulder and ducked left, depositing him on the ground.

Ha! That should teach you!

Then I galloped across the field to Paddy and Dee and Robbie and Snickers.

"I don't think this is going to work," Paddy hissed through clenched teeth when we all met up at the barn. It looked to me like he was going to hit Ben. "This horse will not be going to the Maryland Hunt Cup."

Not going!

I couldn't eat my feed that night and didn't want to leave my stall.

It's true! I know it now. I'm destined for great despair, not great glory. It isn't fair!

I tried to sleep, but all night long I thought of all of the failures in my life: not running fast enough to save my mother; losing the Fountain of Youth Stakes; injuring myself at the Hampton Classic because of stupid lightning; hurting Yuri; hurting Mr. Smith; ruining things; being scared of a silly starting gate; allowing a loose horse to hit me in a race, and getting Wyatt hurt.

I'm never going to get a chance like this to prove myself. I'm old and a failure. It's probably a good thing I'm not going, I'd just get someone hurt.

13
Last Saturday in April

The following morning as streaks of red reached across the sky and we banged and nickered for our breakfast, the purr of an approaching car engine grew louder, then stopped. A car door slammed, then footsteps crunched on the gravel.

Strange — no one usually visits this early in the morning.

I popped my head over the stall door, curious. It was Rick Dunlop.

"Good morning, Rick, what brings you out here so early? Is everything all right? No tooth problems for any of your runners, I hope?" Paddy asked, concerned, holding three small red, blue and green buckets filled with grain.

"No, no, nothing like that," Rick smiled, "I've been up all night thinking. I wanted to catch you before you left for the day. I have something to say that can't wait."

"Hang on a sec." Paddy dumped the grain in each of our feed buckets and placed the small plastic buckets back in the big built-in wooden feed bin in the corner.

"Sorry," Paddy smiled, "we'd have had a riot. I'm listening."

Rick cleared his throat, ran his fingers through his shock of grey hair and drew in a large breath before beginning to speak.

"I think Dee should ride Raja in the hunt cup and I'm willing to vouch for her to get her jockey's license. I already spoke to the hunt cup committee and to the National Steeplechase Association. Paddy, you know he's a good horse and she rides him well. She's green, but she's a natural to a big fence, just like her uncle," he winked.

"She's capable and fearless, but not reckless, and she and Raja have a special bond. I know it's unusual to ride in the Hunt Cup as your first sanctioned race, but plenty of others have done it. Chris Gracie got the ride the week before, just after his 16th birthday, and he won on Swayo. Paddy Neilson won the Maryland Grand National at sixteen. Gene Weymouth, Jonathan Kiser, Henry Cochran and Mikey Smithwick all rode in the Hunt Cup at 16. You know as well as I that Hunt Cup horses don't come around often."

He stopped to cough. "I don't know why I am saying all this. I just believe that everyone deserves the chance to shoot for the stars, especially if that chance is staring you in the face."

Paddy looked at him thoughtfully. "Thank you, Rick. I'll have to admit that the idea crossed my mind, too. Of course, I'll have to discuss it with Dee and her father and get back to you and the committee. Oh my, I think we're all getting a touch of 'Hunt Cup Fever.'"

Rick smiled. "It happens to the best of us this week."

Really? Dee ride me? What a great idea! I think I have Hunt Cup Fever, too!

"Oh my god! A sling! Does it hurt?"

Two days before the race, Wyatt came over as Dee was finishing chores. "I'm fine. I'll be back riding in a couple weeks. It's the third time I've done my collarbone and it wasn't that bad. It's a common break for jump jockeys. Want to see the x-rays? I have them on my cell phone."

Dee shook her head no, shocked. "That's gross."

He grinned at her teasingly. "The question should be…how are you feeling?"

"I feel like I'm going to throw up! I can't do this; I must be insane."

"Don't worry, you'll be fine. Paddy told me that you were going down to walk the course tomorrow. Try to walk it at least three times and once by yourself so that you can visualize your race.

He pulled out a map, motioning Dee closer.

"Seven horses are entered: Raja, Inquisitor, Silver Squire, Abracadabra, Admiralty Bay, TaserferTater, and Cove Warrior. Obviously, Inky is the horse to beat. I think Abracadabra will be tough as well. She's a good jumper. So is Silver Squire. Try to follow either one of them. Stay away from Cove Warrior; he's unpredictable." He smiled, pointing at his sling.

"The hardest fences are the third and thirteenth. They're notorious. They're almost five feet high. Three is tough. It's early and the horses are fresh and hard to rate and there's usually a big crowd at the fence. Raja jumped that high when he was doing the jumpers, so remember that. You don't want to run afoul of a faller, so stay out of traffic."

"How?" Dee asked.

"Mikey Smithwick always told me to ride to the inside flag. There's always room and the yahoos go wide and look for a smaller panel."

Wyatt continued, "The field between four and five will be soft, especially with all of the rain we've had. There's a ridge that stays dry even when the ground is wet. Don't let anyone push you into the boggy spot. Jed will probably try to intimidate you. Don't let him. Just hold your line and pretend he isn't there. Watch out for him — I mean it. He can be a dirty rider and he just hates being beaten by women. He'll think nothing of riding you through a wing, or trying to quarter you. Keep your eyes open and be scrappy!"

Dee's eyes widened as she nodded.

"Sixteen's another big one and by now they've run three miles and they're tired, so Raja will need your support. After 16, the pace will pick up. You still have a long way to go, so be patient. After 20, get going. The finishing hill is a killer. If you're in contention, you'll need to drive hard, but remember that the last fence is a straight up and down board fence, so keep your hands down and let the fence come to you."

"Thanks, Wyatt. Raja would have a better chance if you were riding."

"You'll be fine. Don't be a weenie," teased Wyatt, giving Dee a playful shove.

"Just try to have fun. Riding in the Hunt Cup is one of the coolest things you'll ever do."

"I hope the rain holds off until after the race. The ground is already bottomless — we don't need it any worse," complained Tricia, as she gave me a bath the morning of the race. "How are your nerves, Dee? Just think — the race doesn't go off until four. You have all day to feel sick and terrified," she teased.

Dee didn't answer. She looked very nervous.

"What on earth are the boys doing?" she asked, looking out the barn doors at three boys crawling in the grass on all fours.

Paddy looked up and burst out laughing. "They're looking for four-leaf clovers. You can never have enough luck. What a lovely, wet, Irish day. 'Tis a good thing Raja's a mudder."

I think Paddy wishes he were riding today.

"Wyatt called. Silver Squire colicked last night. He scratched. That leaves six."

April, Glyndon, Maryland

Inquisitor looked over at me derisively as Dee led me into the stall next to him in the pre-race stabling area. The energy in the air was so thick you could practically touch it. Every horse knew this was the big day, the biggest day of the year.

The day of the Maryland Hunt Cup!

"Well, if it isn't flat boy! After the show you put on at the Grand National, I can't believe your owner is running you over jumps, especially in this race. People can be really stupid." Inquisitor nodded his head, then snorted, as if I were an insect he wanted to squash. "Well, maybe you can take out a horse or two and clear out the race for me when you fall at the third."

I just smiled at him.

Good luck today. May the best horse win.

Jed walked over to Dee. "You look nervous."

"I just hope I'm fit enough."

"How fit do you need to be to ride three fences?" He laughed meanly and turned to walk away, "this isn't a sport for little girls."

Wyatt signaled for Dee to come over. He spoke in a hushed tone so that none of the people milling around the stabling area would hear.

"Remember, the fences are all no problem if you're in a rhythm. Six strides out, squeeze with your legs and soften your hands and it will all come out perfectly. Just pretend you are foxhunting." He smiled. "Have fun. I'm jealous. Here's a four-leaf clover. Put it in your boot." He looked at the sky. "Let's hope the rain holds off."

Tricia hurried over carrying a canvas bag, which she handed to Dee.

"Dee, it's time for you to go to the jocks' tent to put your silks on and weigh out. The scales are next to the paddock. The shuttle, the guy in the golf cart, will take you. See, over there? Jed's getting in. We'll see you in the paddock. Good luck!"

"Good luck, Dee!" Paddy shouted from my stall, where he was brushing my tail.

After a few minutes, Paddy saddled me, with the help of Wyatt and Tricia. I could feel the tension in the air as some of the other horses skittered and bucked as they were saddled.

It's almost time!

"Take your horses to the paddock," a tall dark haired man wearing a tweed coat with a clipboard in his hand commanded, repeating it several times in the stable area so that everyone heard.

"They're on their way," he barked into his radio.

I jigged with anticipation as the horses walked in a procession across the field.

The Maryland Hunt Cup!

It was all so exciting. I could barely contain myself. I was fit and ready to go — this felt like old times. A fleeting moment of doubt passed as I looked around at the other horses. They all were great athletes and they all had a lot more experience racing and jumping big timber fences at speed. I knew I was fast and a good jumper, but could I put it together? Did I have the endurance to go four miles? What if Dee got tired or panicked going into a big fence and misjudged it?

I hated to admit it, but I wondered if Dee truly was ready. Jed might be right. This is a rough sport and people get hurt. She was by far the youngest rider in the race.

Look at what happened to Wyatt at the Grand National — and he's experienced.

People dressed in bright colors covered the hillside above the course — a field of pinks, yellows, greens. The grey overcast sky and rich green grass made all the colors deeper, more intense. To our left, several hundred tailgate picnics were underway — I caught whiffs of delicious food smells. I took it all in: kids tossing balls to each other across the yellow carpet of dandelions and buttercups, ladies in dresses eating pieces of fried chicken, and the stream of people flowing toward the paddock entrance.

Is the rain going to hold off for the race? The sky looks dark.

The loudspeaker crackled to life. "Welcome to the Maryland Hunt Cup. The horses are arriving at the paddock. We have twenty minutes until post time."

We entered the paddock and walked around as a crowd of people watched. I jigged impatiently. Cove Warrior, in front of me, was about to explode.

"Heads up, heads up. Mind your back!" a shout went up, as he suddenly reared up and plunged forward.

As I walked, I suddenly saw familiar faces smiling at

me out of the crowd. Beth and Diana waved and signaled "thumbs up" to me. Next to them, with his big crooked grin, stood Yuri.

Yuri!

On the other side, I saw Bob, Michelle and Speedy. They all smiled and started cheering when they saw me walk by. "Good luck, Raja, you look beautiful!"

The Murphy boys stood with Harper and Sam.

"Go Raja! Go Dee!"

Tricia stood next to a handsome, kind-looking man in a suit, flanking Dee, who clutched her racing whip nervously and paced back and forth as she waited.

Is that Dee's father?

"Riders up," came the call from the paddock judge.

It's time to go!

Paddy kept me walking while Tricia walked alongside and gave Dee a leg up. "Good luck, Dee. The nerves go away as soon as you're on course. Have fun."

We walked another turn. I could tell that Dee was nervous — I felt her hands trembling as she tied a knot in the reins.

Should I be worried?

A stone began to form in my stomach.

I hadn't noticed how dark the sky had been getting.

A rumble of thunder echoed in the distance. I felt a drop of rain.

Thunder! I don't feel good about this.

The outrider led the first few horses out of the paddock and started cantering toward the start. As I followed them, I suddenly smelled it.

Gardenias and peppermint!

I stopped abruptly and looked around. "What is it,

Raja?" pleaded Dee, panicking, while she tried to kick me on to catch up to the others.

I stood still and took another look around. In the middle of the paddock, surrounded by two strong-looking men with dark glasses, I saw her. She caught my eye, smiled and blew me a kiss. Then she mouthed the words, "You can do it."

Princess Ayesha!

I happily cantered off to join the others at the start.

We were all in line, the flag was up, and then we were off, galloping slowly to the first of twenty two fences.

I feel good, keen. Ready to go, go, go!

Why are we going so slowly? This is a race, not a horse show!

Dee strained to hold me as I tossed my head annoyed at the constraint.

Let's get going!

But she held me. Up and over we went as a pack. Now, the second fence.

Pretty big — I'd better pay attention.

Up and over again. I heard some timber-rattling behind me as we jumped. Now, across the dirt-covered road. Then I saw the third fence.

WHOA! It's enormous! HUGE!

It was every bit as big as the fences in the Jumper Classic I had won with Oakley at Wellington — only these were big, solid, rails. They looked like telephone poles!

NOW I knew what Inquisitor meant.

Are all of the fences like that? This is harder than I had thought!

A hush came over the crowd of people lining the fence as we approached. All I could hear was my heart beating and the thundering hooves of six horses.

Six strides out, I raised my head, looked at the fence, measured the distance and shortened my stride. Admiralty Bay was next to me, with Inquisitor and Jed two strides ahead, aiming for the inside panel. Time seemed to slow down. Then I moved toward the fence, lengthening my stride decisively to meet it. Dee sat quietly, with her legs steady and hands soft. I rocked back and sailed it.

Perfect! That was big.

The steep landing surprised me, but I was ready.

Dee patted me. "Good boy."

Admiralty Bay left the ground with me and hit the fence with his hind legs, pecking on landing. Out of the corner of my eye I saw his jockey come off, a flash of yellow and green rolling on the ground. I looked up quickly to see where he was.

Just what I need, a loose horse!

Five of us were left in the race: Cove Warrior, TaserferTater, Inquisitor, me and Abracadabra, the good jumping grey mare. I looked for her, remembering what Wyatt had told Dee about trying to follow her.

I didn't want to get messed up by following a faller!

We were tightly bunched, heading for the fourth. I jumped, flanked by Inquisitor and Admiralty Bay, who was now riderless and running alongside us. All of us made it over. Inquisitor and I rounded the corner heading to the fifth fence galloping head-to-head. I felt the ground starting to get muddy and noticed that Jed was trying to push us to the left, into the deeper ground.

It's the boggy spot Wyatt had warned Dee about!

Dee kept a tight hold on her right rein, keeping me on the dry ridge. We ran so close to Inquisitor that I felt Dee's

stirrups clanking against Jed's.

Good girl! Hold your ground, don't give in.

I stayed straight, running on the ridge.

"Hold your line little girl, I'm warning you," Jed growled menacingly, raising the hand holding his racing whip, threatening to hit her. We headed into the fifth, stride for stride, still clanking stirrups. I could feel Inquisitor's sweat as we ran, inches apart.

Look, steady, lock on, one — two — three — up and over!

As we took off together, Jed veered to the left, pushing us into the wing. Dee held me straight and yelled back, "You hold YOUR line!"

CRASH!

Inquisitor bumped me in mid-air, hitting me hard. I lost my balance and stumbled, trying to regain my breath, while Jed galloped away in the lead.

Wow, that surprised me. It hurts.

Dee was now out of the saddle and up my neck, clinging on with her arms. I felt her slip off to the side.

She's going to fall!

By now, the other horses had caught up and I was galloping in the middle of the pack. With his reins dangling over his head, Admiralty Bay swerved dangerously close to us, then scooted across our path, narrowly missing bumping us.

Whoa! That was close.

If Dee falls, she'll be trampled by four horses!

There was nowhere to get out of the way. Sweaty, galloping horses surrounded us, hooves churning urgently, blind to all but the fences and horses in front of them. Dee slipped again as she clung onto my mane, trying fiercely to stay on. I raised my head a bit to help her.

Is she getting tired?

We galloped around the turn as a group, heading toward the gigantic sixth fence. Wyatt had said this was the biggest fence on the course.

It's huge — and uphill.

Suddenly, I felt Dee clasp her hands together around my neck and swing her body under it, using the momentum to heave her leg to the other side. Next, she hooked her knee up and over my withers. This felt familiar.

She's doing the "Under-the-Neck Switch"!

I lowered my head to help her as she pulled herself up the other side. At the critical moment, I raised my head, throwing her back into the saddle, as I had done with Yuri when we practiced the stunt.

We were four strides away from the fence.

Dee gathered her reins, but there was no time to find her stirrups. She sat lightly in the center of my back, as though she was cantering bareback into the big post-and-rail fence next to the barn at home. I measured the distance, rocked back, and jumped, catlike. She grabbed my mane, following me perfectly.

I heard the sound of wood breaking behind us and out of the corner of my eye again saw another flash of color rolling on the ground.

Bright pink —that's Taserfer Tater — another loose horse to think about!

Now four horses were left in the race.

"Good boy," she patted me. Then she reached down, ran her hand along the stirrup leathers, found the bouncing stirrup and got back into position. Inquisitor was ahead by ten lengths, with Abracadabra, Cove Warrior and me behind. After the sixth, Dee and I suddenly clicked.

I relaxed and started galloping in an easy rhythm. Even though we were going faster, time seemed to slow down. We galloped another circuit, sitting fourth, keeping the same relaxed, balanced rhythm.

Gallop, gallop, gallop, jump. Gallop, gallop, jump.

At each fence, I rebalanced six strides out, opened my stride and then met it perfectly. Like the jumper class with Oakley, I focused, concentrated, and suddenly it became effortless and graceful.

Now, the huge 13th was ahead. The crowd at the fence surged closer as we approached. We sat three strides behind Cove Warrior. At the fence, his rider made a big move, asking him to take off early, out of stride. Thrown off balance, Cove Warrior put in an extra short stride, jumping awkwardly, and slipping on the landing side. It was too late to move over to jump another panel.

We're going down!

Dee jammed her heels down and grabbed my mane. I took a deep breath and then jumped as high as I could over the fence and the horse on the ground, extending my legs so that I wouldn't hit him as he got back up.

We cleared him — barely!

Now there were three of us left: Inquisitor, Abracadabra and me, with three loose horses running alongside of us. As Wyatt had predicted, the pace of the race started to pick up after the 16th fence. We had gone three miles, with one mile left to go. Dee and I stayed in sync, galloping easily, jumping perfectly, waiting to make our move on Inquisitor, who was now leading by five lengths. Abracadabra jumped with us, head-to-head, a perfect pair. Seventeen...Eighteen...Nineteen. We headed for twenty.

The sky was getting darker and darker. Now the

raindrops I had felt at the start got heavier. Thunder rumbled in the distance. We moved closer to Inquisitor, jumped fence number 20 and looked up the hill toward the final two fences and the finish. I heard a ripping sound, as though the sky was being torn apart. Suddenly, a flash of light hit one of the trees lining the course.

LIGHTNING!

I forgot about Dee, Inquisitor and the race. I bolted, heading toward the tarmac road bordering the course. Inquisitor and Abracadabra stayed straight, heading up the hill toward the water fence and the finish. Stumbling in the rough, uneven ground, I crashed through the tall grass, almost falling.

In my mind a jumble of images played out. My mother silhouetted against the sky while lightning reached down to strike her; the starting gate at Gulfstream Park; the man in the cowboy hat; and Rob's friend jeering as he held the cattle prod.

Then I heard Dee's voice, "Easy, my love, it's OK."

She reached down and patted me, calmly and deliberately. I kept running, blind.

Then she began to sing in a clear thin voice, growing stronger with each stride, "Don't worry, about a thing, 'cause every little thing is gonna be alright." She kept singing and patting me. As she sang, I heard voices and saw faces:

Speedy, singing to me the night of the storm, "Ah'm so in love with you."

Beth, at the auction, "This one is special. He has the 'look of eagles.'"

Bob, "I hope that you finally get your chance for greatness."

Yuri, "This isn't a horse. This is a dream, a poem — out of a legend."

Michelle, "He's the smartest and most athletic horse I've ever sat on."

Oakley, "You are the most incredible horse I know."

Paddy, "Nevah give in, nevah, nevah, nevah."

Princess Ayesha, "Raja, you are my only true friend."

Max, "Of all of us, you're the one who will really make a mark."

And my mother, "You have greatness in you. Always remember that."

Suddenly, I took a deep breath and looked up, as though waking from a dream.

Dee felt it. "Good boy. Let's go finish the race."

She turned me and pointed up the hill, toward Inquisitor and Abracadabra, who were heading to the water fence, 30 lengths ahead of us. The finish was half a mile away and by now it was raining hard. Dee took a stronger hold and gave me a kick. All of my fears disappeared as I stared up the hill. Both Dee and I knew what to do.

I exploded forward in a giant surge, ignited by something nameless, something more powerful than fear. Then I turned on the afterburners.

Faster, FASTER!

Everything melted away except the path ahead. No past, no future, only the present existed. I put my head down and went as fast as I could. All I could hear was the wind rushing past my ears and the sound of my hooves pounding out their mighty rhythm. All I could feel was the strength of my rippling muscles and powerful legs working together in perfect harmony.

Faster, FASTER!

Dee grabbed onto my mane and tucked her face close to my neck as we roared up the hill. We blended into one being, focused on going forward and going fast, the ultimate speed machine. Devouring the ground as if we were flying over it, we rapidly closed the gap between us and the other horses.

Faster, FASTER!

Dee sat still, squeezed her legs and jammed her heels down for the water fence. We flew over it without slowing, barely noticing it. We passed Abracadabra. Inquisitor had cleared the last fence and was heading up the stretch, alone, ten lengths ahead.

Faster, FASTER!

I kept running, digging deeper into the muddy ground. We met the last fence perfectly, jumping in a giant, powerful leap, gaining ground. We approached the stretch with the crowd lining each side of the finish. A blur of faces turned toward us, screaming and cheering in a tumultuous frenzy. "Come on, Raja, come on!"

Now I could hear the announcer, "And here comes Raja. Inquisitor leading by six lengths, but Raja is coming on strong. RAJA! Closing in, showing an incredible display of speed. Ladies and gentlemen, this is a race for the history books. Inquisitor is still in the lead, but Raja is gaining ground. Can he make it?"

Dee held on tight and concentrated on staying with me as we flamed up the stretch. I didn't need any urging. My body was running on instinct now, generations of speed and athletic ability distilled into this moment.

"Come on, Raja, come on!"

Now we were five lengths behind, now four.

It was a long uphill finish. The delirious energy of the

crowd embraced me, drawing me forward.

"Come on Raja, come on!"

I dug deeper still.

It was a tough slog through the deep, sticky ground. I thought of Max beating Annapurna in the mud at the Belmont Stakes.

Never, ever, ever, ever give in.

We drew alongside Inquisitor, stirrups clanking and sweat mingling. Jed turned to Dee and snarled again,

"I'm warning you, little girl."

I looked Inquisitor in the eye and then drove past him in a final burst of power, splattering him with mud as we went under the wire.

"It's Raja! Raja, in hand and in command. Raja has won the Maryland Hunt Cup! Inquisitor is second, Abracadabra, finishing third."

The crowd went wild. As we pulled up and walked back to the finish, Tricia and Paddy and the boys ran up to us, hugging me. Dee threw her arms around me before dismounting, taking the saddle and lead pad off my back and walking toward the scales to weigh in. She was shaking and crying as everyone crowded around us. I was a little dazed myself.

I just won the Maryland Hunt Cup!

Finally, I won something big. It felt wonderful — strangely calming, as if the victory had always existed and had been waiting for me.

"Your mother would be so proud of you. I'm so proud of you," exclaimed Dee's father, hugging her and helping to take off her helmet.

Paddy kept me walking. "Raja, you did it! You won! I knew you could."

Photographers flashed their cameras in the grey light and soggy rain and I didn't notice the flashes. A bolt of lightning struck a tree in the distance and I didn't care.

Lightning didn't matter anymore.

We were sharing — savoring — the sweet victory.

Dee came back to give me another hug as Tricia kept me walking. "Raja, you are the best horse in the world." She could barely speak through her tears of joy.

"Watch your back, coming through!" a shout rose up.

I looked up to see Sam, Wyatt and the Murphy boys carrying a bucket of water.

Splash!

They poured it over a surprised Dee, laughing. "It's a tradition. You get wet when you win your first NSA-sanctioned race," grinned Wyatt, "I think we cleaned some of the mud off. Hey, don't forget to weigh in."

At the stable area after the race, it was like the best dream I could ever have. All of my old friends I had glimpsed before the race when I was walking around the paddock came to congratulate me.

"Raja, you finally had your chance. I knew you were headed for greatness!" exclaimed Bob as he patted me.

Michelle gave me a sugar cube from her wheelchair. "You jumped like a stag. You were the best one out there. You could have gone to the Olympics, there's no doubt in my mind. You are the best horse I've ever known."

Speedy scratched the tickly spot above my eyes and fed me a corn chip. "Raja, you got some speed, I know, like when you saved the girl's life on the farm. I loved watchin' you win. I wish Oakley coulda seen it."

Beth gave me a big hug. She had tears in her eyes. "I read about your point-to-point win in the Steeplechase

Times and I called Paddy. He told me you were headed here and I hunted down Yuri in New York. He just introduced me to Princess Ayesha. She's going to join our board AND give us a big donation to expand our rescue operation. She's donating to Michelle's therapeutic riding program, too. I knew you were a special horse from the moment I laid eyes on you. You've always had the 'look of eagles.' I can't tell you how happy today makes me. Well done, Raja."

Yuri walked with a slight limp as he approached me and patted me on the neck. "This is the best day of my life. Sasha, you are amazing, but I always knew that. I tried to find you when I got out of the hospital, but you had disappeared." He bowed gallantly, looking me in the eyes with his crooked grin. "It has been an honor to have you in my life and I miss you. Now that I know where you are, I'll come and see you. I'll be visiting to help Beth work with her 'off-the-track' rescue horses and won't be far," he promised.

Finally, Princess Ayesha came over to me, smiling and tear-stained, her long hair bedraggled from running in the rain. She hugged me tightly, reached into her handbag, found a peppermint, and fed it to me.

"See, Raja, what did I always tell you? You are the most perfect thing in the universe and I will always love you."

Raja Glossary

Part One

Chapter 1: Mark of the Chieftain

Triple Crown: Winning the Kentucky Derby, the Preakness Stakes and the Belmont Stakes is the most important racing prize, with only 11 winners and none since Affirmed won it in 1978.

Bay: A brown coloring with black mane and tail ranging from a light "blood bays" to dark brown.

Chestnut: A reddish-brown color encompassing a range of red, gold and liver shades. A chestnut never has black points, mane or tail.

Sent to stud: Racehorses are often sent to stud for breeding when they stop racing. Horses with winning race records can command high stud fees, making them more valuable as studs than as racehorses.

Chapter 2: Youngbloods

Tack: Equipment used when riding a horse. In simplest terms, this consists of a saddle, a girth to secure the saddle, and a bridle for the horse's head as a means of controlling and steering.

Farrier: A horseshoer — someone who trims horses' hooves and puts horseshoes on them.

Working or Breezing: A fast gallop. Racehorses are usually worked once a week.

Two-minute lick: A galloping pace that covers a mile in two minutes.

Wash stall: A special stall for washing horses.

Cold-hosed: Equine leg injuries are often treated by running cold water on the injured area for an extended period of time in order to reduce swelling.

Chapter 3: Road to the Roses

Hall-of-Fame trainer: Fewer than 100 racehorse trainers have been honored by nomination to the National Thoroughbred Racing Hall of Fame in Saratoga Springs, New York.

Shipping bandages: Bandages for protecting horses' legs while shipping or travelling.

Hay net: A cotton or nylon webbed net used to hold hay.

Backstretch: The part of a racetrack that is farthest from the grandstand and opposite and parallel to the homestretch. "Backstretch" is also used to describe the barn area adjacent to a racetrack where horses are stabled and cared for.

Poultice: A thick, clay-like medicinal salve that is put onto horses' legs after hard work, or, when injured, in order to draw heat from the horses' legs.

Stakes race: A prestigious category of race in which nomination, entry and/or starting fees contribute to the purse. Stakes races are typically graded, with Grade One stakes being the most competitive.

Railbird: Avid horse racing fans who stand next to the track rail to watch horses train and race.

Suspensory ligament: A main supportive ligament in a horse's lower leg.

Wire-to-wire: A horse usually crosses under the finish line, an overhead wire, several times during a race, with the final pass being the finish to the race. A horse that wins wire-to-wire leads for the entire race.

Parrot-mouth: A parrot-mouthed horse's top incisor teeth are farther forward that that of the lower teeth.

Call to the Post: A special call played on a bugle used to signal the horses to the starting gate.

Girth: A leather, cotton or nylon strap that holds the saddle on a horse's back.

Overgirth: A stretchy, elastic girth that goes over the saddle and under the horse's belly, ensuring that the saddle doesn't move if the regular girth breaks.

Quarter Pole: A striped pole on a racetrack used for marking the quarters of the track.

Under the Wire: Crossing the finish line, designated by an overhead wire.

Grade One Stakes Race: The most competitive of all races, offering very large purses. Grade One Stakes horses are the best racehorses in the world.

Laminitis: Commonly called "founder," laminitis is a painful inflammation of the soft tissue surrounding the coffin bone in the hoof, resulting in severe lameness and, in severe cases, rotation of the bone through the sole of the hoof.

Gelded: Castrated. Male riding horses are generally gelded.

Part Two

Chapter 4: Jumpers

Warmblood: Over the last hundred years, thoroughbreds have been crossed with draft horses to breed warmbloods, horses suited for pulling carriages, show jumping and dressage.

Short stirrup: A horse show division for junior riders beginning to jump courses.

Pony hunter: Classes for ponies judged on their movement, jumping style and overall performance. Classes are both over fences and "on the flat."

Equitation: Classes judged on the rider's position, smoothness and effectiveness. The horse is not judged outright, but the horse's performance reflects the rider's capabilities.

Selle Français: A French sport horse known for its abilities in show jumping, racing and eventing.

Dandy brush: A soft-bristled brush used for grooming horses.

Scope: When riders speak of a horse's scope, they are referring to the animal's ability to jump fences easily. A good, athletic jumper is said to be "scopey."

Oxer: A jump that, with two sets of standards, is wide as well as tall.

Gymnastic: A series of jumps set in a line, usually at one- or two-stride increments, used to teach a horse how to jump, and for honing jumping skills.

On the Flat: A horse's work at the walk, trot and canter.

Dressage: An equestrian discipline that develops, through progressive training, a horse's natural athletic ability. Dressage horses compete by performing a series of movements in an arena, and are judged on the quality of the horse's movement, precision and harmony with the rider. See www.usdf.org.

Aids: The means by which a rider communicates with the horse. Natural aids include hands, seat, legs and voice; artificial aids include spurs and crops.

In-and-Out: Two or more fences that are placed one, two or more strides apart from one another. Also called a "combination."

Jumping faults: Penalty points that are accrued in competition when a horse knocks down a rail or refuses to jump a fence.

Braiding: Horses' manes and tails are braided for hunter and equitation classes or other formal events, such as three-phase events, dressage shows or foxhunting.

Vertical: A jump consisting of one set of standards and a pole or poles.

On deck: Next to go.

Half-Halt: A barely visible, almost simultaneous coordinated action of the seat, legs and hand of the rider in order to increase the attention and balance of the horse.

Jump-off: In jumper classes, when two or more horses do not incur jumping or time faults, they then complete a timed jump-off of a shorter course to determine the winner of the class.

Chicken Coop: A triangular-shaped obstacle that is built on an A-frame. It is a common obstacle in the hunt field and is usually an inviting, natural jump.

Figure-eight noseband: A type of noseband that prevents the horse from opening his mouth. The noseband crosses over the nose and attaches in two places, resembling a figure eight.

Timothy: A type of hay commonly fed to horses.

Withers: The ridge between the shoulder blades of a four-legged animal. In horses and dogs it is the standard place to measure the animal's height.

Timber: Steeplechase races over solid wood fences, usually post-and-rail. The Maryland Hunt Cup and the Virginia Gold Cup are famous timber races.

Grand Prix: The highest level of show jumping and dressage, typically drawing international-caliber horses and riders.

Wellington: A major winter showing center for hunter/jumpers (and dressage and polo) in Florida. Wellington hosts a number of Grand Prix jumper events.

Pull a rail: To knock down a rail.

Chapter 5: The "A" Circuit

"A" Circuit: A series of hunter/jumper shows that are rated "A" and sanctioned by the United States Equestrian Federation (see www.usef.org). Shows recognized by the USEF are rated C, B, or A, with A shows most competitive.

Dropping a horse: To suddenly release rein contact with a horse's mouth right in front of a fence, thereby throwing the horse off balance.

Getting left behind: A rider failing to follow the horse in the air as he jumps, throwing the horse off balance and jerking him in the mouth with the reins.

Hoof dressing: An oil-based liquid that is brushed onto horses' hooves both to promote hoof health and improve appearance.

Thrush: A bacteria infection characterized by a foul odor, thrush, or hoof rot, is a condition that develops when the hooves are not cleaned out.

Medal/Maclay: The USEF Medal and ASPCA Maclay Championships are two prestigious and highly competitive national equitation awards for junior riders.

Big Eq: Slang for horse show equitation classes in which riders show to qualify for national championships, especially USEF Medal and ASPCA Maclay Championships.

Bowed tendon: An equine leg injury that tears the fibers that make up a horse's tendon. When the tendon is damaged, it thickens, giving it a bowed appearance.

Chapter 6: Change of Fortune

Belgian: A Draft breed. See Draft horse.

Fetlock: Technically, the term for joints on a horse's lower leg, often referred to as the "ankle." The tuft of hair growing near the joint is also called the fetlock.

Draft horse: Large, strong, heavy-boned horses bred for pulling wagons or farming equipment or logging. Typically characterized as "coldbloods," draft breeds have been cross-bred to produce sport horses. Draft breeds include Percherons, Belgians, Clydesdales and Shires.

Chapter 7: The Man in the Cowboy Hat

Palomino: Palominos have golden coats and light manes and tails.

Percheron: A Draft breed. See Draft horse.

Registered Paint: The American Paint Horse is a breed that combines both the conformational characteristics of a stock horse with a spotted Pinto coat pattern of white and dark colors.

Run for a tag: To enter a horse in a claiming race.

Claiming race: A type of race in which the horses entered are subject to being purchased, or "claimed," for a specified price determined in advance of the race.

Bran mash: An easily digested mixture of bran and other feed, moistened with hot water, often given to horses after a long work or travel day.

Rolex: Ranked Four stars in difficulty (the most difficult) and held in Kentucky every April, Rolex is the most prestigious three-day event in the United States, typically drawing top international competitors. See Eventing.

Cross ties: Two ties used to secure a horse for grooming while standing in a stable aisle.

Steeplechase: A race for Thoroughbred horses requiring them to jump over fences. Steeplechase races are run over hurdles, brush obstacles, or wooden timber fence. See www.nationalsteeplechase.com.

Grand National: A famous steeplechase race held at Aintree in England each March. The most difficult steeplechase in the world, the race was featured in the 1944 film "National Velvet" starring 12-year-old Elizabeth Taylor.

Yoke: A neck strap often used while riding racehorses.

Leg yield: A movement in which a rider uses their leg to move the horse in lateral direction while maintaining forward motion.

Cross rail: A small X-shaped jump.

Rain rot: A skin condition caused by bacteria often as a result of improper grooming, or damp conditions.

Scratches: Also called "mud fever," scratches is a condition caused by bacteria often as a result of standing in mud. Horses' lower legs become scabby and inflamed.

Eventing: A three-phase competition that consists of dressage, stadium jumping (a course over fences in an arena) and cross-country (a course over natural obstacles outside of a ring, including water, ditches and banks). See www.useventing.com

Northern Dancer: One of the most influential sires in Thoroughbred history, Northern Dancer has produced multiple champion racehorses and outstanding sires.

Secretariat: Nicknamed "Big Red," Secretariat won the Triple Crown in 1973, the first to do so in 25 years. Secretariat set course records in the Kentucky Derby and The Belmont Stakes, winning the latter by 31 lengths.

Hand gallop: A slow gallop.

Chapter 8: Ten-Foot Cop

Morgan: An American breed known for their versatility and toughness. Morgans were used as cavalry horses during the American Civil war. Morgans are used under saddle for multiple disciplines and for driving.

Quarter Horse: Originally bred for racing short, quarter-mile distances, the American Quarter Horse is used for all Western disciplines (roping, ranching, barrel racing, reining) and most English ones (eventing, hunter/jumper, foxhunting).

Clydesdale: A Draft breed. See Draft horse. The Budweiser Clydesdales are famous for pulling the Budweiser wagon in parades, shows and Super Bowl commercials.

Shoulder-in: A movement in which a horse bends around the riders inside leg, resulting in the horse's front legs moving on a more inside track than the hindquarters. A shoulder-in encourages suppleness and engagement of the horse's hind end.

Cossack: A Slavic people from southern Europe, Russia and Ukraine noted for their horsemanship and military skill; Cossacks formed an elite cavalry corps in Czarist Russia.

Quarter sheet: A wool or fleece horse blanket used while riding in cold weather to protect the horse's flanks or hindquarters.

Tying-up: The common term for azoturia, a condition characterized by muscle cramping in a horse's hindquarters — often caused by not properly cooling a horse down in cold weather.

Flying-lead changes: Changing the leading leg at the canter without breaking the gait. Lead changes require the horse to balance on its hindquarters and rearrange the order of its front legs.

Part Three

Chapter 9: The Ice Storm

Pony Club: An international youth organization teaching riding, mounted sports, and the care of horses and ponies. Pony Club organizations exist in over thirty countries worldwide. See www.ponyclub.org.

Racing plates: Light aluminum horse shoes used for racing.

Chapter 10: The Murphys

Piebald: A horse with black-and-white coloring.

Maryland Hunt Cup: An historic and very difficult timber race known for its big fences.
See: www.marylandsteeplechasing.com.

Gone to ground: A term describing a fox returning to a den or fox hole.

Pick-up hounds: Signaling to the hounds that it is time to go home after a day's hunting.

Cubbing: The period of the foxhunting season before the formal season. Cubbing usually takes place early in the morning from August to early November.

Master of Foxhounds (MFH): Masters are typically appointed or elected by the members of a hunt club to lead the club and make the decisions regarding the proper care and handling of hounds, relations with landowners and hunt members and the hunt staff.

The Meet: The location from which a hunt is set to convene.

Wool cooler: A light wool blanket used in cold weather to keep a horse warm as it is cooled out after exercising, or dries after being bathed.

Hurdle race: A steeplechase race over hurdles — fences comprised of a padded roll-top fence topped with plastic "brush" that allows horses to "brush through" while jumping at speed.

Outrider: A specially trained, mounted race assistant. Outriders lead horses to the start of a race and catch loose, riderless horses.

Point-to-Point: An early season steeplechase race, typically without purses and organized by a hunt as a fundraiser and community event.

Judges' stand: A tower where race officials and judges manage a race meet.

Turn of foot: An expression describing a sudden burst of speed in a horse.

Win picture: It is typical to take an official "win picture" after winning a race.

Chapter 11: Timber!

To break (in): To train a horse for riding or driving. In company: With other horses.

Cross/Double bridge: Two terms for holding both reins together in a "bridge" with both hands.

Hurdle fence: A fence used for hurdle races consisting of a steel frame stuffed with plastic "brush" standing about 4 feet, 6 inches high. A foam-rubber roll, covered with green canvas, is placed on the take-off side. Hurdle fences are more forgiving than timber fences.

Wing: White plastic "breakaway" or wooden panels on either side of a steeplechase fence.

Timber fence: Wooden fences constructed of boards, logs or posts and rails. Timber fences are five- to six-panels wide and 3'6" to 4'6" high (Maryland Hunt Cup fences are 4'11").

Chapter 12: The Big Sticks

Timber bandages: Stiff bandages that protect the horse's hind legs from hitting timber fences.

Beacon: A flag or cone or other marker designating the race course. Failing to "honor" a beacon will result in elimination and fining for going off-course.

Cover up: Placing a horse directly behind another horse while racing or galloping in order to slow it down.

Clipping heels: Galloping so close to a horse in front of you that you interfere with the other horse's movement. Clipping heels can be very dangerous in a race.

Sanctioned/Under Rules: Races that are sanctioned by the National Steeplechase Association and run under their regulations.

Chapter 13: Last Saturday in April

Mikey Smithwick: Hall-of-Fame steeplechase trainer and winner of a dozen National Steeplechase Association championships. Before becoming a trainer, Smithwick was a top amateur steeplechase jockey and won the Maryland Hunt Cup a record six times.

Ride through a wing: To intentionally swerve in front of another horse or push the horse over in the air so that the horse is forced to go through the wing.

To Quarter or "Put someone down": To intentionally adjust your horse's speed so that he jumps with another horse next to his hindquarters, causing the other horse to take off early and fall, or be "put down."

Colic: Technically, "colic" is a term for any equine stomach/intestinal disorder and can range from impactions, to gas, to intestinal twists. Colic is the number one natural killer of horses.

Mudder: A racehorse that performs well in muddy conditions.

Weigh out: To officially weigh for the assigned weight before the race with tack and the correct lead weights if needed.

Post time: The official assigned time for a race to begin.

Weigh in: To officially cross the scales after a race in order to ensure that correct weight was carried in the race.

Steeplechase Times: The leading newspaper covering Steeplechase Racing in the United States.
See www.st-publishing.com.

Anne Hambleton *Author*
Lifelong horsewoman, retired amateur steeplechase jockey and USPC graduate "A," Anne Hambleton has been active in a number of equestrian disciplines including Eventing, Jumpers, Polo and Foxhunting. A renewable energy and corporate sustainability consultant, Anne graduated from Middlebury College and The Paul H. Nitze School of Advanced International Studies. She lives on a farm in Vermont with her family and several ex-racehorses she actively trains and competes. *Raja* is her first novel.

Margaret (Peggy) Kauffman *Illustrator*
A fine art bronze and pastel sculptor, Peggy Kauffman is internationally known for her portraits of both animals and people. She has completed over seventy-five bronze commissioned portraits. A lifelong horsewoman, Peggy has competed in Eventing at the intermediate level and has spent many years working with Hunter/Jumpers. Peggy has illustrated two published books: *The Fox's Morning* by Anne McIntosh and *Clayton in the Moonlight* by Jessi McQuilkin. Her work has received awards from the American Academy of Equine Art and the Kentucky Derby Museum and has been featured in *Spur, Equine Images* and *Country and Abroad* magazines. Peggy studied at Bennett College and at the Maryland Institute in Baltimore. She lives on a farm in Millerton, New York with several ex-racehorses. *peggykauffman.com*

Cappy Jackson *Cover Photo*
A lifelong horsewoman and USPC graduate "A," Cappy Jackson has been a professional photographer for more than 40 years. She is best known for award-winning equestrian photography. Her work regularly appears in the pages of *Western Horseman, Horse & Rider Magazine* and *Practical Horseman.* Her most recent awards include the 2002 AQHA Photo of the Year and the 2002 Photo of the Year from US Equestrian, Inc. Cappy has a BA from Middlebury College. She lives in Glencoe, MD, where she rides as much as she can. *cappyjacksonphotos.com*

Sally Stetson *Book Designer*
A graphic designer focusing on print communication and packaging, patterns for fabric and rugs, interior color consulting and print making. Sally is a lifelong animal lover and currently owns three rescue dogs and three event horses in various stages! She and her husband live on a ranch in Stowe, Vermont and spend as much time as possible working from Southern Pines, NC when the snow starts to fly so she can continue training. *sallystetson.com*